Gambling with the Earl

The Earls of the North
Book 1

Elizabeth Heights

ARE YOU SIGNED UP FOR DRAGONBLADE'S BLOG?

You'll get the latest news and information on exclusive giveaways, exclusive excerpts, coming releases, sales, free books, cover reveals and more.

Check out our complete list of authors, too!

No spam, no junk. That's a promise!

Sign Up Here

www.dragonbladepublishing.com

Dearest Reader;

Thank you for your support of a small press. At Dragonblade Publishing, we strive to bring you the highest quality Historical Romance from some of the best authors in the business. Without your support, there is no 'us', so we sincerely hope you adore these stories and find some new favorite authors along the way.

Happy Reading!

CEO, Dragonblade Publishing

Chapter One

Year of Our Lord 1296. A remote fishing village on the wild north-east coast of England.

MOONLIGHT SPILLED THROUGH the open window, illuminating the shabby furnishings in the once beautiful parlour of Shoreston Manor.

When Kitty was a child, her mother's titled relatives had gathered here twice a year to eat sweetmeats and try to convince the stubborn Lady Isabella to return home to Answick Castle. Back then, candlelight had sparkled in the looking glass, making everything appear bigger and brighter than it really was. Now the rug had been half-eaten by moths, and a thick layer of dust coated everything. There was no coin to spare for a fire in the grate of such a large room and so the door was usually kept closed. Only the tall, dark wood dresser remained unchanged. One cherished heirloom from her mother's past.

With a steady hand, Kitty placed her candle on the dresser and surveyed the row of tiny drawers which nestled beneath the larger cabinet doors. *Drawers for secret things,* her mother had laughingly told her.

If only her mother was here now, to see her prophecy brought to life.

"Are the jewels still there?" Rosalind whispered, twisting her long fingers together nervously. Her pale face was puckered with an anxious frown which Kitty longed to dispel.

"Patience, dear sister," she admonished gently.

The central drawer was smaller than the rest. You could be forgiven for not noticing it at all. Her mother had shown her how to apply just the right amount of pressure to the engraved cross on the front panel to pop it open. Kitty held her breath and steadied her trembling fingers. In another moment, they'd discover if their worst fears had been realised.

She pressed the cross, and the little drawer sprang out. She held the candle closer, struggling to make anything out in the darkness. From beyond the window came a distant shout and a roar of laughter. Rosalind flinched and drew her woollen shawl tighter over her slender shoulders.

Kitty reached into the drawer and breathed a deep sigh of relief when her fingers encountered a familiar cloth bag. She traced the line of hard edges beneath the softness of the cloth, releasing a faint trace of her mother's scent into the air. She closed her eyes and shook her head, dispelling the fancy. Mother had been dead for ten years now. Her fragrance had long since disappeared from Shoreston, along with the silver and the sweetmeats.

"They are still there," she said, her pronouncement echoing against the bare walls.

"Oh, thank goodness." Rosalind clasped her hands with relief. "I knew Lizzie was wrong. Father would never be so reckless as to gamble away the last of our inheritance." Her voice shook with the indignation of youth as she flicked back the neat braid of hair that had fallen over her shoulder.

Kitty shot her a look. Her little sister had seen fifteen summers. How could she still be so naïve? A shaft of moonlight fell on Rosalind's upturned face. With her delicate features, fair hair and pearly skin, she was a younger, slighter version of their beautiful mother, whereas Kitty had inherited her long limbs, red hair and freckled complexion from her father's side of the family. Years ago, the difference had bothered her. Now she had more important things to worry about.

"I'm not sure about that," Kitty said carefully. "When Father goes to the tavern, the very devil comes upon him. There's no telling what he might do."

Rosalind tossed her silvery blonde head. "I know. But I don't worry as much as you do, because I have you to worry for me." Her unswerving loyalty made Kitty's lips curl into a smile. Meanwhile, Rosalind stifled a yawn. "Can we go back to bed now?"

"Yes, we can," Kitty said, closing the drawer and standing back from the dresser, disliking the way the shadows dipped and flickered around them. She wished there was some way she could secure the jewels further, but this was the best hiding place in the house, and it had served them well until now.

Lizzie, one of just two remaining servants at Shoreston, was waiting for them in the hall. Her greying hair was neatly pinned under her cap, but her apron bore the stains of a long day's work.

"Is all as it should be, miss?" she enquired, as soon as the two sisters appeared.

"All is well," Kitty assured her, knowing how the older woman fretted. "But you did right to wake us, Lizzie, thank you."

"I'm that glad." The old woman put a hand on the simple cross-shaped pendant she always wore around her neck. "Alfred brought back some terrible tales from the tavern." Her voice shook with a mix of nerves and almost feverish excitement. "He's gone back there now to keep an eye on things."

Rosalind stiffened and Kitty laid a comforting hand on her narrow shoulder. Kitty and Lizzie did everything they could to shield Rosalind from the hardships that had befallen Shoreston Manor. Rosalind had the choicest vegetables from their garden, along with the warmest woollens, but her bones still jutted outwards. Despite all Kitty's hard work and efficient savings, there simply was no longer enough coin to go around. Especially when their father, Owain, was determined to gamble away everything he could get his hands on before drinking himself into a stupor every night.

"Hopefully Father will fall into a ditch and sleep off the worst of it before morning," she said. The sentiment was harsh but deserved.

Lizzie met her eye over the flickering flame of the candle. "God willing, he will stay away tonight," she said. "But you should know this. The menfolk of Rossfarne won't let any harm befall the two of you. They remember your mother and the kindness she showed them when she first came here."

Reassured, Rosalind yawned loudly, making the candlelight jump. Kitty's own response was more complex. Her body was strong, her mind was sharp and she was still young at just twenty-two years of age. She didn't want charity from the people of the town.

"Let's go up." She raised her candle to illuminate the bare wooden stairs. "Thank you again, Lizzie."

The servant bobbed into a small bow which made the corners of Kitty's mouth twitch once again. On most days, Kitty could be found working side by side with Lizzie to scrub the floors, peel the home-grown vegetables and beat the fading rugs. She had long since abandoned the airs and graces associated with her birth. Yes, she was a blood relative of the Duke of Answick, but she was also the child of a fisherman. She had always fancied it was the lowly side of her lineage that showed the strongest.

This was why she had put away Mother's jewels for Rosalind.

She stood back to allow her younger sister to go ahead of her up the stairs. Pretty Rosalind would not befall the same fate as she. Of that, Kitty was determined. Her sister's hands would stay soft and white. She would learn her lessons and make a suitable match when the time came. Mayhap not with anyone from the titled gentry, but Kitty hoped a local farmer or landowner might express an interest in the beautiful and ladylike Miss Rosalind Alden—helped, of course, with a dowry from Isabella's jewels.

If things had been different, if Isabella had survived the difficult birth of a poor, ill-fated third child, Kitty would have hoped for more for herself. She had fond memories of a magical childhood spent riding horses and playing happily in the grounds of Shoreston. A singing tutor had come twice a week, and Kitty's voice had been highly praised.

"A voice that could charm the birds from the trees," her mother had teased. *"A voice that will bring the suitors running."*

The very idea made Kitty snort with derision. There were certainly no suitors running to woo the oldest daughter of Owain the drunkard. No eligible young men breathing kisses over her work-roughened knuckles or whispering terms of endearment into her tousled hair as she kneaded the next day's bread. Not that she cared. She had neither time nor yearning for love. The only thing that mattered was Rosalind.

A gust of air blew down the stairs and settled around Kitty's neck and arms, making her shiver inside her chemise. She should have brought a shawl from their bedchamber. Shoreston Manor was crumbling, and although it was early summer, the nightly draughts streaming through the windows and roof retained the chilly sting of winter. Tiredness clung to her bones, as she had been up at sunrise to help Lizzie feed the chickens. In a few hours it would be time to rise again, but until then she could enjoy some undisturbed rest. Her eyelids were already closing as they turned the corner into their shared bedchamber, and she started in surprise as a frantic hammering rose up from the floor below.

Rosalind gripped her arm, unsteadying the candle. "What's this now?" Her face was tight with trepidation.

"I don't know." As calmly as she could, she loosened her sister's viselike fingers and crossed the room. "Who is it, Lizzie?"

Below she could see the older woman drawing back the bolts from the big front door. Alfred, their one remaining manservant, burst through before Lizzie had the door properly open.

"Where are they—Miss Katherine and Miss Rosalind? We don't have long."

"We're up here." Kitty took matters into her own hands, stepping onto the landing and peering over the worn, splintering banister.

"You must hide, Miss Katherine." Alfred, a man who had worked hard all his life and was no longer young, ran a few steps up the stairs and then retreated back down. "Not up there. That's the first place he'll look. Lizzie, where can they hide?" he beseeched his fellow servant as he twisted his cap in his capable hands.

"In the pantry, behind the salt barrels," Lizzie answered quickly, as if this was something she'd given previous thought to.

"Is that really necessary?" Kitty raised her eyebrows, reluctant to abandon the prospect of her warm bed.

"It's worse than you could have ever dreamed." Alfred dragged a hand through his wispy curls. Kitty opened her mouth to protest further, but he cut her off with a frantic shout after glancing back through the door. "Quickly now. They're coming."

Rosalind appeared at her side and with one accord they joined hands and rushed down the stairs. Lizzie led them along the narrow servant's passage and through the kitchen to a rickety door at the back. Behind this was a small, cold, stone-flagged room which housed their pickles, preserves and the big wooden barrels used for salting meat. As she ushered them into the claustrophobic space behind the barrels, Kitty heard the march of a dozen approaching footsteps and the low rumble of a carriage. She crouched down next to Rosalind and reached for her hand.

A door banged and Rosalind whimpered in fright, but Lizzie shushed her. "Not a word," she urged. "Stay as still and as quiet as you can. Please God they won't find you here." She clasped her hands together in a familiar, pious entreaty.

"What do you think is happening?" Rosalind whispered, as soon as the servant had retreated.

Her breath was warm against Kitty's shoulder. The darkness was absolute. Kitty imagined spiders scurrying around them, but this was no time for childish fears.

"I've no idea," she said firmly, closing her mind to desperate imaginings. The sisters were so close their foreheads were touching. "But we'd better do as he asks. Alfred would never do anything to harm us."

Rosalind silently nodded her agreement. Years earlier, Alfred had carried them on his back when their little legs had grown tired. He'd pulled them on a sledge made by his own hands and smiled at their gleeful screams when they coursed down the nearby hills covered in snow. He was as loyal and honourable as the day was long—and Kitty and Rosalind were just as devoted to him as he was to them. Just last year his arm had been cut by an axe, but with Kitty's careful nursing, the old man had pulled through.

For a moment all was quiet, but both of them tensed as they heard their father's unsteady voice booming through the downstairs rooms.

"Katherine, where are you?"

He was drunk, that much was obvious. His words slurred together. A door slammed shut with such force the whole house rattled.

"Katherine, come to me now."

Her heart jumped in her chest. Why would father single her out? Rosalind was his favourite, the double of the wife he'd loved. Kitty, he treated little better than a servant. But why would he shout for either of them at such an hour?

Rosalind gripped her hand and Kitty leaned closer to her sister, reassuring her that she would not reply. Footsteps overhead announced their father had entered their bedchamber. They heard him curse when he found the room empty.

"Damnation, Katherine. Show yourself."

He was angry now. An angry man who was accustomed to getting his way. A great clatter told them he had pulled over their woollen chest. Rosalind stifled a sob and Kitty wriggled until she could put an arm around her, hardly daring to breathe.

The footsteps retreated but sounds of smashing glass and splintering wood still reached them. Kitty put her hands over Rosalind's ears to protect her from it. Her father had returned from the tavern the worse for drink many times. Lately, his gambling habit had begun to spiral out of control, but thankfully they had little of value left for him to lose.

Would he come to the kitchen? Whatever did he want with her?

Owain never usually ventured into the servant's quarters. Despite his lowly birth, he held himself in too great esteem to trouble himself with the workings of the house that had been bought with coin grudgingly given by his wife's family.

Kitty placed her forehead on her knees and breathed deeply, calming her thoughts. Her father had drunk too much ale, that was all. Most likely he wanted her to attend to a tear in his tunic or to prepare him a broth. They would sit here and wait for him to fall asleep. In the morning, all would be back to normal.

All she could hear was the frantic hammering of her own heart. The silence stretched for so long it was almost unbearable. Then came the unmistakable sound of the bolts in the front door sliding shut. Kitty couldn't wait a second longer. She stood up, stretching her cramped limbs, and nudged open the pantry door. The kitchen was flooded with moonlight and both girls blinked until their eyes adjusted. Rosalind's clean white chemise was smeared with dust. Kitty would have to scrub it in the morning.

"Has he gone?" Rosalind whispered, her voice high and shaking.

Kitty paused. The house felt peaceful once again. "I think so."

She indicated for Rosalind to stay where she was and crept slowly forwards herself. They both jumped with fright as a looming male figure appeared in the kitchen doorway, but relaxed as Alfred spoke up.

"Come and see, both of you." His voice was bone weary.

They followed the tall man and his flickering candle back down the passage and into the parlour, wincing at the cold of the floor. Kitty stopped abruptly when she saw the drawers of the dresser standing open. The cabinet doors had been ripped from their hinges and flung across the room. Had father opened the small drawer and taken the jewels? Her body trembled with cold and worry, but Alfred was already ushering them towards the window.

"Stand here," he insisted. "And don't fret. Master or not, we won't be letting Owain back in. Not tonight. Not ever." He shook his head in disbelief. "Everything has changed."

Kitty looked at him searchingly, but Alfred refused to meet her eyes. He held back the heavy, mouldy-smelling drapes, motioning for her to squash in beside Rosalind, before letting them fall and encasing them once again in darkness.

She frowned at the scene before her. Their usually quiet country lane was thronged with men holding lanterns and torches. The men were quiet, although their faces were set and determined. In the midst of them all stood a great, black carriage.

"The Earl of Rossfarne," Rosalind yelped. "The carriage is his. Look at the coat of arms."

"The Earl of Rossfarne is dead," Kitty replied without think-ing, shuddering a little at the memory of the evil man who had plagued their small village with his debauched, barbaric ways since before she was born. Tales from Rossfarne Castle could make the most hardened fisherman blanche.

"Miss Rosalind is right." Alfred's voice came from behind the drape. "The new Earl of Rossfarne has now taken up residence in the castle."

"I didn't even know he had any family," Rosalind mused. "Still, I hope he's a kinder man than his father was."

Kitty frowned at her sister. Kindness didn't come into it. The Earl of Rossfarne had been a danger to all right-thinking men and women. Especially women.

Protected as she was, it was important Rosalind was aware of such things. But Alfred spoke before Kitty could put these complicated thoughts into words.

"Not his father, his uncle," he corrected her gently. "The new earl is his nephew. And he has not yet demonstrated any kindness or leniency," he added with a break in his voice.

"What's Father doing?" Rosalind interrupted.

Kitty pressed forward until her breath clouded the glass. Owain was walking unsteadily up their front path towards the carriage. He staggered from side to side, but not one of the watching men extended a hand to help him. As he reached the carriage, the door swung silently open and Kitty flinched backwards as a shaft of moonlight fell upon the outline of a tall, muscular man. She caught sight of a chiselled jawline and gleaming dark eyes, before Owain held up a small cloth bag with shaking arms and all the blood drained out of her body.

"Mother's jewels," she whispered, the awful reality hitting her.

"Your mother's jewels," Alfred repeated steadily. "He lost them in a game of dice."

"To the Earl of Rossfarne?" Kitty's mouth was as dry as sand.

"That isn't the worst of it," Alfred mumbled, but Kitty wasn't listening. What could be worse than the loss of their inheritance and Rosalind's best chance of a future?

Owain handed over the cloth bag and anger unfurled in Kitty's chest as the Earl slowly inspected its contents. What did a man as rich as he need with their mother's precious jewels? He would most likely forget he had them by morning.

An unfamiliar voice, low and masculine, spoke from the carriage. "Is that all of them?" His words were clear despite the distance. It was a voice of authority, accustomed to giving commands. A voice which sent shivers down her spine.

"Every last one, my lord." Owain ducked into a half bow and Kitty heard a great roaring sound in her ears, as if the sea was crashing upon the rocks in a mighty storm. Her vision blurred and she had to grip the drapes with white-knuckled fingers to stay upright. The next part of the conversation was lost to her, but she saw Owain hold his hands up as if in apology and the earl sniff contemptuously.

"By morning, I swear to it," her father was saying when she tuned back in.

The earl motioned him away. "No matter." The door swung

closed and after a second, the carriage rolled back down the lane.

"What did he mean?" Rosalind asked breathlessly.

Kitty's head was pounding so much she feared she might fall over. "We've lost the jewels," she croaked. It was all she could think of.

"The men are forming a circle around Father." Her sister wriggled free of the heavy drape, pulling it away from Kitty in the process, but there was no cause for secrecy now. "Alfred, what's happening?" Rosalind persisted.

"Owain is being escorted out of Rossfarne." Alfred folded his arms across his once muscular chest, shifting from one foot to another with uncharacteristic nerves. "If he goes peacefully, he won't be harmed."

Kitty watched dully as the crowd of men gathered behind her father, their lanterns bobbing in the darkness. Slowly but surely, they urged him forwards, away from his house and his daughters and anyone he could harm further. Not a word was spoken, not even by Owain. Maybe even he knew that this time he had gone too far?

"Father's really going," Rosalind said. Her voice was faint with disbelief and Kitty reached for her hand, unable to offer any other form of reassurance.

The glow of yellow light from the assembled lanterns grew dim and distant. The carriage had long disappeared out of sight and the events of the night felt unreal, like a bad dream. Like a cool glass of water might clear their heads and make it all go away. But Kitty knew this was a dream they would never wake up from.

Silence enveloped them. Rosalind stood as if frozen and Alfred waited, his head bowed respectfully.

Kitty allowed her knees to buckle. She slid down the wall until she was sitting on the hard wooden floor. Coldness settled into her bones as the last of her hope drained away.

"Father's really gone," she confirmed, hardly caring of the fact. "And worst of all, so have the jewels."

Chapter Two

KITTY AWOKE WITH the cock's crow, weary but resolute. The morning sun peeked between the shutters, shining brightly enough to strengthen her newly formed convictions.

She would not allow their father's recklessness to define them anymore. The menfolk of Rossfarne had shown Owain from the village. Now it was Kitty's turn to step up.

Rosalind slept on beside her, her rosebud lips slightly parted and her golden hair streaming across the thin blanket. Kitty moved slowly, anxious to prolong her sister's repose after such an eventful evening. The wooden floor creaked as she put her weight upon it, so she crossed the room on tiptoe, pausing only to scoop up Rosalind's shawl and drape it around her own shoulders.

She would not dress as usual, not yet. Her chores beckoned but just for once, thought claimed precedence over action.

Evidence of Owain's rampage was everywhere. An atmosphere of devastation hung over Shoreston Manor, with doors hanging off their hinges, belongings carelessly scattered and furniture overturned. Kitty was a stickler for tidiness and couldn't bear to see so much as a chair out of place, but this morning she closed her mind to the chaos and walked with calm determination down the stairs towards the back kitchen door. The stone-flagged floor was cold against her bare feet but her wooden pattens were nowhere to be seen. Sighing, she slipped back the bolt and stepped out into the fresh morning. Immediately, she felt better. She could breathe more easily and some of the worry weighing on her shoulders abated. She tilted her face up towards the sun and closed her eyes, basking like a cat on a hot day.

Standing like this, she could almost believe that her plans, formed during an anxious night, had some small chance of success. Although the idea still made her stomach churn.

Could she really journey to the castle and converse with an earl?

She had to try, no matter what.

The blackbird had already begun the morning chorus. Kitty breathed deeply and let the lilting melody wash over her. If she concentrated, she could hear the roar of the sea from beyond the fields. A faint tang of salt clung to her lips and a gentle breeze caressed her tired limbs.

Yes, she had to try.

There was nothing to ponder, not really. She couldn't stand back and do nothing. Not when Rosalind's only chance of a bright future hung on the Answick jewels. Without them she would have no dowry, and no chance of a good marriage. Kitty didn't have to swing her gaze to the wattle-and-daub manor behind her to know that the roof was sagging. With their mother's meagre inheritance all but spent, there was no coin to keep up repairs to the house. The awful truth was that the Alden sisters could not live on at Shoreston for many more years, eking out an existence between a fertile kitchen garden, a clutch of chickens and the charity of the townsfolk.

Charity. Kitty's lip curled in disgust. How she hated that word.

She had already accepted more charity from the people of Rossfarne than was proper or right. She knew many of the locals had written off Owain's gambling debts in deference to the wellbeing of his daughters. It was some time since either Lizzie or Alfred had received the coin they were due, and she recognized pity in the gazes of the fishing families as she browsed their market stalls every Tuesday. Since her mother's death, she was no longer beheld as the daughter of Isabella of Answick. Instead, she was the daughter of Owain the drunkard; the fisherman who hadn't stepped on a fishing boat since his wedding day.

Worst of all were their weekly trips to chapel. The first pew was always reserved for the Aldens, even though the most genteel family in the village was now, indisputably, the Erkines—farmers who owned land at the other side of the river. Mrs. Erkine had been a regular caller at Shoreston when Mother was alive. She would sit in the parlour and converse with Isabella, bouncing a chubby toddler on her knee. Now, every Sunday, the same kindly woman sat diagonally behind Kitty casting sympathetic glances at her shabby dress and faded bonnet.

Kitty still tried to keep up appearances, for Rosalind's sake, but with each passing year it became harder.

She closed her eyes. Enough. She would take the necessary action. Even though the prospect filled her with dread.

She walked further into the garden, ignoring the dew that clung to the hem of her chemise and enjoying the springy feel of the early summer grass. The ground was soft and muddy from recent rain. She would have to wash her feet before setting off for the castle, although that was the least of it. She would also have to put on her best dress and pin her hair and somehow find the right words to further her cause with a man she didn't know and already feared. But she would willingly do all this and more for Rosalind.

Her heart beat faster as she remembered the man in the carriage, his chiselled jawline and low, authoritative voice. She would have to lay claim to her mother's name, which meant remembering how to be a lady, how to speak, how to stand and how to address an earl.

She paused at the edge of the pasture where the ground began its downward journey towards the sheer cliffs and the sparkling sea. She shaded her eyes and gazed towards the horizon. On a clear day like today, the dark battlements of Rossfarne Castle sprang out sharply against the endless blue backdrop. Two hundred years earlier, the old Earl of Rossfarne had insisted on building his home on a small island, separated from the mainland by a thin strip of seawater. When the tide was out, two thousand paces would take you from Rossfarne Cove to the castle gatehouse, although few folk from hereabouts would elect to.

People who left for the castle didn't always come back.

Walking meant there was a chance of being cut off by the tide. It would be safer to go by boat, Kitty mused, but her father's boat was no longer seaworthy. She would have to walk. Although the destination was as perilous as the journey towards it.

"What are you doing out here, Miss Katherine?"

Jolted from her thoughts, Kitty turned to find Lizzie standing beside a pair of blossom-filled apple trees.

"I am judging the tides," she replied, as steadily as she could.

"For what purpose?" The old woman frowned. Her servant's cap was starched and neat, but her watery blue eyes were still creased with tiredness.

Kitty held her gaze. "This morning I will walk over to Rossfarne Castle."

"No," Lizzie cried, dropping her pail of chicken feed in distress. "You mustn't do such a thing."

"I must." Kitty was emphatic. "I will speak to the earl and recover Mother's jewels." Despite her iron will, her voice shook and betrayed her nerves. She looked away from Lizzie towards the low-slung house she'd always known as home.

"Glory be, do you think that monster is just going to hand them over to you if you ask him nicely?" Lizzie shook her head in disbelief as she bent to scoop up the spilled corn.

Kitty swallowed. "We don't know that he's a monster. We shouldn't judge him by his uncle's behaviour."

"We have evidence enough," Lizzie began, but then she stopped short. She opened her mouth and closed it again, as if there was something she wanted to say but she couldn't find the words.

"It doesn't matter anyway." Kitty folded her arms against a sudden breeze. "Without the jewels, Rosalind has no hope of a good marriage." She shrugged. "I have to try, Lizzie."

The servant's gaze softened. "I know you'd give your last breath to help your sister, but you don't have to take on the evils of the world all by yourself." She ploughed on before Kitty could interrupt. "Trust the Lord above and the good folk of Rossfarne." She stepped forward and placed one gnarled hand on Kitty's shoulder as the other clutched her crucifix. "We'll see you right."

More charity, which she didn't want to accept. Kitty took a deep breath and placed her hand over Lizzie's. "The people here have already been too kind, given us too much." She squeezed her fingers. "I'm young and strong, Lizzie. When the time comes, I can work in the farms or in the fields and do whatever it takes. This pretence at gentility is for Rosalind's sake, to better her prospects for a good marriage. You know that. She deserves the future she would have had if Mother hadn't passed away." She broke her gaze, unable to bear the sympathy flashing in Lizzie's eyes. "And to that end, I will go to Rossfarne Castle and ask for our jewels to be returned. The worst he can do is say no." She smiled to hide her fears.

Lizzie looked anguished. Her healthy cheeks were pale and her eyes wild. "Oh, Miss Katherine, he'll do far worse than that once he's got you inside that castle."

"I'm going, Lizzie." Kitty made her voice calm and resolute. "Just as soon as the tides allow it."

BARELY AN HOUR later she had laced up her cleanest kirtle, persuaded her wilful red hair to stay pinned neatly beneath her hood, and trooped down the stairs to the front hall where her sister and Lizzie waited with sombre faces. Rosalind held up a small oval looking glass so she could see the effect.

"You look lovely, Kitty," her sister said, "but you don't have to do this. I don't need Mother's jewels for a dowry. I want to marry for love."

Kitty cupped Rosalind's smooth cheek with her own rough hand. "That isn't how it works. I wish it was."

"Then I'll just stay here for the rest of my life with you and Lizzie."

Kitty wanted to say they wouldn't be able to stay in this big house for many years longer, certainly not for the rest of their lives. The coin chests were almost empty, and the roof was letting in damp. But she pressed her lips together and said nothing. There was no need to cause extra alarm on a day like today. She gazed at her reflection in the oval glass, surprised at the difference a tidy dress could make. The young woman looking back at her could be on her way to meet friends in the marketplace. She looked like someone accustomed to laughter and ease and fun. Not a drudge with a prematurely aching back and no prospects.

Kitty motioned for Rosalind to put the looking glass away. Her reflection made her miserable.

Alfred walked in from the kitchen and dropped the heavy load of firewood he was carrying when he caught sight of Kitty.

"You're never going to him?" he said.

Kitty turned in surprise. It was unlike Alfred to drop anything and even further out of character for him to question her decisions.

"I'm walking to Rossfarne Castle while the tide is out, and there isn't anything you can say to change my mind," she said sharply, hoping to deter any debate.

"But dressed like that." He gestured to her snugly fitting kirtle. "You'd be better off in your apron with smuts on your face."

Kitty's eyebrows shot upwards. Had the events of last night turned Alfred's mind?

He acknowledged her bewilderment and turned to Lizzie with a frown. "You haven't told her, have you?"

Lizzie wrung her hands in her apron. "Lord help me, I haven't found the words," she wailed, sinking down into a hard wooden chair beside Rosalind.

"What words?" Kitty interrupted, her pulse beginning to pound. "What haven't you told me?"

The two servants glared at one another in a silent battle of wills and Kitty held her breath. What fresh bad news awaited them?

"She needs to know," Alfred barked, his hands on his hips.

Kitty bit her lip to prevent herself crying out in frustration.

"Mercy, I can't do it," Lizzie sobbed into her clean apron.

Alfred sighed and rubbed his eyes. "Miss Katherine. The truth is, the jewels aren't the only thing your father gambled with last night."

Kitty laughed. She couldn't help it. "We hardly have anything else."

He avoided her gaze and didn't smile back. "It was a high stakes game. Just Owain and the earl left in. When your father proposed his jewels, the earl said he couldn't vouch for their quality." The manservant ran out of words and fell silent.

"And?" Kitty prompted. Her stomach was a tangle of anxiety but she didn't allow a trace of it to show in her voice.

"And your father suggested his eldest daughter in addition to the jewels," Alfred said in a rush.

At first the words made no sense but as the meaning sank in, she knew the hottest, deepest flush of embarrassment she had ever experienced. Heat rose through her tightly strung bodice to sting her cheeks. "You don't mean..." she trailed off. Beside her, Rosalind's eyes opened wide.

"I'm afraid so." Alfred looked anywhere but at her. "Your father lost the game. Which means that you belong to the Earl of Rossfarne."

Bile rose in her throat. Her stomach heaved and she pushed past her sister, desperate to be outside. Once through the back door she took great lungfuls of fresh air, but the tang of the sea and the gentle breeze didn't calm her as it had earlier. She might never be calm again. Deep, debilitating shame had taken root inside her heart.

She belonged to the Earl of Rossfarne.

She knew what that meant. It meant he could do as he pleased with her, in all ways. Although she wasn't too sure what those ways might be. Her mother had died before she could explain the mysteries of the marriage bed, leaving Kitty to puzzle things out for herself. But she knew that years ago, when she was still a child, young women from Rossfarne had been lured to the castle by the old earl and most of them were never seen in the village again. Worse, they were spoken of with derision, as if by entering the castle gates they had abandoned all honour and standing.

But she'd heard whispered tales that were even more awful than that. The old earl's insistence on the right of Prima Nocta, the first night with any bride on his lands. The unexplained mystery of a high tower room. Women shamed, jumping off the harbour wall to avoid a life of torment.

Why had she thought that the new earl would behave differently?

Kitty couldn't help herself—she began to tremble so violently her teeth chattered together.

Rosalind crept up beside her and slipped a cool hand into hers. "You don't have to go. We could run away." The wind caught hold of her shawl and it streamed out behind her.

Kitty looked down, shaking her head. "You're not running anywhere," she replied woodenly. Her intentions had been so clear just moments earlier, but now it was as if a fog had settled over her brain.

"Don't ruin your life just for me." Rosalind spoke with more passion than Kitty had ever heard from her before.

Kitty looked at her in surprise, noting the pink of her cheeks and the painful jutting of her shoulder blades. "It's too late for that. Don't you see? My life is already ruined." The words came blurting out before she could stop them.

Rosalind tossed back her golden hair which she'd pinned back behind her ears. "It doesn't have to be."

Kitty fought an urge to pull her hand away from her sister's. There was so much about the world that Rosalind simply didn't understand.

"You still have choices," her sister added pleadingly.

"Do I?" She raised her eyebrows. It didn't feel like she had choices. But all the same, Rosalind's pronouncement had sparked the beginnings of an idea.

"I heard what you said to Lizzie this morning." Rosalind traced circles with her bare toes in the damp grass.

"You followed me out here?" Despite everything else going on, Kitty was still cross that Rosalind had risen early after such a restless night.

"Why shouldn't I? You treat me like a child but I'll be sixteen soon."

"Not soon, Rosalind. Your sixteenth birthday falls on Michaelmas Eve."

Rosalind made an impatient gesture. "You told Lizzie that you could find work anywhere, in the fields or on a farm. And it's true. You could do anything. We could go anywhere." She leaned forward to pluck a sprig of fresh mint and the pungent scent filled the air.

Kitty stared at her sister, her mind racing. "What did you say?"

Rosalind frowned back, crumpling the mint between her fingers. "What do you mean?"

"Just now. What did you say just now?" Kitty clutched her skirts to control her mounting excitement.

"That you could do anything." Rosalind shrugged. "You don't need me to tell you that."

"I could find work as a maid or servant." Kitty tried out the words and found she didn't hate them.

"If you wanted. But you shouldn't have to. You're a direct

descendent of the Duke of Answick." Rosalind's voice grew loud and high.

Kitty held up a hand to stop her. "Would you say I could find work as a serving maid here in Rossfarne?" She held her breath. The plan forming before her eyes was bold and daring, but was it workable?

"Of course." Rosalind screwed up her pretty face. "Although it's unlikely anyone in the village would have enough coin put by to hire a maid. And they probably wouldn't hire you out of respect for Mother." She unclenched her fingers and let the crumpled mint fall to the ground. A small garden bird hopped forward to inspect this surprising offering, then flew off into the apple tree.

Kitty folded her arms tightly across her chest, conscious of her restrictive clothing. On the distant horizon she could just make out the battlements of Rossfarne Castle. A gull cried mournfully overhead, spurring her towards a decision.

"I imagine the Earl of Rossfarne has plenty of coin," she said.

Her sister looked up sharply, her blue eyes squinting against the weak sunlight. "You can't mean what I think you mean."

"Why not?" Kitty swallowed. "It's a way out of this." She paused, still testing out the idea in her head. "I can't go to the castle and ask for the jewels to be returned, not now that I know what Father did. But I can go to the castle in disguise, find the jewels and bring them back to you."

"No." Rosalind shook her head so vigorously her hair came unpinned. "It's far too dangerous."

"I'd be as good a servant as anyone." Kitty inspected her square nails and scuffed knuckles, fighting down a ripple of anxiety. "And the new earl has only just come to Rossfarne, so it's likely his household is not yet complete," she thought aloud.

"You'll be recognised." Rosalind grasped at the trunk of the apple tree, as if she could no longer support her own weight.

"No, I won't." Kitty had already thought of this. "No one from the village works at the castle. The old earl brought all his servants from over the county border. And they scarcely ever come across to the mainland."

"True enough mayhap, but it's still a terrible idea. The earl will be looking for you." Rosalind faltered and her cheeks flushed even pinker than before.

Kitty spoke quickly to cover her discomfort. "I'll give a false name. He has no idea what I look like." She lifted her chin defiantly. "Who knows, he may have even forgotten about Father's wager." She bit her lip as a new wave of embarrassment washed over her. "But we know he definitely has the jewels. And we need them back."

"But your hair," Rosalind blurted out, her eyes open wide in a mute appeal for Kitty to see sense.

Her sister's words gave her a moment's pause. She couldn't deny that her tumbling locks of red hair would give her away as her father's daughter to anyone who had laid eyes upon him. They shared the exact shade of burning copper, rarely seen on these shores. And the resemblance didn't stop there. She had also inherited his height, his flashing sea-green eyes and his infamous stubbornness.

But despite all that, she wasn't about to turn back now.

"I shall keep my head covered," she promised. "Besides, I won't be there long enough for anyone to start caring who I am or where I come from."

KITTY HELD BACK her tears until she had hugged her sister goodbye and was striding across the sandy beach in a direct line towards the thin causeway. A slight breeze buffeted back the floppy straw hat she had borrowed from Lizzie. She was obliged to use one hand to hold it in place while the other clutched at the skirts of her rough woollen servant's dress. With every step she took away from Shoreston, she lost a little of her courage. Twice she nearly turned back, but the memory of Rosalind's face kept her going.

A group of small children were playing on the sands, searching for shells and daring one another to run into the waves. Their happy shrieks put her in mind of her sister as a carefree young girl and she walked on with renewed purpose. Luckily no one was about to witness her journey to the Isle of Rossfarne. If anyone had tried to stop her—or worse, recognised her—she would have wilted to the ground with shame. Alfred's words still echoed through her mind.

You belong to the Earl of Rossfarne.

What would the earl have done to her if Alfred hadn't run back from the alehouse and warned them to hide?

She shuddered so violently her pattens slipped on the wet stones and she very nearly fell. Once again, she looked towards home with a lump in her throat. It wasn't too late to turn back.

She breathed deeply to quell her rising panic, but the grief in her heart refused to be denied. All of the pain and upset of the past evening reared up inside her. Father's anger, Rosalind's fear, Lizzie's helpless worrying. Her fingers clutched at her skirts as she remembered Alfred's staunch bravery, especially when he had drawn the bolt against the master of the house. Such kindness and love she had known, and now she was walking away from it, to the castle of a monster.

She closed her eyes. These thoughts would get her nowhere. She was like an overtired youngster, growing more hysterical by the minute. She must think and act more positively, like a young woman taking steps to secure her family's future. To secure Rosalind's future.

Mother's jewels were beautiful. A necklace of gleaming sapphires, bluer than a summer sky, a hair pin tipped with pearl and an oval amber brooch. But the piece they prized above the rest was a cross-shaped pendant embedded with blood-red rubies. Mother used to hold it up to Kitty's neck and laugh at the similarities in shade and colour between the precious stones and her daughter's hair.

"This one is for you, Kitty," she'd promised. "Your dowry."

Kitty had believed her. The future had been bright and magical then. But within five years of her mother's death, she'd hidden the jewels inside the dresser and determined they should all be destined for Rosalind's dowry. Every last one. Even the ruby pendant. By then, the funds inside the big coin chests in the basement were running low. Father had gambled away the silver which mother had painstakingly saved. And the Duke of Answick was no longer prepared to support their family, now that his niece was dead.

It was down to her. She had no one else to rely on.

Kitty straightened her back and shaded her eyes from the bright late-morning sunshine. Without meaning to, her gaze focused on the battlements of Rossfarne Castle, which reared out of the haze like some mythical creature of the deep. Her heart began to beat wildly once again, but instead of submitting to her emotions, Kitty refused to break her gaze.

It was but a castle. A stone dwelling, like any other. What harm could a mere building cause her?

Immediately, a hundred stories and warnings flashed before her eyes, but Kitty batted them away. Those stories all pertained to the old earl, who was dead and gone. She wouldn't let fear of a man no longer living keep her from doing what needed to be done.

She would not be led by fear.

Feeling stronger, she took a deep lungful of fresh, salty air. Her mother may have been Lady Isabella of Answick, but her father was a fisherman. She came from a long line of healthy, hearty peasants who had prospered on these shores. And she wasn't like those poor girls who had been lured to the castle in times gone by. She was prepared. She was on her guard. If the Earl of Rossfarne thought he could best her, he would have a fight on his hands.

As if simply thinking his name had conjured him up, the

outline of a tall, muscular man astride a powerful horse came into view. She gasped out loud, dropping her skirts and putting her hands to her heart in fear that it may jump outside her chest. He was there, before her. The Earl of Rossfarne. It could only be him. None other hereabouts could have his bearing, his brooding presence, his looming authority which radiated across the shallow sea.

Her pulse slowed. She must have fallen victim to some trick of the hazy light, for the man on the horse was not before her. He was at the other end of the causeway, standing as still as if he had been hewn from rock.

Surveying his estate. Surveying what was his.

Surveying her?

Her stomach heaved as if she might be sick, yet still she couldn't take her eyes from the apparition. She was drawn to him, despite all she knew. He looked so masterful, full of power, easily dominating the heavy warhorse he sat astride. She imagined the set of his shoulders, his powerful arms, the muscles in his calves, gripping the warm flesh of the horse.

Her face flushed and she stumbled back a few paces. Where had that notion come from? Kitty was not accustomed to picturing men's calves nor any other part of them. It was the lurid tales of the old earl that had got into her head. Tales she must banish if she had any hope of succeeding in her quest.

For a moment she once again considered flight. To continue meant walking towards the terrifying figure at the other end of the causeway. Meant serving him, in his castle of ill repute.

Kitty lifted her chin, rammed her straw hat more firmly down on her head and strode onto the damp stones of the causeway. She would reclaim her family jewels and take them home for her sister. She would succeed, for she had no other choice.

Chapter Three

GUY SAT ASTRIDE his charger and watched from the cliffs as the swirling sea gradually retreated from the mainland, exposing the narrow causeway linking his home to the fishing village of Rossfarne.

He had never set foot in these parts until six days prior, but what he found had pleased him for it was a wild, beautiful landscape and the rhythmic crashing of the tides eased the knot of tension inside him. In the narrow gullies on the far side of the castle, the waves sounded as loud as thunder, like an external manifestation of his own anger and pain. If he must endure several months of enforced inactivity, he would choose to endure them here, where the physical barrier of the sea and the social barrier of his uncle's grievous reputation combined to keep prying eyes away.

Prying eyes and thieving fingers, keen to exploit his temporary vulnerability.

As if sensing his master's surge of emotion, the horse beneath him shifted. Guy sat deeper in the saddle and wrapped his long legs around the horse's warm belly to steady himself. He must use balance and intuition until his useless left arm had healed.

The surgeon had told him to rest completely. But Guy was a knight, used to physical extremes and constant action. He lived for the adrenaline rush of galloping across a battlefield, sword in hand. He could no more lay in bed all day than he could dance a jig.

At least his sword arm was unharmed.

The tide had drawn back. It was time to leave. Guy had no real urge to explore the mainland and risk coming into contact with villagers or farming folk, but the claustrophobic confines of the island were already plaguing him. More importantly, he had a job to do. One that he would be pleased to put behind him.

He had left the castle unannounced, dressed plainly in a linen shirt and a soft cap. With any luck, no one would recognise him. It was only the coat of arms on his carriage that had given him away at the tavern last night.

Last night. How he regretted the impulse that had propelled him into a misjudged game of dice in a grubby alehouse. He had gone in search of mild distraction and instead, had borne witness to the depravity of the human soul. The evening had sickened him.

He nudged his horse forwards, adjusting in the saddle as the long strides threatened to unseat him. A familiar surge of pain travelled from his wrist to his shoulder, and he held his body tense until it passed. Pain was good. Pain meant his arm was not fully dead and that there was hope it might recover. And then, one day, he could re-join his band of brothers on the battlefield.

Although the first thing Guy would do was track down the no-good thief who had stolen his bag of coin while he lay helpless on a hospital bed. Coin that had been hard-earned in battle against the Scots.

His muscles twitched at the memory and the powerful horse broke into a trot. Guy clenched his teeth and drew back on the reins with his remaining good hand. He must keep his emotions better under control. In all his years fighting under King Edward, he had never shown weakness. His horses could always trust him to remain calm in the face of chaos.

He turned in the saddle to look back at Rossfarne Castle. Two fortified towers reared towards the sky while roiling waves crashed continuously against the outer wall. His eye travelled over the crenelated stonework looking out for tell-tale cracks, but it all appeared sound. The castle lacked luxury, but it was weatherproof. Only the gatehouse, standing to the east of the bailey, needed attention. The marshal had told him of a ferocious winter storm that sent a tree crashing straight through the roof. If Guy still had his bag of silver, he could have set about ordering repairs right away.

The horse trotted forwards, ears pricked, easily eating up the ground. Guy found his face breaking into an unexpected smile. He'd feared any pace faster than a walk would unsteady him, but so long as he ignored the jolting pain in his shoulder, no one would ever guess that one side of his body had been slashed right through to the bone. The jagged scar ran from his navel, over his ribs to his shoulder blade. Guy inspected it every morning when he dressed. Not through vanity, but to ensure it continued to heal. He was counting the days until he could return to the life he loved in service of the king.

Maybe that day was closer than he dared to dream? Guy scanned the causeway as it stretched out before him. A straight path featuring just one bend. For as far as he could see, it was empty. Of course it would be. No one ever came here. The villagers lived in fear of the notorious Earl of Rossfarne. Guy had long ago disowned his family and in so doing, shrugged off the ghosts of his scarred upbringing. He believed in action, not sentiment—and he certainly had little sentiment for the terrifying old man who he had visited only once as a child. But while he was here, he intended to exploit his uncle's dark reputation. It would ensure his days passed without the scourge of uninvited visitors, but more importantly, it would keep thieves and opportunists away.

How he hated his current state of weakness.

With no one ahead of him and the ground level, it was the perfect time to urge his horse into a canter. To see how far he was from full fitness.

The three-beat staccato rhythm brought a new surge of discomfort. A nagging ache encircled his torso and hot sparks of pain shot down his ruined arm. Guy gritted his teeth, but he was not a man to admit defeat. Wincing with effort, he transferred the reins into his feeble left hand, all the while keeping contact with the horse through his muscular calves. Reins secure, albeit only just, he lunged out with his sword hand, mimicking a sword thrust in battle. Sweat sprang out on his brow, but he had done it. Just.

Light-headed with pain and exultation, Guy sat up straighter in the saddle and drew back steadily on the reins. That was when he saw her. A young woman, tall and curvaceous, with a purposeful stride and a face that filled with fear when she saw the horse careering towards her.

"Whoa," Guy instructed, his voice calm and deep. But he had not yet taken the reins back into his good hand and the horse, panicked at the insufficient contact with his master, veered sharply to the left.

The sudden movement knocked Guy off balance. For a long moment he hung precariously to one side, but his years in the saddle had given him an instinctive feel for a horse's movements. He righted himself and grasped the slack reins, pulling the horse up short. At the same time, the girl darted forwards, pale hands outstretched for the bridle.

What madness was this?

Startled again, the horse reared, front legs thrashing at the air. Guy clung on, his face twisted in a grimace of pain.

"Steady there, steady," urged the girl. Her straw hat fluttered to the ground releasing a surprising wave of hair the colour of autumn leaves.

The horse snorted and landed heavily. The jolt sent pulses of pure anguish shooting up Guy's wrist. His shoulder was on fire and his back was damp with sweat.

"What in heaven's name are you doing?" he demanded. His voice was low and calm because of the horse, but he imbued the words with all the authority of his newly acquired rank.

He expected her to flee, but instead she met the full force of his gaze. Her eyes were like a still sea on a summer's day. Her chin tilted upwards in a small gesture of self-assertion he recognised from his own younger days. A small part of him noted that this was a woman of courage.

"I am steadying your horse," she replied. Her voice was sweet and clear, not coarse like he'd expected. She may be clothed in a poor woollen dress, but she spoke like a noblewoman.

"My horse is no concern of yours." The force behind his words lessened as he gazed down at her honest face and captivating green eyes. She was tall, unusually so. He estimated she stood just a half head shorter than he.

Undaunted, she reached out once again and stroked the snorting, foam-flecked creature. Instead of veering away, the horse exhaled with something like relief and dropped his head. Guy sensed the moment that all the fright and flight went out of the animal and simultaneously experienced something similar himself. He felt the warmth of the sun on his face, heard the calling of the gulls overhead and the gentle breaking of the waves behind them.

What was happening to him? Witchcraft?

"Do you know who I am?" he demanded, straightening up.

Immediately she sank into a surprisingly graceful obeisance. "I believe I do, my lord."

She knew who he was, yet she did not run in fear. Was this bravery or foolishness? Despite his reluctance for human contact, he was intrigued.

"What business do you have on my land?" His voice was softer now.

She swallowed, betraying her fears. "I am come looking for work." Her eyes darted to the ground and rested on her fallen hat.

He was surprised. His household staff was small. The marshal had explained that few locals were willing to come there. He'd suggested it was due to the isolation of the island, the fierce storms, the separation from the mainland. Guy knew that none of these things would dissuade the villagers from steady employment and regular coin. The truth was, the people of Rossfarne would rather face starvation than seek work from his uncle.

He looked at her closely. She had no possessions and only a shabby woollen dress to protect her from the elements. A dress which clung tightly to the womanly curves of her body.

"Have you travelled far?" He averted his eyes from her figure with effort, fixing them instead on her heart-shaped face.

"Oh yes," she nodded eagerly. Mayhap too eagerly. "For many nights now."

It was a lie. This woman had bathed recently. He could smell the lemony freshness of her hair. And despite its poor quality, her dress was neat. He did not believe she had been sleeping rough in the fields.

Why the deception? Was she come to do him harm? His mouth twitched upwards. He'd faced mighty warriors on the battlefield and would enjoy any challenge issued from a green-eyed maid with a steely backbone.

If only the foolish man he'd faced last night had shown half her character.

The memory of his morning's errand made his face harden and suddenly the spell that had been woven silently between them fell away, like a tide withdrawing from the beach.

What care did he have for the running of a household he would not be staying in long?

"You are welcome to enquire with the marshal," he said dismissively.

"Thank you, my lord." This time her obeisance was low and deep, and it unlocked something inside him.

Was she a noblewoman fallen on hard times? Should he extend the hand of chivalry? But if that were so, why would she tell him an untruth? Perhaps she was the bastard child of his uncle, come looking for some inheritance?

Well, let her try.

With a brusque nod, he urged his horse on, away from the bewitching young woman and her bewildering tale. The marshal would no doubt offer her employment. She would not starve. And her presence at the castle might enliven his long, dull days of convalescence. Something about her called to him, like a distant memory which could not be fully recalled; the seductive sway of her red-gold hair, her calm air of confidence.

He shook the notion away. It had been too long since he'd known the pleasures of female flesh. And he had higher priorities than bedding a serving girl, no matter how sparkling her eyes. His body must heal so that he could return to duty on the battlefield.

But before that, he had a far less pleasant undertaking.

HE SLOWED HIS horse to a walk as they approached Shoreston Manor. His left arm was grieving him terribly now and he kept it tucked close to his body. He had done too much, pushed himself too hard. But he must return the cloth bag of jewels to the family of the drunkard before he could turn back to the castle.

He shouldn't have taken them in the first place. But he had won them fair and square in a roll of the dice witnessed by more than a dozen villagers. Guy had been dumbstruck when the red-faced, overweight man before him had raised the stakes in what had been a harmless game, giving name to the Answick jewels.

He knew of the Duke of Answick and dimly remembered the tale of a distant cousin wedding far beneath her, against the wishes of her ancient family. He'd gazed down at the small table, pungent and sticky with spilled ale, and sensed a chance for him to recoup what he had lost. The bulging bag of silver that he'd needed for tithes to the king as well as repairs to the castle. He should have turned away, but the thrill of competition ran hot in his blood. He'd never been able to back down from a challenge.

Though was it likely that here, in a grubby alehouse in a small fishing village, he would recover an equivalent fortune to that which had been stolen from him? Instead of drinking down his ale and bidding farewell to the gamblers gathered around him, he had leaned back in his hard wooden chair and declared that the so-called Answick jewels were not enough.

"What do I know of their quality?" he'd demanded, expecting the addition of livestock or more coin.

When the drunkard had named his eldest daughter, Guy had been seized with cold disgust.

As soon as the first rays of morning sunlight had woken him from a troubled, uncomfortable sleep, he'd known he must return the jewels. Thank heavens he didn't have to return a daughter in the bargain. A daughter whose life could have been marred forever by the greed of her father.

He patted the leather saddlebag beside him inside which he had hidden the Answick jewels. Last night, they had sparkled inside the darkness of his carriage, surprising him with their beauty. With their undoubted authenticity. He'd hoped for trinkets of some little value, instead he was holding the means to elevate the life of the girl who now, by rights, belonged to him. He couldn't keep them in good conscience. Each time he looked at them he would be reminded of the evening in the tavern and the awful depravity of the man known as Owain the drunkard.

Although he'd seen it only by moonlight, the winding country lane was familiar, as was the approach to Shoreston Manor. He urged his horse into a trot once more, accepting the pain in return for getting this over with quickly. He turned into the driveway, noting the weeds and the tumbled down boundary wall. The house had once been welcoming, he could see it in the set of the mullioned windows and the sweeping steps up to the front door, but now it was rundown and neglected. Just one piece of the jewellery in this bag would pay for a new roof and more. How had the jewels remained unsold?

It was no concern of his. His jaw tightened as a clucking chicken scurried away from the horse's hooves. He would hand over the bag and get out of here as quickly as he could. He only hoped Owain had sense enough to stay out of his way.

But no servant opened the door on his approach. The house stood silent and closed off to the world. He turned in the saddle to survey the farm buildings. No one was around. Shoreston Manor was apparently deserted.

"Hello," he shouted, his voice gruff and loud.

No response, save the scratching and clucking of the chickens.

His mouth curled with disgust at a wasted journey. Could he leave the jewels somewhere they might be found? It was tempting to get them off his hands and put the whole incident behind him. But he already knew he couldn't. He must ensure they passed directly to Owain's daughters, and he knew better than anyone how thieves lurked around every corner.

With a low growl of displeasure, he spun the horse around and set off for the causeway at a gallop. The speed pained his body but set his mind free. He was one with the horse, one with the wind, one with the foaming sea, which was already closing over the far edges of the causeway as they clattered home. He had misjudged the tides and how little time they allowed him. No wonder his uncle had kept a carriage and horses on the mainland.

His horse was battle fit and unfazed by their journey, but Guy's legs were weak as he dismounted and handed over his reins to a stable boy. His left arm was a long streak of pain and his ribs ached as if the enemy sword had cut them afresh. Had his exertions opened his scar? He cursed his own foolishness and then ground his teeth in frustration at his ongoing physical failings.

Must he live in this cursed place like an invalid? To do so was against his very nature.

"Welcome back, my lord," the marshal nodded from the gatehouse.

Guy grunted a reply. He wanted only to retire to his solar and close the door. To spend another day with nothing but his pain for company.

Irritation surged inside him that his life had narrowed so drastically. Just weeks earlier, he had been a trusted knight of the king. Now he couldn't even gallop a few paces without whimpering like a babe. The dark battlements of the castle increased his displeasure. He walked through the courtyard as if he were about to enter a prison.

A prison of his uncle's making. This castle had known neither laughter nor joy in many years. A dour misery had seeped into the very walls, infecting the servants and even the furnishings. It reminded him of the wretched childhood he'd worked so hard to escape. Phantoms that he'd banished long ago were rising within him, threatening everything.

Suddenly his need for human contact became overwhelming. He pivoted on his heel and marched back to the marshal.

"Did a young woman come here today looking for work?" he demanded.

"Yes, my lord. I sent her to Cook. She always has need of extra help."

"What was her name?"

The marshal thought for a moment. He was a small man with a weathered face. "'Twas Kitty, I believe."

"Kitty." Guy turned the name over in his mind. He recalled her tumbling curls, the colour of autumn leaves. Her sea-green eyes. The hypnotic sway of her hips. He pressed his lips together and tasted salt from the sea. "I look forward to seeing more of her." He paused. "Mayhap have the girl bring luncheon to my solar, if Cook can spare her from the kitchen."

Chapter Four

THE CASTLE KITCHEN was filled with steam from the big pot on the stove. Red-faced and perspiring, Kitty leaned over and stirred the thick vegetable broth, closing her eyes and relishing the delicious smell that rose up to meet her.

"Keep on until it boils," shouted Cook, who was rolling pastry on a big stone table at the other end of the room. She was a small woman with a sharp face, but her nut-brown eyes revealed a kind nature and Kitty had taken to her instantly. "Then you can go on up and tidy his lordship's bedchamber while Thomas is in the armoury."

Kitty nodded her assent, keeping her head down so no one would notice the excitement in her eyes. This was her third day of service in Rossfarne Castle. She'd been hired as a housemaid with barely a second look from the marshal. But with only the earl himself in attendance at the castle, her duties had been confined to the kitchen so far and she was unlikely to discover her family jewels amidst the roasting spits and food barrels. On her first day, she'd been thrilled to be summoned to the solar, wildly imagining that she might lay her hands on Rosalind's inheritance within the hour. But a dark temper had hung around his lordship, and he'd curtly dismissed her just as soon as she placed her heavy tray on a polished walnut table. She hadn't even had the chance to so much as raise her gaze and glance around the room.

She straightened up and wiped her hands on her stiff apron. "Are there specific instructions?" she asked.

Agnes, a tall, stooped servant some years older than Kitty snorted in derision. "Make sure he's not still in there. You don't want to be left alone with him." She nodded emphatically before returning her attention to a brown sack of muddy potatoes.

Kitty's eyes opened wide. The man she'd met on the causeway had given her little cause for concern, but she still had much to learn about life in Rossfarne Castle.

Cook flapped her floury hands. "Don't listen to her," she told Kitty impatiently. "She's remembering the old earl. His lordship isn't like that." She turned her disapproving face towards Agnes. "And I won't have smutty tales told in my kitchen."

Agnes rolled her eyes before plunging the potatoes into a bowl of water. "It never hurts to be careful."

"I'll be careful," Kitty reassured her, remembering the dark carriage and the deep, commanding voice which had sent shivers down her spine.

"And don't be caught with your back turned," Agnes quipped.

Cook held out her large knife threateningly, and Kitty quickly looked away from both of them. She didn't want a ruckus caused on her behalf. It would be better by far if they hardly noticed her. Then they wouldn't miss her when she'd gone. And more importantly, no one would ever trace her back to Shoreston Manor. She'd already broken her promise to give a false name, but the incident on the causeway had left her shaken and disorientated. All she could think of was the tall, brooding man on the powerful charger. The way his muscles had rippled under his shirt and how his dark eyes had bored into hers. When the marshal asked for her name, she found herself reciting the pet name she'd been known by since birth.

Kitty. It was a good name for a servant. Simple, sensible, no frills. It suited her.

"Go on now," Cook urged, wiping her hands on her apron and bustling over to take the wooden spoon from Kitty. "Make haste or else his lordship will be back from his morning ride and looking to change."

Kitty didn't need further encouragement. With steady hands, she removed the heavy pot from the stove and settled it on the scrubbed wooden table to cool.

"You'll need a broom for the rushes," prompted Agnes, perhaps regretting her earlier, unhelpful words. "Sprinkle them with dried lavender."

Kitty tucked her errant curls more securely under her cap and found all she needed. The kitchen took up most of the lower ground floor. To leave it, she had to ascend a spiral stone staircase which led directly into the vast, echoing great hall. It was a room meant for feasting and gathering, but with so few people in attendance at the castle, the long trestle tables had been pushed up against the bare stone walls and the dais was bare. Four circular pillars reared up towards the vaulted ceiling, and in the far corner stood the raised lip of a deep well, situated inside in case the castle was ever held under siege. Kitty pressed her lips together at the thought. Rossfarne had known peace in her lifetime, but the troubled borderlands were not far away, and the earl had no army to protect them against marauding raids.

Shaking the thought away, she glanced around her to get her bearings. The earl's solar was situated in an alcove on this floor and the grand bedchambers were above. She walked past the cavernous fireplace, balanced her broom against her shoulder and opened a creaking door to the tower stairs. She had not yet been higher than the ground floor of Rossfarne Castle. The steps in front of her were narrow and slippery and her heart began to beat loudly beneath her apron as she climbed. She paused beside a window to catch her breath as the turbulent sea crashed repeatedly against the mighty castle walls. Out there, gulls cried and fishermen from the village plied their trade, but the forceful, elemental waves had power over them all.

How could she, a mere girl from the village, hope to better the formidable Earl of Rossfarne?

Kitty swallowed down her fears and turned resolutely from

the cheerless view. So much wilderness all around only served to underline her own physical weakness. But she was so close. She must hold her nerve for just a little longer.

She reached a tapestried gallery with a door set into the stone wall beside another narrow window. This must be the earl's bedchamber. Squaring her shoulders, Kitty hesitantly knocked on the door. The last thing she wanted was to walk in unannounced and discover he had returned unexpectedly. Worse, to find him waiting for her, his fierce eyes flashing, his powerful body coiled like a spring.

She closed her eyes to banish the image and listened hard, but no sound came from the thick-set doorway. Pulse-pounding, she turned the handle and pushed. The door refused to yield.

It was locked.

Kitty darted backwards as if she had been burned. Was it the wrong door? She looked left and right, but all she could see were more steps going higher.

Heart quaking, she began to climb again. These steps were even narrower than the last and she feared her large, ungainly feet may slip at any moment. If only she had Rosalind's dainty limbs. But then Rosalind would not make a convincing servant. She'd never been taught to light a fire or turn a joint of meat.

Kitty clasped her hands tightly in a bid to control her spiralling thoughts. All she had to do was find the earl's bedchamber. She wasn't trespassing. She had every right to be here. But it was as if her true intentions were writ large across her face. And despite Cook's reassurances, she couldn't help remembering the stark warning Agnes had delivered.

Don't be left alone with him.

The servant's words mingled with Alfred's awful pronouncement and made Kitty's courage flail.

You belong to the Earl of Rossfarne.

She hadn't been recognised, and she had no reason to fear that might change. But still, she was keenly aware that one false step on her part could lead to disaster. Kitty would no longer be a respectable serving girl, stirring broth in the kitchen. She'd be like the long-ago women lured here by the old earl, never to be seen again.

The narrow steps ended at another arched wooden doorway. This one set right against the head of the stairway so there was nowhere else to turn. Kitty rapped on the wood, louder this time, but she didn't need to turn the brass handle to know that this door was also locked. It had the look of a door that had not been opened for some time. A door hiding dark secrets. One that should remain closed.

Her broom clattered to the floor as her hands flew to her face. Was this the locked tower room in the Castle of Rossfarne? Had she stumbled on that den of iniquity without meaning to? Kitty's heart beat so loudly it rivalled the crashing of the mighty waves. Images flashed through her mind, half spun from hushed gossip in the village. Women flushed and disrobed. A man edging closer, his hands outstretched towards pearly flesh.

Cheeks burning, she spun on the spot and flung herself back down the stairway, uncaring now of the narrow stone steps and her large, ungainly feet. She wanted only to be back in human company, watching Cook wave her wooden spoon and hearing Agnes sniff with displeasure. The winding stairs circled on relentlessly and the stone walls seemed to close in around her, mocking her fears.

All at once she stumbled out into the light and barrelled into something tall, solid and unmoving. Her senses flooded with a masculine scent—leather and salt from the sea. Her eyes travelled upwards fearfully, already knowing what they would rest upon.

The chiselled jawline and imperious stare of the earl. Her head came to just below his broad shoulders. He was clad in riding breeches and a soft shirt which clung to the rigid walls of muscle in his chest.

"Kitty, I believe?" He arched his dark eyebrows.

"Forgive me, my lord." She immediately dipped her head, making an obeisance with grace as she had once been taught, and realising too late that servants only bobbed their heads. She righted herself as heat flooded her face and neck.

He must step aside. Dismiss her. She couldn't walk around him. His looming frame took up all the space in the small gallery. It felt as if all the available air was taken up, drawn into him.

His scorching gaze flickered past her. "What were you doing up there?" His tone was mild, but his masterful voice still resonated around the tapestried walls.

Her heart beat even faster. "I was in search of your bedchamber."

His eyebrows arched again, and a quiver of amusement flashed over his handsome face. "I see."

"To clean it," she added, lifting her chin defensively.

"The room at the top of the tower is out of bounds," he stated. "As is my bedchamber, to all but Thomas, my manservant."

His shock of dark hair was dishevelled from exercise and the salty air. Spray still clung to loose curls around his stubble-coated jaw. She forced herself to look away, but he was too close. He was all she could see. A warm wall of hard muscle. His lips twitched upwards as if he was sensing her discomfort. All at once the implicit superiority in his face ignited something deep inside her.

"Thomas is busy in the armoury. I was sent in his place."

He folded his arms and a painful wave of embarrassment all but felled her. What was she thinking? She should scurry away, but the new heat of his gaze compelled her to stay.

"I see. And so I deprive you of your purpose."

He was mocking her.

Her heart thudded like the beating of a drum. She should excuse herself and leave. Return to the safety of the kitchen. But her jewels could be secreted just beyond that locked door and she may never again get such an opportunity to establish their whereabouts.

"I will not disturb anything, my lord. I will merely put your chamber in order."

She wrenched her gaze away from his finely-carved face and rested her eyes demurely on the handle of the locked door, as if an air of calm expectation might bend the situation to her will.

A beat passed. She could almost imagine him unlocking the door and stepping back to allow her inside. Unbidden, her eyes flickered upwards to take in his impassive expression, his faint stubble, his dark, dangerous eyes. A shiver travelled through her, not of fear, but of something primal that tugged at her insides.

He watched her steadily. A wolf, confident of its prey.

"Are you so keen then, to see inside my bedchamber?"

Her courage drained away. She was a captive of his magnetic gaze. All at once the airless gallery was far too small. She heard Alfred's words, "You belong to the Earl of Rossfarne."

And here she was, demanding entrance to his private room. Alone with him, beside a locked door.

"Forgive me, my lord. I will leave you at once."

She darted forwards, uncaring of the contact she was forcing between them, but he shot out an iron grip and stopped her in her tracks. She felt his solid height and warm breath against the top of her cap.

"Why the sudden haste? I begin to see the benefits of such an eager serving girl."

His hand on her wrist was warm. The heat of his flesh travelled along her arm. She focused on the stone-flagged floor and bade her legs to stay strong and hold her up. She couldn't hope for notions of propriety to moderate his behaviour. This was the Earl of Rossfarne. Fear burgeoned, swamping all thoughts of her family's jewels and Rosalind's inheritance. A sob escaped her, and she ducked her head further down so he wouldn't see fright in her eyes.

Her terror would only inflame him, as it always had with her father.

But no sooner had this thought sprung into her mind than he dropped her wrist like a burning ember from the fire.

"If you are so keen to serve me, I bid you to attend to my

solar. It has not been cleaned for several days now."

He shifted around her so his back was to the locked chamber door. She could see the winding staircase and the light from the great hall below.

He was going to let her go.

Relief swelled up inside her although her wrist still tingled from the warmth of his fingers. She dared not look up and expose her flaming cheeks to his scrutiny. Instead, she gave him a small, deferential nod, one worthy of a castle servant, and tripped clumsily down the stairs without another word.

Once she reached the relative safety of the great hall, she pressed her back against the cold, jutting stones and covered her hot face with her hands. She had escaped, unscathed, but the encounter had left her reeling, as if all her strength had left her limbs. All feeling and certainty had abandoned her, leaving her with nothing but a swirling fear deep inside her stomach. It was a fear which leapt into a feverish kind of excitement when she remembered the pressure of the Earl's fingers around her slender wrist. Her determination to recover the jewels had led her to lift the lid of a forbidden chest, to push herself into a place she would never usually inhabit. Now she was safely on the other side, but it was no thanks to her foolishness.

Foolishness which must never be repeated. She would tread more carefully from now on.

She forced herself to breathe more slowly, to unclench her shoulders and lift her head. Cautiously she moved away from the security of the wall, grateful to find that her legs still supported her. Her body was recovering from the shock and fright, though her mind still raced. She must calm her demeanour. If anyone was to come across her like this, they would think the worst. The rumours would begin, baseless as they would be. Rumours that could ruin her reputation.

He had let her go.

He had toyed with her. Touched her. Barred her path. And then lost all interest. Was it her plain features and servant's garb that had put him off? Or was the new Earl of Rossfarne a man of some honour after all?

No. The answer came to her with sudden ferocity. A man of honour would not have robbed a family of its rightful inheritance. Or played a game of dice for the rights to a fisherman's daughter.

Anger sliced through her body like a sword. The strangeness of the last few days had affected her mind. She must keep her thoughts clear and focused on finding the jewels. Nothing else mattered.

The solar. She had the earl's permission to enter his private chamber. The room where he spent most of his day. Mayhap the jewels were secreted somewhere there? Her instincts told her otherwise, but it was worth a look.

The broom. Her heart sank as she realised her mistake. Her sweeping brush was still at the top of the tower, beside the locked door. Her pulse pounded anew. She couldn't bear the thought of retracing her steps to recover it.

So be it. She hadn't come to the castle to clean.

Kitty walked purposefully across the stone floor and continued into the solar without hesitating. The earl himself had ordered her to tidy his personal chambers. She kept her back straight and banished her fears. She was a housemaid about her daily chores.

But the beauty of the empty room brought her up short. She hadn't expected such welcoming cheer to exist in the otherwise austere castle. It was as if she'd entered another homestead entirely. A fire crackled in the grate, laid by Thomas no doubt, and above it hung a brightly patterned tapestry. She stepped closer, intrigued. Elsewhere she'd seen drab and faded depictions of hunting or battles, scenes which did nothing to pique her interest. But this tapestry showed wildflowers blooming in a meadow beneath luminous rays of the rising sun. It was beautiful. Her breath caught in her throat as she traced the delicate outline of a bunch of cow parsley. Such care and attention had gone into the work.

The earl's walnut desk was positioned by the high windows, with rose-coloured drapes gathered behind it. The desk was tidy, the rushes on the floor were clean and two high-backed chairs were neatly arranged by the fire. Kitty pursed her lips. What would a real housemaid do in here?

Her hand went to her apron pocket and pulled out a polishing cloth. She could buff up the candlesticks if nothing else. It would give her a reason to stay in the solar and to search for any places where the earl may have hidden her jewels. The candlesticks were heavy and elaborately carved. She rubbed the silver carefully as her eyes roamed about the room, increasingly curious about the new Earl of Rossfarne. Was he a cruel, base man, like his predecessor? The charm and colour of his personal chamber said not. But he had entered into a wager against a daughter's life. What sort of a man would do that?

She replaced the candlesticks on the mantel and rubbed her temples, where a faint throbbing indicated a headache that threatened to erupt. There were too many questions and not nearly enough answers, but the only question which should concern her was the whereabouts of the jewels. Her pulse quickened as her eye alighted on the edge of a wooden chest which had been pushed into the corner by the window.

Glancing behind her to ensure no one was watching, Kitty crossed the room and held her breath while she tugged at the lid. She half expected it to be locked, but it swung open with an audible creak. She bit down on her lip and leaned over, her heart beating wildly against her ribs. A mass of folded fabric met her gaze. Puzzled, she ran her hands over the rippling silk. The material was soft, luxurious. She pulled it out and gasped as a beautiful blue gown, embroidered with gold thread and pearl buttons, unfolded before her.

It was the gown of a lady, in every way except the cut. Kitty blushed as she beheld the immodestly shaped bodice. Was this some fashion of old? She couldn't imagine her gracious mother ever displaying so much of her own creamy flesh. She reached for the next gown, this one trimmed with fur, and shook her head in confusion as the same revealing neckline sprang into view.

She carefully laid the gowns beside her and plunged her hands back into the chest, her fingers searching beneath the fabrics for the familiar cloth bag. Nothing. She sat back on her heels, disappointed but not surprised.

The jewels were in the earl's bedchamber. She knew it in her bones.

She must fold the gowns and place them back exactly as she had found them. Although why the unmarried Earl of Rossfarne had a chest filled with ladies' gowns in his solar, she simply couldn't imagine. Especially ones cut just so. Kitty ran her fingers along the neckline. Her own generous bosom would surely spill over the top of such a dress.

All at once she realised what she was holding in her hands. Sickened, she pushed the slippery fabric into the chest and closed the lid, not sparing any time to fold the gowns neatly.

Kitty was too nauseated to fold.

How had it taken her so long to work it out?

Those were not gowns for ladies. Not real ladies, like her titled relatives who had occasionally come to Shoreston to dine with her mother. Those were gowns for ladies of a different persuasion altogether. Gowns for ladies who wanted to display their flesh for the perusal of men.

For the perusal of the earl.

She winced as if she had been slapped. To think she had questioned his reputation. The man was every bit as base as the uncle who had gone before him. Unless, of course, the gowns were from the era of the old earl. Mayhap they had nothing to do with the man upstairs? It was a tempting thought, but she had no way of knowing for sure.

She straightened up, her legs trembling anew. She should leave this dreadful place at once. To stay was to become as much a gambler as her father. But what then would become of Rosalind?

Lost in her thoughts, she didn't hear the heavy wooden door to the solar swinging open. She didn't see the tall, brooding man standing in the doorway, watching her.

It was only when he spoke up that she jumped in surprise.

"What the devil are you doing in here? I should take you out to be flogged."

Chapter Five

Guy DAMPENED HIS washcloth in a bowl of warm water and rubbed vigorously at his torso. His scar was puckered and dark, a sharp contrast to the smooth, bronzed skin on his right side. But it was healing; that was all that mattered.

Naked from the waist up, Guy crossed his bedchamber to the high, latticed window. His gaze travelled out over the sparkling sea and then returned back to the castle grounds. If he listened carefully, beyond the crashing of the waves he could make out raised voices coming from the outer courtyard. Guy grimaced. The stable master was unused to spirited horses and his favourite charger, though usually a kind animal, was increasingly restless. At first, Guy had assumed that like his master, his horse was struggling to adjust to life away from the battlefield. But this morning's ride had planted a new fear in his mind—that the horse was responding to Guy's own inner turbulence.

He clenched his left fist tightly and swore in frustration. His grip was still feeble. Too feeble. He needed to recover fully, for his horse's sake as well as his own.

The stark walls of his bedchamber mocked his plight. Guy was used to a knight's transient lifestyle and had picked up few possessions of his own. Those he had, now graced the solar downstairs. But this room was unchanged. His pitiless uncle had slept beneath the dark canopy of the bed and picked out the sole cheerless tapestry hanging by the door. Today's brightness only served to highlight the lack of warmth and colour inside. Dust danced in the sunlight streaming through the window and the rushes on the floor were beginning to smell stale He should have let the maid put the room to rights, but he had sworn to allow no one in here but his manservant. Thomas was a dour soul, but he had served Guy faithfully for many years. After the theft of his coin, Thomas was the only person Guy could trust.

With a roar of frustration, he slammed the wooden shutters closed, casting the room into shadow. That was better. He could hide in the gloom, safe from the phantoms which the familiar granite walls were raising from their slumber.

He rummaged in his closet and found a long tunic that would suffice for the day. Pulling it roughly over his head, his fingers encountered a familiar knot of scarring across his clavicle. There it was. The tangible proof that he must return to the battlefield with all possible haste. This old injury had not threatened his life in the same way as his newest scar, but it was the one that he spent his days running away from.

He remembered the flash of cruelty in his father's grief-stricken face when he'd released the dagger.

"Never again lower your guard," the older man had growled, his pink lips curling back in satisfaction as deep red blood pooled in his son's clavicle.

For all his brutality, his father had been right. Guy had found kinship on the battlefield and over the years, he had begun to let down his guard. And this new trust in humanity had led to the loss of his silver.

Guy had learned his lesson now. All locks would be fastened. All shutters barred. He would never again forget the cruel lesson his father had imparted in the aftermath of his younger brother's death. A death he'd carried the burden of since his miserable youth.

A hammering on the door jolted him from his reverie.

"Come," he shouted, lifting his chin to straighten the tunic.

Thomas stalked into the room. He was unshaven and carried a faint whiff of polish from the armoury. Guy beheld him with displeasure. It was true that they did not expect visitors to the castle, but certain standards should still be maintained. Thomas's grey hair needed combing and his shirt was missing a button.

"What is it?" he asked.

Thomas nodded behind him. "I found her lurking in your solar, my lord."

Guy raised his gaze over the servant's balding head and encountered the flashing green eyes of the serving girl from the causeway. Kitty. The one so keen to enter his bedchamber. Well, she had finally gotten her wish.

"I see." Surprise stole his capacity for any further comment.

"I told her she should be flogged for insolence." Thomas sniffed, his beady eyes lighting up at the prospect.

Did the man have a streak of cruelty running through him?

Kitty opened her mouth as if to speak and then closed it again. He could see a tumult of emotion crossing her face. Denial, frustration and most intriguingly of all, a faint sparkle of authority. She would like to put Thomas in his place. He could see it as plain as day. Although she would do so calmly. Guy couldn't imagine Kitty ever losing control. She radiated a quiet certitude.

Instead of offering an explanation, Guy simply pursed his lips. "And what do you have to say for yourself, girl?"

For the briefest moment her eyes clashed with his, steel on steel, before her expression dropped demurely to the floor.

"I was merely carrying out your orders, my lord."

"Orders," spluttered Thomas, but Guy held up a hand to stop him.

"My orders," he confirmed. "That's quite right. No harm has been done." He cleared his throat. "No one shall be flogged today."

Again he caught a flash of green. A surge of watchful, determined patience.

"But she wasn't working, she was just standing there," Thomas protested.

This time the serving girl couldn't help herself. Her gaze shifted warily, and her lips tightened. If he hadn't been watching her closely, he would have missed it.

What was her story, Guy wondered. How had she come by such inner poise and confidence? Again he puzzled over what had brought her to these shores, to the infamous castle of the Earl of Rossfarne.

It was a puzzle he would like to solve.

"I begin to think I have tasked you too severely, Thomas," he said. "We will permit Kitty entrance to the solar. She will be responsible for it, from now on." He waved his hand in the air, not completely sure what was involved in a chambermaid's duties.

Thomas looked displeased but knew better than to question his master. "Very good, my lord." He ducked his head and ushered Kitty from the room.

Guy turned towards the window. "I would like you to stay, just for a moment."

"Me, my lord?" his manservant queried.

"You may go, Thomas."

He kept his back turned until Thomas's shuffling footsteps had left the room and the chamber door was closed once again. Silence stretched between them, but he waited patiently. Who would break it first? As a servant, this wench should know not to speak before he did.

"How may I assist you, my lord?"

Not a trained servant then. She had given herself away. Guy whirled around, ready to confront her, but the sight of her downturned head and neatly folded hands made him pause.

"I wish to know more about you, Kitty." He took a step forward and was struck by her lemony scent. He breathed it in. It was a fragrance he could lose himself in, if circumstances were different.

"More about me, my lord?" Her voice rose with alarm.

"Yes." He stopped a few feet away from her and folded his

arms. "Where did you say you were from?"

She swallowed, clearly uncomfortable. The skin of her cheek was smooth with a faint clustering of freckles around her upturned nose. An auburn curl had sprung loose from her cap to sit upon her slender shoulder.

"Not far from here."

"But you said you had travelled for many days," he countered quickly.

"I did." She straightened up and met his gaze levelly. He thought again that he had never beheld such beautiful sea-green eyes. "But I did not come directly to Rossfarne. I asked elsewhere for work first."

That made sense. He was almost convinced. But an air of mystery still surrounded her. Surely no serving girl would stand so tall and speak with such refinement?

"Where else did you enquire?"

At this her eyes darted to the side and a faint flush brought colour to her sculpted cheeks, but she answered readily enough. "With the Duke of Answick."

Again, the reply was reasonable. The duke lived some miles distant, but a healthy young woman could walk there and back in a matter of days.

"It is a blessing for us that you were turned away," he said drily.

"Thank you, my lord."

He should dismiss her, but this conversation was the most interesting one he'd had for several days now. With no company bar the cheerless Thomas and his uncle's former servants, Guy was increasingly alone with his troubled thoughts. Thoughts which he desired respite from.

"And are you happy in your work?"

"Very happy, my lord." Her voice was uneven, piquing his curiosity further.

"The other servants treat you well?"

"Extremely well," she paused, seemingly searching for words.

"Like family."

This he could not believe. His uncle's servants seemed to have been hand-picked for their morose ways. Or maybe it was the gloom of Rossfarne Castle which could quell the sparks of the most buoyant soul.

"I am pleased to hear it." He let his arms fall to his sides, wincing at a jolt of pain from his injured wrist. Their conversation was at an end. He must release her back to her chores and her fellow servants, those who treated her like family.

Family. He had never known the joys of it, except briefly with his younger brother. But that happiness had quickly turned to grief and then to a hardened wretchedness from which he could never escape.

"I must let you return to your work," he said stiffly.

Relief washed over her wide-set eyes. "Thank you, my lord." She bobbed her head and turned to leave.

He didn't want to let her go. "Just a moment," he called.

She halted immediately. Did a faint tremor pass over her? "What is it?"

"I think you have forgotten something." He walked with measured footsteps until he stood in front of the door. Kitty's gaze was fixed on the floor, but she worried at her lower lip, betraying her anxieties. Her hands fluttered to her apron pockets. "I am no expert, but I believe you will require a broom to sweep my solar."

"Of course." She looked up at him and almost smiled. He found he wanted to see her smile and watch those beautiful eyes light up with something other than determination. "I will fetch it now."

"No need." He didn't want this innocent young woman further exposed to the darkness of his uncle's tower room. "I shall recover the broom for you."

Her pale hands fluttered upwards as if to stop him, but he marched from the chamber and up the narrow stairway before common sense could intervene and demand to know why he was extending the hand of chivalry to a serving wench.

Too fast. He had moved too quickly and underestimated the tight turns of the spiral staircase. His left side clenched with warning, and he gritted his teeth in frustration. Damnation. Could he not even ascend a flight of stairs now?

The broom was laying on the floor, just out of reach. He had no wish to punish himself further by leaning downwards, but he could draw it closer to him with his foot.

Alas, he again moved too sharply, and the handle of the broom flew towards him. He ducked to the side and a hot flash of pain traversed the length of his scar. Breathing hard, Guy leaned against the cold stone wall and waited for the agony to pass.

Footsteps behind him increased his discomfort. He didn't want anyone to see him like this, especially not a young woman with entrancing eyes.

"Are you well, my lord?" Her voice was hesitant.

"Clearly not," he shot back.

She had come to a halt just behind him, and he cursed her for it. Now they must cross paths on the impossibly small landing. Pain seared through him, blurring his vision and stealing his breath.

"Is there anything I can do?"

"You should have waited downstairs."

It was too late now. There was nothing for it but to stagger sideways and allow her to see how he clung to the castle wall.

Perspiration sprang out on his forehead as his heel teetered dangerously on the top step. He was accustomed to physical fitness, not this debilitating weakness, but the hard ride this morning intended to steady his horse had pushed his tentative recovery too far.

"You are ill." She ducked down until he could see the concern in her face.

"I am injured," he corrected her with a growl. "But I shall be fine in just a moment."

She bent to pick up the broom with enviable ease. "I didn't

know," she faltered.

Of course she didn't know. No one here knew, bar Thomas. It was better that way. If news of his fragility spread further, all manner of scoundrels may descend upon them, and he had not yet fully secured the castle. His uncle's staff barely managed the household. There were no guards except the marshal who kept watch at the gatehouse.

He shot out his good arm and gripped her wrist. "You must tell no one of this."

He heard her swallow, though his vision swam before him. "I won't." Her voice was steady, and he implicitly believed her. "Will you allow me to help you back to your chamber?"

No. He wouldn't accept help from anyone.

"Return to your work," he told her, dropping her wrist.

"But I can't leave you here."

"Leave me," he barked.

She didn't leave. He could sense her, even as the world dissolved into a swarm of hazy colours. Damn her defiance. He should have her flogged after all.

"I once nursed a man back to full strength after he was cut with an axe." She paused. "I could help you, my lord, if only you would let me."

Guy forced himself to stand upright and lift his gaze from the floor.

"I don't need help," he enunciated slowly and clearly. "I haven't asked for it and I don't want it." His hand grasped for purchase on the rough stone behind him. "Now get back to your work."

NIGHT FELL SLOWLY this far north. Guy had been drawn to the window seat of his solar by the luminous colours of the sunrise, and there he had stayed. It was surprisingly comfortable on the padded cushions and as the shadows lengthened around the battlements, he had discerned a further benefit to his locale.

With the heavy drapes closed behind him, no one could see where he was.

A plan had sprung into his mind, perfectly formed and impossible to resist. He would wait on the window seat until the servants divined he had retired for the evening. When the maid came in to clear the room, he would emerge from his hiding place and insist upon an audience. He could have saved himself all of this trouble and simply sent for her, but then there would be questions asked in the kitchen and he couldn't risk even the scent of gossip.

He twisted his signet ring around his thick-set knuckles, angry and frustrated in equal measure. That he should sink to such depths to speak to a servant appalled him. But he must ensure her silence. Earlier on, debilitated by pain, he had not been able to impress upon her the importance of it. But by God, she must understand, and she must submit.

That was the crux of it. Not his desire to spend more time in her company, to look into her bewitching green eyes and enjoy her quick-witted conversation. He cared for none of this. Only her promise of silence.

The remaining embers of the log fire glowed faintly, the only light in the room. He'd watched the tallow candles flicker their last some time previous. His legs ached from their cramped position and his scar throbbed, reminding him of the doctor's advice to remain in bed, but still Guy waited.

At last, a faint click announced the door latch being raised. Guy struggled to his feet, ready to stride out and take Kitty unawares. A cramp had taken hold of his left arm, but he had another. His hand twitched the drape aside and in the light of a newly arrived candle he made out the outline of the maid he was waiting for.

Kitty walked lightly into the solar, as graceful as a noble lady entering a ballroom. She had removed her cap and apron, convinced no doubt that her quick evening rounds would not be disturbed. Her abundant red-gold curls cascaded down the back of her plain grey servant's dress and her slim hips sashayed as she crossed from the desk to the fireplace, straightening cushions and replacing candles ready for the morning. All at once, it was as if Kitty was the mistress here. He was the interloper, hiding behind a drape, intent on mischief.

He swallowed, unable to resist the lure of her feminine curves. Curves that were usually hidden beneath an apron and were still partially obscured by her modest dress. But curves that were undeniably present. Guy couldn't take his eyes off her. He moved backwards to ensure the drapes concealed him and watched.

Kitty reached for the tall wooden candlesticks atop the fireplace and audibly tutted. Her dextrous fingers explored the wax that had dropped down them and she began to rub one against her dress. Guy's breath caught in his throat as he felt a flicker of unbidden desire.

Desire that must be quashed. He was not his uncle. He would not bed the servants, nor any other maid from common stock hereabouts.

Get a grip on yourself, he thought. *Go out there and tell her what she needs to know.*

But then Kitty began to sing.

Quietly at first, her surprisingly beautiful voice grew stronger until it soared around the vaulted chamber. Guy didn't recognise the words or the melody, but it didn't matter. Her singing was his undoing.

All at once, his remaining strength deserted him. He sat back heavily on the window seat, feeling as if Kitty had reached her slender hand into his very soul and pulled it out. He was drained, but at the same time he was replete. A calmness descended over him and the tight knot of tension he carried in his gut unclenched.

Kitty dropped to her knees to position the fireguard and her singing quietened. Guy strained to hear more, but she sat back on her heels as she gazed at the glowing embers, apparently lost in thought.

Sing again, he wanted to beg her. *Don't stop.* But all he could do was sit as still as a mouse and wait.

Finally she sighed, straightened up and smoothed down her dress. Guy held his breath, hoping for more, and his patience was rewarded when she picked up the tune once again. This time she hummed, but the soothing magic of her voice was just as potent even without words. He closed his eyes and rested his head against the granite wall, luxuriating in the rise and fall of the melody. A heaviness came over him as Kitty's voice washed his worries far away.

He could rest. He could even sleep. Her singing had brought him peace.

She walked to the door, lifted the latch and closed it behind her. The melody stopped, and Guy was momentarily bereft.

He remembered their first encounter on the causeway and his thoughts as she magically calmed his frenzied horse.

Witchcraft.

Was she a witch come to charm him? He'd never before entertained such superstitious notions. But with a voice like that, she could do with him whatever she wanted.

Guy's lips twitched into a smile. He had discovered one secret of his enigmatic serving maid and he already wanted more. Before long, he would unpick the rest.

Chapter Six

"MY LORD, RIDERS have been sighted on the causeway. At least twenty men. They will be at the castle within minutes." The marshal had run all the way from the gatehouse to deliver his message. He put a hand to his chest, his ribs visibly heaving beneath his grey tunic.

Guy stood up from his desk as quickly as he dared, instantly on high alert. The morning sun had already risen high in the sky, and he had been sitting in the solar alone in a kind of trance, allowing his thoughts to wander to the beautiful serving maid with an equally beautiful voice. But here was danger, or at least the scent of it, and his knight's instincts came rushing to the fore. "Did they carry a standard of any sort? Or a coat of arms?"

"Aye, sir." The marshal leaned back against the door jamb, still trying to recover his breath. "I saw it clearly. 'Twas a golden lion on a red standard."

Immediately some of the tension left Guy's shoulders. "Those are the colours of Darkmoor," he announced with relief. "The earl is a cousin of mine, and his son Otto is a good friend." He half smiled as he remembered a distant boyhood summer spent roaming the fields of Forbisher with young Otto, a willing accomplice in youthful mischief.

But for the marshal, the name had darker associations, and he visibly blanched. "You don't mean Otto Sarragnac…?" His voice was disbelieving.

Guy waved his hand, half amused by the man's reaction.

"Known as the *Feared One*?" he finished for him. "Yes, the very same. He'll be delighted to learn that news of his exploits has spread this far east. Though you should not believe everything you hear, my good man. Otto is a skilled warrior, no more, no less." His fearlessness had been apparent at a young age, Guy recalled, when they had faced one another with wooden swords, mounted on willing, if diminutive, ponies.

The marshal crossed his arms, his head on one side, clearly not reassured. "Should I close the gates?"

This was evidently the correct course of action in the man's mind. Guy held his gaze, closing his ears to the plaintive calling of the gulls outside. It was a sound eerily reminiscent of the wailing of a child. "The Darkmoors will have already overcome a great many obstacles to ride all the way here from the western shores." As he spoke the words, one question bubbled at the forefront of his mind. *Why did they come?* But he kept his voice light and unconcerned. "Do you consider a closed gate to be an effective deterrent against the *Feared One*?"

"Then what are your orders, my lord?"

The marshal's unease was rubbing off on Guy, despite his initial reaction to the news. He couldn't help but weigh up his own physical strength, depleted as it was, against that of his infamous cousin. Otto Sarragnac was the mightiest of warriors. His father, Lord Ulric, had a fearsome reputation of his own. And Guy was an injured knight who could not yet ride his horse without debilitating stabs of pain. He could not hope to stand against the Darkmoors, whatever the purpose of their visit. Therefore, his only choice was to make them welcome.

"Throw open the gates and ready the men to receive their horses," he barked. "Tell Cook we shall expect refreshments." He grimaced, unable to stop himself adding more. "But warn the female servants to stay out of sight until I send word." It was the least he could do, to keep them safe. The enigmatic maid, Kitty, amongst them. Though he would wager the Darkmoors had come with peaceful intent, that didn't mean that the female servants were entirely out of danger of a particular sort.

He considered his cheerless great hall and weed-covered courtyard, a far cry from the comfort and style of his childhood home of Forbisher; an even further cry from the elegance of Darkmoor Castle. For the first time, Guy felt a wave of regret for not doing more to brighten up his recently inherited fortress. But it could not be helped now; he had but minutes to spare. Besides, this was his convalescent home, and he had not anticipated receiving visitors.

Burying his unease deep inside, he rang for Thomas and asked him to fetch down a heavily embroidered deep blue tunic which was a more fitting costume for an earl than the plain shirt in which he'd dressed that morning. Once appropriately attired, he strode into the courtyard to welcome his unexpected guests. The clatter of approaching horses' hooves was like a deafening drum roll as the gleaming armour-clad soldiers poured up the causeway and through the arched entrance in the outer castle walls. Guy stood as tall as he could, wishing he had somehow found the coin to hire castle guards for Rossfarne. He could not rely on the tides as a deterrent, he realized. Not against men like Otto Sarragnac. Guy flexed his fingers around the hilt of his sword. If hostility was shown, he would not go down without a fight.

But his concerns were eased when a heavily armed warrior on a bright chestnut horse cantered through the ranks towards him. The man reached up to remove his helmet, revealing nut-brown curls, and smiled widely in greeting. "Guy," he exclaimed, towering above him on his prancing horse. "So the rumours are true! You are here in Rossfarne."

"The rumours are true," Guy confirmed, reaching up for the reins as his boyhood friend slid off his horse. "It's good to see you, Otto."

He hoped that were true. Otto's relaxed demeanour and the casual stance of the Darkmoor knights gave him no cause for immediate alarm.

"You too, my friend. It has been too long." Otto flung an arm around Guy's shoulders and squeezed him tightly, making him wince with pain, though he didn't let it show.

"To what do I owe this pleasure?" Guy looked levelly at Otto Sarragnac, the Feared One, only son of the Earl of Darkmoor. Otto was a towering giant of a man, all muscle and brawn, wearing a mail shirt topped with polished plate armour. Guy would hate to face him across a battlefield. But close up, he could still see the warmth in his brown eyes and the sincerity in his smile.

"I apologise for our sudden arrival," Otto said immediately, grimacing in recognition of his lapse in etiquette. "I should not have blamed you if we had met up with armed guards on the causeway." Guy inclined his head, swallowing the urge to confess to Otto that he had no armed guards at his disposal. "We had business with the Duke of Answick, and thought to call on you, being so close to your new home."

Guy pursed his lips. The story was plausible, but something about Otto's strained voice told him it was not the full story.

"You are welcome, of course," he said. "Is your father with you?"

Otto indicated a distant trio of riders picking their way slowly over the final cobbles of the causeway. "That is him coming now." He took Guy's arm and led him a few steps away from the Darkmoor knights, who were dismounting from their horses and stretching weary limbs. "May I speak frankly?"

"I wish you would," said Guy, matching his old friend's bluntness as he looped the horse's reins through a hook affixed to the stable wall.

Otto smiled, giving Guy another glimpse of the boy he had once known. "In truth, my father is tiring. We had hoped to make it as far as the western mountains today, but within an hour of leaving Answick, he was stooped over his horse's neck." A shadow passed over his handsome face. "I tell you this in trust, Guy, in recognition of our kinship and the friendship we once shared, even though it is many years since we last broke bread together. I have come to ask for food and shelter for the night. And I admit, it pains me to ask for anything."

A wave of relief washed over Guy. "I thank you for your honesty," he said. He didn't need Otto to spell out the implications of Lord Ulric's ill health. Darkmoor occupied prime lands, and many an opportunist would be willing to take a chance on ousting the Sarragnacs if word got out that the earl was failing. "Of course, I will say nothing of what you have told me." He put his arm across his heart to demonstrate his faithfulness.

"Least of all to my father." Otto ran a hand through his tousled dark hair. "He grows cantankerous when forced to confront his failing health. I have told him we are here for my pleasure, so that I might catch up with an old friend." He clapped Guy on the shoulder once more, luckily not his injured one.

Guy reached out and clasped Otto's hand. It was many months since he had felt the calloused knuckles of a warrior, and the feel of his skin combined with the smell of horses, leather and clean sweat, made him momentarily weaken with nostalgia for his old life. "Tell your men to make themselves comfortable in the barn," he said. "I will have food and water sent out to them. You and your father will dine with me tonight. I will ensure the best rooms are made ready for you."

Otto laughed. "We are two men, both accustomed to sleeping rough when the occasion demands it. Even my father, ageing as he is. We have no need of luxury, my friend."

"I am glad to hear it," Guy told him wryly.

HOURS LATER, GUY sat with Otto beside a roaring fire in the great hall. A long trestle table had been pulled out and positioned in the centre of the stone-flagged room. Guy had dined alone in his solar since taking up residence in Rossfarne Castle, but tonight would be different. Candles had been lit and positioned around the four ornate pillars, casting a flickering light into the distant corners of the bare walls. It was far from cheerful, but for the first time, Guy could begin to see how Rossfarne Castle could be brought back to life. If that was what he wanted.

The two men stretched their legs before the fire, reclining in ornately carved wooden chairs. They were drinking good wine, and the potent liquid was helping to make Guy feel comfortable and relaxed. He should not have regarded his old friend with such suspicion, he mused, as Otto relayed a humorous tale about a recent joust. Fear and distrust of good men could be as dangerous an enemy as weakness or bad judgement.

"Do you joust at all these days?" Otto asked suddenly, his darkly stubbled face half illuminated by the dancing flames.

"I am injured, my friend," Guy answered, surprising both of them with his honesty. "But I hope to return to full health in time."

Otto acknowledged his confession with a nod of sympathy. "And then you shall return to service with the king?" he asked, taking a long swig of wine.

"Of course." Guy gazed into the fire. "I know of no other life." His gaze flickered over to the heavily-muscled warrior by his side. Even in repose, Otto's body hummed with energy. "Have you never considered it?"

"The life of a serving knight?" Otto raised his eyebrows. "You think I am worthy to fight the king's battles? This is praise indeed, coming from Guy de Vray, first son of Forbisher." He spoke lightly, evoking Guy's full name and the title he had abandoned long ago. But his brow clouded quickly when he saw how his words affected his cousin. "Forgive me. I spoke unthinkingly."

Guy waved his hand to dismiss the apology, leaning forward to pour a liberal helping of wine into both of their goblets. "There is nothing to forgive. That is indeed how you once recognised the winner of our many contests." He winked at Otto as he sat back in his chair.

Otto laughed. "You did not win every time." He pursed his lips. "You could beat me for speed, of course. And your skills with a sword were exemplary, even then. But for sheer brute force, I reckon I was usually the winner."

Guy raised his glass to his friend. "For sheer brute force, no man in the land can hope to outclass Otto Sarragnac." He drank deeply, enjoying the moment of camaraderie.

"Except, of course, on those occasions when we both held back to allow Angus to win," Otto said softly.

Guy stilled, his goblet resting on his knees. Images of his younger brother crowded his mind. Angus had been but a small child, barely more than a toddler, during the long summer when Otto and Guy had shared a tutor at Forbisher. He'd trailed after them, desperate to join in with their games, laughing uncontrollably at Otto's clownish antics. Guy swallowed hard, quenching the swell of grief. "Aye, except for then," he forced out. "I try not to remember those times, to be honest."

"It was a terrible thing that happened," Otto murmured, his fingers beating a tattoo on the arm of his chair. This was a man who had faced innumerable horrors on the battlefield, but he still displayed palpable grief at the injustice of a child taken from the world too soon. "Do you never go back to Forbisher?"

"Never," Guy said, more harshly than he intended. "My aunt has taken up residence there. She collects the tithes and considers herself lady of the manor. I say she is welcome to the lot." He shifted in his chair, keen to change the subject. "You have not yet answered my question about joining me as a knight in the king's service."

Otto breathed out heavily, glancing up at the door to ensure they were still alone. Lord Ulric had retired to his room soon after arriving, and Thomas had carried hot water up to him for a bath. The old earl had sent word he would join them for dinner, but he had yet to arrive in the great hall. "In truth, there is nothing I would like more." He inclined his head, looking Guy fully in the eye. "But alas, I fear I am needed at home."

Guy considered this for a moment as a log sizzled in the flames. "Does Darkmoor not know peace?" he asked, keen to keep the conversation far away from the painful topic of his past.

"Aye, it does, for now." Otto scratched his chin, flickering a sideways look at Guy. "Though I fear my father is on the cusp of hostility with our nearest neighbours, for no better reasons than pride and avarice."

A beat fell. Both men were seasoned warriors who well knew these were no reasons to spark bloodshed.

Guy leaned forward, ignoring a stab of pain in his arm. "You know you can always call on me in a moment of need." He laughed to dispel the sudden tension. "Though in truth, I am not much good for anything right now."

Otto took a swig of wine. "Your body will heal," he said emphatically. "Of that, I am sure. But Darkmoor does not lack muscle. We have an army of well-trained knights. What I need, mayhap, is a friend I can trust." His sincerity was evident. Guy's chest swelled with fellow-feeling, but he failed to find the words he needed to express his deeply felt emotions before Otto continued. "I will call on you, Guy, at such time as I need to. Though I hope and pray it will not come to that. My father is still a great and powerful man. Only a fool would rise against him."

A movement to their left made both men startle. The door swung open and Lord Ulric, Earl of Darkmoor, came striding into the great hall. Like his son, he was a man bred for battle. Tall and strong, with a formidable bearing and a sharp glint to his eye, despite his age and ill health. His once dark hair was now liberally streaked with grey, but the muscles on his arms still bulged beneath the heavily embroidered tunic he wore over light-coloured breeches.

"Father." Otto stood up to greet him, the candlelight throwing his body into sharp relief. He was dressed more modestly than his father, in a plain dark tunic that hung from his powerful shoulders. "Are you well-rested?"

"I suppose I am." The Earl of Darkmoor stopped before Guy

and inclined his head in greeting. "It is good of you to offer us hospitality with such little notice. I told my son it would not do for an army of men to arrive at your door unannounced, but he was determined to have his evening of wine and reminiscences with an old friend." The man stood tall and proud, no doubt well aware how the reputation of the knights of Darkmoor had preceded them.

"I am pleased to see you both," Guy said, diplomatically. For a moment the three of them stood facing one another as the flames danced and the shadows lengthened. Guy felt a chill of apprehension crawl up his spine, reminiscent of his unease earlier that day when he awaited the warriors, not knowing what brought them to his door. While he had chatted with Otto, it had been like old times, with the strength of their kinship and shared history glowing between them. But now, he was once more aware of the inequality between his poorly guarded household and the well-trained soldiers outside. Lord Ulric could order his men to seize the castle, and Guy would be able to do nothing to stop him. He cleared his throat. "Please take a seat. I will ring for dinner, if we're ready?"

Lord Ulric nodded his assent and sat down at the head of the trestle table, as if this was his right. Guy felt, but did not see, Otto tense beside him. They were both keenly aware of this breach of manners. But Guy would not allow an old man's rudeness to spoil his evening. He waved Otto to a seat on his father's right and made his own way to the other side of the table, further from the warmth of the fire. Lord Ulric sniffed with displeasure over the freshly baked bread and finely carved meats, but his eyes gleamed with interest when Kitty—commandeered to serve at the table due to the shortage of castle servants—carried a tray of sweet figs into the hall.

What was it about this particular maid, Guy wondered. Her hair was pinned under her cap. Her dress and apron were neat. There was nothing to set her apart from the other servants, yet somehow, she stood out, like an eagle amongst pigeons. It was her grace and bearing, he thought afresh. She looked at the world with the measured gaze of a lady.

She was a puzzle he was determined to solve. And she had also attracted the eye of his guests.

"Over here," Lord Ulric commanded, cupping his fingers to beckon her over. Guy watched as Kitty hesitated, then turned to position her tray within easy reach of the Earl of Darkmoor. "What else have you got down there that could please an old man?" he asked.

Kitty's cheeks turned pink, but her balance was steady as she dipped her head politely. "I shall go and enquire, my lord."

"Bring us more wine, if you please," Guy spoke up, hoping to dispel the awkwardness and perchance divert Kitty from the hall for longer.

All three men watched as Kitty walked gracefully out of the hall, and Otto cleared his throat. "I see you have no shortage of beautiful women, here on your wild island." He spoke lightly and Guy swallowed down his instinctive flare of irritation.

"I do not dally with the servants." He wagged a finger at Otto before taking another long drink of wine.

"Of course not." Otto too drank deeply from his goblet.

"So what have you in the way of entertainment?" Lord Ulric demanded belligerently. "Are we to sit here in silence?"

"Is it not pleasant to sit and talk, Father?" Otto put in.

Lord Ulric sniffed loudly. "For you two, maybe. Not for me. Have you no minstrels? Musicians?" He fixed Guy with a questioning stare.

Guy quelled his rising impatience, reminding himself that Lord Ulric was suffering ill health and mayhap even injury as well. "I'm afraid not," he answered calmly. His mind flooded with memories of Kitty's beautiful singing voice, but he would sooner face a cavalry charge than divulge her hidden talents to a vulture like Lord Ulric.

Lord Ulric's displeasure was evident in his furrowed brow and wrinkled nose, but his expression brightened somewhat when Kitty re-entered the room. She kept her eyes cast down as she approached the table.

"Very nice, very nice," Lord Ulric muttered. "Fill me up." He gestured grandly to his goblet.

In a sudden flash of premonition, Guy knew that if Kitty approached the end of the trestle table, Lord Ulric would put his hands upon her. He wouldn't hurt her, but he would touch her in some way. Perchance he would take a hold of her wrist. Mayhap even put his wrinkled hands in the vicinity of her derriere. Guy couldn't allow it. Blood rushed to his head as he searched his mind for a reason to delay her.

"That wine is no good," he announced, startling Kitty as much as the men he was dining with. "Take it away, immediately."

Confusion washed over Kitty's previously composed features, and Guy cursed himself for speaking so abruptly. If he could only explain that he was trying to keep her away from wandering hands.

"This wine, my lord?" She nodded at the earthenware jug clutched in her trembling fingers.

"I want only the best wine for the Earl of Darkmoor." Guy took a breath. "You must ask Thomas to fetch it up."

"Very good, my lord." Kitty bobbed her head and all but ran from the room.

Guy fought an urge to go after her. Otto raised an enquiring eyebrow, but his father seemed to find nothing amiss. "Your wine is good," he allowed. His long fingers tapped on the trestle table. "But I know not how you can spend so many long evenings alone here without taking leave of your senses."

Otto's eyes sent an unspoken apology in Guy's direction. "Mayhap I came here to recover my senses," Guy suggested. "I find the peace restorative." A gust of wind rattled the windows as if to bely his claim.

"I am sure the views are considerable, especially from the tallest tower. Do you go up there?" Otto asked.

It was a decent stab at conversation, but unfortunately Otto had again hit upon the wrong subject. "I do not," Guy replied. "The tower room was the preserve of my uncle. Though mayhap you are right. I should consider making better use of it."

Lord Ulric harrumphed, and the room fell into uncomfortable silence. Guy risked a glance at his companions. Beneath his suntanned face and youthful vigour, Otto looked tired and drawn as he toyed with a cut of meat. He was known throughout the north as a fearless warrior and a wealthy man, with no cares to speak of. But here he sat, clearly beset with worry for the future. And as Lord Ulric twitched with impatience, Guy could see why. The old earl was like a powder keg, likely to explode at any moment.

"We have consumed much wine," Otto observed, gazing into his drained goblet. "I may have a sore head in the morning."

Guy smiled in response. "You have no cause to leave early. Please, stay as long as you wish."

Otto looked serious. "Thank you, but we must ride at dawn. We have been absent from Darkmoor overly long already."

Lord Ulric harrumphed once more, fixing his son with a steely glare. "You should have thought of that earlier, mayhap when you concocted this foolish plan to spend a night in a draughty castle with no way to pass the time easily." He picked up his goblet with an unsteady hand and drank deeply.

Was the man drunk, Guy wondered. A flush in his cheeks and a faint slurring of his words indicated as such.

The outer door opened once more and Guy's heart sank as Kitty reappeared, this time holding a pale earthenware jug. She seemed to keep her gaze deliberately from him as she approached the table, and Guy could think of no good reason to speak up.

"This is more like it." Lord Ulric sat back in his chair and gestured to Kitty. "Come here, young miss. I grow weary of this meal, but you offer me some diversion and perchance the opportunity to pass a more pleasant evening. Come and sit beside me."

Kitty placed the wine down on the table and folded her hands demurely in her apron, clearly at a loss as to what to do. Guy's fingers tightened around the edge of the wooden table as he watched the events unfold, feeling frozen in place.

"Come now," Lord Ulric urged. "Otto, go find the maid a chair," he barked at his son.

"Father, you're embarrassing the girl," Otto said firmly. "She's a servant doing her job. Let her be."

Lord Ulric raised a steely gaze to his son. "If I'm not mistaken, I'm still the Earl of Darkmoor, and you are my son. You will do as I say. The servant will spend the night with me."

His words pierced Guy's stupor, and he jumped to his feet, his chair scraping back against the flagstones. Time slowed down as Kitty raised an anguished face to him in a silent plea for help. A plea he had already determined to answer. "That will not do," he announced, uncaring of Lord Ulric's flash of anger. "No one will make a claim on Kitty."

The tension in the room grew palpable as Lord Ulric also rose to his feet. Guy wondered when the earl had last been denied his every wish. Mayhap not for many a year.

"And why is that?" Lord Ulric asked, one hand going to the sword at his hip.

Otto's eyes flickered between the two of them. Guy knew that his old friend would be cognisant that Lord Ulric had erred, but if he had to make a choice, he would side with his father.

Guy fixed his eyes on Kitty, who was now visibly trembling. Whatever happened, he would not abandon her to the unwanted attentions of Lord Ulric. She was in his employ and deserved his protection. But more than that, the thought of any man touching her caused him inexplicable discomfort.

He could see but one way out of this. Switching his gaze from the pretty wench to the furious old warrior, Guy summoned an insincere bark of laughter. "Why? Because she is mine, Lord Ulric. And I confess, I am possessive over my women."

Did Kitty flinch, or was it his imagination? Guy couldn't afford to spare her so much as a glance. His attention was firmly fixed on Lord Ulric, most especially the hand on the hilt of his sword.

For a second, the old man's gaze still conveyed his wrath, but then his lips creased into a smile, and he sank back down in his chair, reaching again for his goblet of wine. "Fair enough, my good man," he allowed. He gave a small chuckle. "You really should have said something earlier."

"Forsooth, Guy." Otto also reached to refill his wine, his eyes dancing with a mix of merriment and relief. "What was that you said about not dallying with the servants?"

Guy sat back down in his chair, his knees weak and his stomach still jittery with nerves. "Every rule needs an exception," he stated, finally looking away from Lord Ulric and raising his eyes to Kitty. Did she know that he acted purely to save her?

"And what an exception." Lord Ulric raised his glass to the red-faced serving maid still standing by his side.

"You may leave us now, Kitty," Guy said. Her obvious shame made him almost regret his actions, but then she flashed him the smallest of smiles and he knew she was grateful to him. His relief was almost as great as when Lord Ulric released his sword. Relief which mingled with the buzz of adrenaline and intoxication from the wine. He suddenly needed to be near her. "Hold on," he ordered, just as she reached the door. With a nod at his amused companions, Guy stood up from the table and crossed the hall to meet her. She smelled of freshly baked bread and something sweeter. A strand of hair had escaped her cap, and Guy had to control his urge to push it back behind her shell-like ear. The poor girl still trembled like a leaf, but he could not put an arm around her shoulders to offer comfort. "Finish up in the kitchen and go straight up to your chamber," he told her in a low voice that only she could hear. Her green eyes grew wide as saucers as she looked up at him in alarm. He leaned closer. "Then bolt your door from the inside and allow no one admittance."

Relief washed over her features, removing the lines of worry and leaving her beautiful once again. "Thank you, my lord," she whispered.

"You shall always be safe in this castle," he breathed, unable to prevent his hand brushing lightly against her arm. "For as long as I am Earl of Rossfarne."

Chapter Seven

THEIR UNINVITED GUESTS left soon after sunrise. They took with them supplies for the journey, skins of wine and great hunks of freshly-baked bread, but were in too much of a hurry to break their fast at Rossfarne Castle. Kitty stood at the small window in her chamber and watched them leave, the clatter of their horses' hooves ringing through the dense castle walls.

Thank goodness, she thought. Her skin still burned with shame as she recalled the way Lord Ulric had so casually announced that he would spend the night with her. As if she were worth nothing. It had taken all her self-restraint not to flee from the table, but she'd known a real servant would stay in the great hall until she was dismissed. Fear, though, had knotted her stomach. The Earl of Darkmoor was an old man, his hands trembled and his cragged face was creased and lined, but he was a warrior still. His toughness was apparent in his every move. Despite her youth, she would have been no match for him in strength. And his son positively burned with energy and might. 'The Feared One' Agnes had called him, downstairs in the castle kitchen. Then she had nudged Kitty's arm and said she was sure she'd feel no fear in his arms. Cook had shaken her wooden spoon at the both of them, even though Kitty had played no part in Agnes's smutty talk.

The Earl of Rossfarne had saved her.

It was an unexpected twist. The man she thought would ruin her honour had in fact defended it. What should she make of that?

Kitty worked through her morning chores, deeply lost in thought. What concerned her most of all was how her eyes had instinctively flown to him for help. She had known, somehow, that he would not let Lord Ulric near her. She had felt protected in his presence, more so when he bade her to bolt her door from the inside. Was he a man of integrity, after all? She shivered a little at the memory of how he had jumped up from the table, anger flashing from his dark eyes. "She is mine," he had said. And even though that sentiment flew scarily close to the secret truth, her heart had gladdened at his words.

She had never thought to have such a handsome protector.

Kitty leant her sweeping brush against the wall and put her hands to her flushed cheeks. What fresh madness was this now? She had no time for such flights of fancy.

The big castle kitchen always knew a moment of quiet directly after luncheon. Cook would sink into an overstuffed chair pulled near the fireplace and close her eyes. Agnes would slip outside to meet Gwen the laundress, and Kitty, up until now, would retire to her narrow bedchamber and pace the floor in a flurry of nerves. Not today though. Today begged to be different, especially after the conflicts of yesterday.

Kitty ached with desire to leave the restrictive, grey castle walls. She longed to feel the sun on her face and sand between her toes. For almost a week her every waking thought had been consumed with recovering Rosalind's jewels, but her focused efforts had gotten her nowhere. The jewels were not secreted in the solar. She'd been able to overturn every inch of the room over the last few days. The castle did not have vaults, and her discrete enquiries had failed to uncover where the silver and coin chests were stored. Surely there must be a room dedicated to them? But for as long as she had known, the earl had always been a single, unmarried man with no family. Mayhap no stash of treasure was kept here? Mayhap that was why the new earl had been so keen to get his hands on her family's remaining jewels?

Kitty pushed such thoughts from her mind. She would grant herself a short break from all jewel-related worries and wonderings. For the next hour, until the belltower tolled, she would remember what it was to be something other than a chambermaid in the Castle of Rossfarne.

Katherine. Her real name was Katherine. As a child she had worn elegant gowns and travelled in a carriage. She had a tutor who had taught her music and praised her singing. A maid had combed her unruly mop of hair and told her she was pretty.

Kitty hung her apron on the hook by the pantry door and stretched her tired arms above her head. Hours of scrubbing, carrying and helping in the kitchen had left her sore and aching. What she would love to do would be to soak in a tub by the fire. She remembered how Alfred would stoke the flames and Lizzie would fetch them hot water. Those days were gone now.

Not gone, she corrected herself. She would return to her old life and the people who loved her just as soon as she found the jewels.

She shook her head in amusement. Despite her best efforts, it was impossible to stop her thoughts circling back to the real reason she was here.

She was about to walk outside when her name was called down the servant's staircase.

"Kitty."

The voice was masculine and harsh. One she couldn't fail to recognise. Her heart sank.

"I'm here."

She walked steadily along the stone-flagged passageway until she could see up the stairs. Thomas peered down at her, his face made even more querulous with a deep frown.

"His lordship wants to see you, in his solar."

"Now?" She couldn't help herself. The request baffled her.

"No, on midsummer's eve." His voice dripped with sarcasm. "Of course, now. What are you waiting for?"

Should she re-tie her apron, tidy her hair? Kitty had been

preparing to walk on the beach and look for pretty pebbles, not go in front of an earl. But Thomas's snarl made it clear there were to be no further delays. Hastily wiping her hands on her woollen skirts, Kitty ascended the stairs and followed the manservant through the great hall.

"I know the way," she couldn't resist stating as Thomas ushered her past the vast stone fireplace, their footsteps echoing through the empty room which bore no traces of last night's feast. The trestle table had been pushed back against the wall and the grate was dark and empty.

Thomas didn't respond, not even with a darkening of his expression. Kitty knew she shouldn't tease him, but her days were long with little to break the monotony.

"Why do you think he wants to see me?" she asked. Her impish question hid genuine curiosity. She had felt safe in his presence yesterday, but would that have changed with the morning light?

This time he turned, his face thunderous. "Why would any earl wish to see a chambermaid alone?"

His words winded her, but she wouldn't let him see. "To complain about my work, maybe?" she suggested innocently.

Thomas made a noise that sounded like a horse grunting, before knocking gently on the solar door and flinging it open with a flourish.

"Thank you, Thomas. You may leave us now," came the earl's voice.

Thomas's face turned a darker shade of red, but he turned without a word and stalked back through the great hall, his boots clumping against the stones.

"Kitty, close the door behind you, please."

Her composure had left along with the manservant. Kitty did as she was told, her hands trembling, then stood quietly in the corner awaiting further instructions.

The Earl of Rossfarne was sitting at his desk by the window. The afternoon sunlight cast a golden glow all around him, almost like a halo. She remembered his fingers closing around her wrist and the unanticipated pull of attraction in the pit of her stomach. He had willingly ascended the tower steps to find her dropped broom, despite being stooped with pain. The earl was injured, yet none of his household knew. Who was tending to him?

How, in fact, had he come by such an injury? She recalled the low-cut sumptuous gowns secreted in his solar and shuddered. Perhaps a jealous husband had sliced him with a sword.

Such a jumble of thoughts crowded her mind that she couldn't hope to sift through them. This was a man the villagers feared, albeit as a consequence of his bloodline, but there was no escaping the fact of his sordid wager with her father. She should despise him. But he had also shown her glimmers of something else. Honour and maybe even kindness. He'd conversed with her almost as an equal, despite thinking her nothing more than a servant. And yesterday he had saved her from the unwanted attentions of Lord Ulric. What did that mean?

More pressingly, what did he want with her now?

Her heart jumped in her chest like a bird beating its wings against a cage. The palms of her hands grew hot as the silence stretched between them. Still the earl sat at his desk, head down, writing. Seemingly absorbed in his task. He must be a man of learning. A dazzling haze of light obscured his chiselled features, but she could see his long, ink-stained fingers holding the quill. Fingers that she had felt against her own flesh.

She bit down on her lip. She could bear it no longer.

She cleared her throat. "You asked to see me, my lord."

He looked up sharply. "Where did you train as a servant?"

His words took her by surprise and her mind unhelpfully went blank. She could hardly reveal that she had learned all she knew by watching Lizzie at Shoreston Manor.

"A housekeeper helped me," she said at last.

"A housekeeper in which establishment?" He looked back down at the parchment as if her answer hardly interested him.

"A minor manor far from the coast. You won't know it, my

lord."

Immediately he looked back at her, and she shrank backwards under the scorching force of his gaze. Dark eyes boring into her soul. Did he recognise her deception? Was he about to claim her as his own? A prize won in a game of dice, witnessed by many.

She is mine, he'd said last night. Did he actually know this for a fact?

Dread circled around her stomach, and she half closed her eyes against the inevitable shame.

"Try me," he said.

Her heart pounded as she reached desperately into the recesses of her memory for a name. "It was near Belford," she said weakly. "After the crossroads."

She had no idea if there were crossroads at the village of Belford, but the detail seemed to convince him.

"They do things differently there, no doubt." His dark eyes roamed over her face. Looking for what? But he merely pursed his lips and added, "Just as we do here."

"Here, my lord?" She realised too late that her voice rang out across his solar with the clarity of a lady.

He put his head to one side, watching her. "You will have noticed, Kitty, that we keep meagre staff."

Her mind raced again. Was this a challenge? Compared to Shoreston, Rossfarne Castle positively teemed with servants.

She lowered her eyes. "'Tis not my place to notice." She deliberately altered her speech patterns to match those of her fellow servants below stairs. She would have to try harder to mirror all of their ways. How else did she readily give away her true identity?

The earl sat back in his high-backed chair and opened his arms expansively. "Come now," his voice was encouraging. "We have no guards, no musicians, no entertainers." He marked them off with his hands. "No lady's maids of course, for there are no ladies."

He had found her out. Kitty felt the world spin around her.

"Life here is very different to life at Answick Castle, for example," he added.

Her knees sagged. She waited.

"Would you not say?" he prompted when she didn't respond.

"I wouldn't know, my lord." It was hot in here. Too hot. She felt a flush rising through the wool of her dress up her neck and a log crackled in the grate as if to mock her plight.

"How did you pass your time in your minor manor at Belford?"

She clutched her hands together until the blood left her fingers. "I'm unsure of your meaning."

"In the evenings." He rose from his desk and walked towards her like a wolf approaching its prey. "How did you pass your time in the evenings, when all your work was done?"

Was he going to come all the way over to her? He was so tall, his shoulders so broad, that he made her feel small and insignificant. A chambermaid to be trifled with.

Kitty lifted her chin. "A servant's work is never done, my lord."

She spoke with all the authority of her mother's daughter and as soon as the words left her lips, she recognised her mistake. But the earl's expression did not change.

"Much like a knight," he suggested, pausing by the fireplace and glancing down into the flickering flames. "All the more reason to seek pleasure in our rare moments of repose."

The sun passed from behind a cloud, illuminating him with renewed colour. Kitty noticed a flash of sorrow in his eyes. His face, she realised, was quite beautiful. His thick eyelashes curved upwards and a faint covering of dark stubble served to emphasise his jutting cheek bones. So he was a knight. Her mind reeled with this new knowledge. The image did not sit with her old views of the Earl of Rossfarne, but it chimed well with the man keen to protect her from a lecherous guest.

His injury must have been caused in battle. Her eyes widened as she made the connection. Not a drunken brawl or a spat over a woman. An honest battle fought under the king.

"You served King Edward?" she asked, the words leaving her mouth before she could think better of them.

His dark eyebrows lifted a notch. "For many years."

She bit down on her lip. That had been another mistake. Servants didn't ask questions. It would be best to lower her gaze and simply wait to hear his reasons for summoning her.

She was safe, surely, with a knight of the realm?

He had served the king for many years. But how many, she wondered? The earl was older than she, that much was evident. How much older? The depths of his gaze suggested a type of wisdom only acquired with age, yet his hair was as back as night, not streaked with grey. Thirty, she guessed. He could not be less, for men of more tender years rarely had such formidable bearing.

Silence, thick and heavy, enveloped them. Kitty began to feel drowsy with heat from the fire. A fire that was surely unnecessary this far into spring? She longed to relax in the overstuffed chair which sat invitingly just feet away. For all her hard work at Shoreston Manor, she realised now that she had never truly understood what it was to be a servant.

Kitty gave herself a little shake to banish the weariness and found the earl gazing directly at her. His head was lifted with all his usual authority, but his eyes were curious, questioning. She could withstand his customary ferocity, but not this quiet consideration. It made her feel false and deceitful.

What would happen if she simply told the earl the truth about who she was and why she was here?

As if reading her mind, he straightened up, impressing upon her again the sheer size of him. His dark blue tunic clung to his powerful shoulders and once she had noticed, she found it hard to look away. She recalled how she had paused on the beach and pictured his muscular calves wrapped around the belly of his horse and a blush rose to her cheeks. He stood before her, clad in riding breeches which underlined every bulging muscle in his long legs. He was a giant of a man. A warrior. What manner of opponent had managed to fell him?

"It is customary, I believe, for a man in my position to be offered entertainment."

His statement jolted her, and her lips parted in surprise. "I know little of such things."

"No?" His eyebrows raised, questioning her or mocking her? She couldn't decide. "Have you never heard of musicians, jesters?"

Relief washed through her. Kitty's mother had often recounted tales of brightly-lit occasions at Answick Castle, when the duke and his family were diverted by the likes of musicians and jesters. For a moment she had feared the earl might list out other, more scandalous forms of entertainment. Her mind twitched again to the low-cut dresses in the wooden chests, and her pulse sped up.

He was still waiting for her answer. "I believe I have, my lord."

Her words pleased him. He looked at her closely, capturing her in his dark eyes. "Do you sing, Kitty?"

Her heart seemed to stop. "Sing?"

"Sing," he confirmed mildly.

Kitty loved to sing. Since she was a small child, she had burst into a song at a moment's notice. At Shoreston, she sang while she rolled out pastry and beat the rugs, but since arriving in Rossfarne Castle she had deliberately stayed quiet.

Except for that one time, here in the solar. Had he heard her? Dread pooled in her insides.

"I don't, my lord," she answered firmly, despite the sting of heat in her cheeks. Ladies sang in parlours to appreciative gentlefolk, but she was sure that servants did not.

"I should like to hear you try."

Her eyebrows shot up towards her hair. What was happening here?

"I don't believe..." She swallowed, searching for the words. "I don't believe that singing is usually considered part of a chambermaid's duties."

Something flickered in his expression. She wrenched her eyes away from his, conscious once again that she had spoken out of turn.

The earl pursed his lips as if considering the idea. "But you served at the table last night, did you not? Such a thing is also not a typical duty of a chambermaid. Anyway, my castle, my rules."

She blanched as a new wave of heat travelled through her body. He was testing her. That was it. But how should she answer him?

Like a servant, that was how. She bobbed her head, conscious of her hair springing free of her white cap. "If it pleases you, my lord."

"Excellent." He rubbed his hands together. "Return here later this evening and we shall see how a chambermaid's duties may be further amended."

WHAT SHOULD SHE *do?*

Kitty was distracted by that question all afternoon. Her attention wandered so far from her chores that Cook had to speak to her severely to prevent her burning the sweetmeats.

How could she go alone to the earl's solar and sing for him? The very idea was preposterous, yet it was what he had asked of her. And she was a servant in his employ. Again and again her thoughts returned to the conclusion that a genuine servant would have no choice but to comply. Twice she nearly blurted out her problems into Cook's kindly ear, but to do so would invite further conversation which might risk revealing her true identity—and with it, the fact of her father's wager.

She simply couldn't do it. Her shame was too great to say the sordid words out loud.

"Kitty, are you listening to me?"

She dropped the soup ladle in shock. "Sorry, Cook."

"You're away with the fairies this eve," Cook tutted.

"I'm sorry." Kitty bent to recover the ladle then placed her palms down on the scrubbed pine table to centre herself in the room.

"I was asking if you wanted to join Agnes and myself on a trip to the market tomorrow."

Cook's words made no sense to Kitty's tormented mind.

"It's our half day," the older woman reminded her gently. "And market day over in Rossfarne."

Market day in Rossfarne. The notion was from another life entirely. A life she dared not step back into, not yet. What if she saw someone she knew?

Kitty gathered her wits. "It's kind of you to offer, but I must use the time to do some mending." It was true enough. Her stockings were full of holes.

Cook shrugged. "Suit yourself. If you're finished with the soup you can take it up for Thomas."

"No need, I'm here." The earl's manservant shouldered past Kitty in his haste to pick up the tray and be gone from the kitchen.

"I don't think he likes me very much," Kitty remarked as his heavy footsteps resounded up the servants' stairs.

"Thomas likes no one," Agnes stated, spinning a rolling pin between her sticky hands.

"He's devoted to his lordship though," Cook said conversationally. "He served him all through the Welsh wars. It seems neither of them are enjoying life away from the battlefield."

Kitty stopped slicing bread and listened closely. So it was true. The Earl of Rossfarne was a knight.

"He'll be gone as soon as the old man's affairs are in order," Cook concluded.

Agnes shuffled closer to both of them and checked over her shoulder to ensure they were alone. "Gwen told me he'd been robbed."

"Robbed?" Cook wiped her hands on her apron. "Where did she hear such a thing?"

"Thomas told one of the grooms." Agnes swiped a sweetmeat from the platter which Kitty had carefully arranged.

"I told you before, I want no gossip in my kitchen."

Agnes held up her hand. "But it affects us all. If his lordship can't pay his tithes to old Longshanks, we'll all be looking for a new position."

Kitty held her breath. Was this why the earl had need of her family jewels?

"Nonsense." Cook resumed her work. "That Gwen is filling your head with fanciful tales. I thought better of you, Agnes."

Agnes merely shrugged. Kitty had observed before how Cook's scolding washed straight over her.

"How are you getting on with the marzipan?" Cook demanded.

"Terrible." Agnes pursed her lips. "I haven't the knack for it. Mayhap Kitty should try?"

"Aye, mayhap she should. Go on then, off with you, Agnes. Kitty, come here and help me."

Kitty was conscious of time passing. The earl would be expecting her upstairs at any moment, but she had no choice but to follow Cook and take over the rolling of the marzipan, which Agnes had made such a terrible mess of.

"She's a wily one," commented Cook as they both gathered up the sticky dough. "She thinks I don't know what she's about."

Kitty looked up in surprise, and Cook gave her a wink.

"Agnes can dress a cake with marzipan as well as you or I, she just pretends to have no knack for it so she can retire early."

Kitty cut a neat circle of marzipan and spread the cake with jam to make it stick. "It's a fine idea," she commented, biting her lip as her mind started to whirl.

"Fine indeed, but cunning as a fox." Cook sighed. "Thank goodness for you, Kitty. You're a good worker and honest as the day is long."

Kitty hid her flush of shame by concentrating hard on trimming the excess marzipan with a blunt knife. She spun the cake around to check all was level and was grateful when Cook finally bustled off to the pantry.

Alone in the kitchen, she straightened up and carefully positioned the knife on the sideboard. Cook had embarrassed her, but also given her the beginnings of an idea.

The earl had instructed her to sing for him, but that didn't mean she had to sing well. Kitty licked her fingers, liking her plan. She would attend his solar, as requested, but she would make sure he never made such a request again.

Chapter Eight

W OULD SHE COME?

Guy paced the solar as the shadows lengthened around him, waiting to see what fate had in store. His situation reminded him of the time immediately before a battle. You picked the favourable ground, prepared as best you could and then let events play themselves out.

He tried to ignore the critical inner voice which calmly stated that he should never have asked her to come and sing for him, certainly not alone. She was a servant, for goodness sake.

Although she wasn't just a servant. She was a puzzle he was determined to solve.

He paused by the window and allowed himself to look out, even though the view brought him pain. From here, the view of the sea was limited. All he could see were the forbidding granite walls of the barbican and the windswept inner courtyard. The similarities with Forbisher, the great estate where he had spent his childhood, were uncomfortably apparent. That desolate patch of open land stretching out to the gatehouse could be the same grassy knoll where he had played swords with Angus, his younger brother—the only time he had ever willingly given away his advantage.

He closed his eyes to banish the ghosts of his past, yet still they rose up around him. Since coming to Rossfarne, he had seen Angus everywhere. His cheerful smile as he ran across the long gallery; his excitable young voice urging Guy down to the beach.

These were mere tricks of memory, for Angus had never visited this castle. Had never grown old enough to leave Forbisher.

It was only his isolation and enforced inactivity giving rise to such flights of fancy. His lively mind, usually occupied from dawn to dusk, was free to roam into nooks and crannies he had deliberately left long abandoned. Newly empowered, these phantoms were becoming real to him, and it was harder than ever to shut them out.

Which was why he'd asked the girl to come and sing for him. Nay, he hadn't asked. He had ordered.

A tentative knock sounded on his door.

"Come." His voice was a growl. Unexpectedly, he was angry at her for coming. His request had been ill advised and he'd half hoped she would have the backbone to refuse him.

Kitty shuffled through the door and closed it softly behind her, reluctance apparent in her every movement. She wore a clean white apron with every bit of her hair swept up beneath a snugly fitting cap. Her reddened hands were neatly folded and her eyes downcast. She bobbed a slight nod and stood with her shoulders hunched forwards, so different to the graceful, upright posture she usually displayed. Then, nothing. She kept her back pressed to the wall and studied the floor as if searching for a lost jewel.

At the sight of her, something inside him cracked. His anger evaporated like a puff of smoke in the presence of her quiet composure.

She didn't speak up like she had before. Her lips pressed together as if she would keep any words inside her by force. He'd drawn attention to her waywardness, he realised. And now she would stay silent and obedient before him, like any other member of his household staff.

Damnation. That was not what he wanted.

"You have come," he said at last.

"As you requested, my lord."

"Come forwards," he beckoned irritably. "Stand before the

fireplace."

She walked readily enough to take her position while he in turn lowered himself into an armchair. His long fingers beat a drum-like rhythm on the arm but aside from that, the room was as still as it had ever been. Even the flickering flames in the grate seemed to pause.

"Well," he barked. "What are we waiting for?"

Her green eyes widened almost imperceptibly but she kept her gaze focused on the rush-covered floor.

"I am awaiting further instruction."

Frustration swelled within him but at the same moment, he recognised the flash of backbone he'd been hoping for. She was toying with him, like a canny knight leading troops into a trap.

He settled more comfortably into the chair. Two could play at that game.

"Your instructions are to sing for me, if you please, Kitty."

"But I do not know how, my lord." Her voice was without expression. She could have been reciting a line written for her.

He twirled his signet ring, beginning to enjoy himself. "Let's start with a tune from your childhood," he suggested. "Mayhap something your mother sang to you?"

He wasn't expecting his casual proposition to have such a profound effect. Immediately her head lifted, and a surge of defiance flashed through her delicate features.

"My mother?" she repeated. "How do you know that my mother could sing?"

"Merely a guess on my part." He met her gaze levelly. What was she hiding? "All mothers sing to their children, do they not?" He stretched out his long legs and crossed them at the ankle in a show of casual indifference. His mother had never sung, neither to Guy nor Angus. Although he liked to believe the coolness displayed by his parents was the exception rather than the norm.

Kitty's face closed off again. "'Twas a long time ago. I can't remember the words."

He recalled the soaring melodies the girl before him had sung just a few nights ago and once more quelled his impatience. She was like a wealthy baron, lying and misleading to jostle for favour with the king. Her calm confidence was somehow unsettling him, as if he was the visitor in her chamber. He ran a hand beneath the loose collar of his tunic, wishing he had not positioned them both so close to the fire. "Why don't we forget about the words for now? Just hum the tune."

She looked as if she might question him once more, but then began to hum some unidentifiable tune, just as he had requested. The noise coming from her was toneless and grating, one moment deep and the other painfully high. He was at first surprised and then entertained. Rather than speaking up and interrupting her flow, he simply sat and waited for her to draw the performance to a close.

"Well now, Kitty, how did you enjoy that?" he asked once she had abruptly fallen silent.

She opened her arms, her face a mask of innocence. "I don't know, my lord."

"It was delightful," he announced, relishing her look of surprise. It took all his self-control not to crack a smile.

"Really?" She was like a deer caught in the path of a huntsman's bow.

"I should like to hear it again." He leaned forwards with his elbows on his breeches and looked up at her expectantly.

Her mouth tightened. "I am no minstrel, my lord." Her voice was low and full of the authority he'd come to associate with this enigmatic maid.

"I should think not." He pretended to think for a moment, running a hand through his unruly dark hair. "I have seen many a minstrel perform for the king, and not one was as pretty as you."

She started back as if his words had burned her, and he knew a moment's regret. But the game was afoot and he would not be outplayed.

"Very well." She straightened up and lifted her chin in a further display of fortitude. "Would you like a different tune this time?"

"Very much." Guy bit down on his lip to prevent himself from smiling widely.

She started up again. This time the tune was less uncertain, more deliberately dreadful. He kept his expression carefully neutral, until Kitty's voice hit a soaring soprano note which wobbled down to a tremulous, off-key bass and Guy felt his face break into the first genuine smile he had known for many months.

Oblivious to his emotional journey, Kitty soldiered on. Guy rested his forehead on his palm in an attempt to hide his merriment, but when she repeated the same refrain, he couldn't help a snort of laughter from escaping him.

Kitty stopped abruptly and gave him a sharp look. Her sea-green eyes were impossible to read. "Have I displeased you, my lord?"

"Not at all." He straightened up and cleared his throat. "I liked it enormously."

"Really?"

Was her lip twitching as if she too was hiding a smile? Despite her humble attire, Kitty was looking less and less like a chamber-maid. Her back was straight and her hands were folded demurely in her skirts, exactly like a well-bred young lady conversing with her equals.

"Oh yes." He paused, weighing up his next words. "I would beg for a third, though I begin to fear I have already pushed my luck too far."

He had given himself away. He saw it in a flash of her lively green eyes. She was onto him.

Kitty smoothed down her skirts as a faint tinge of pink stained her cheeks. "I believe I must rest my voice, for a little while at least."

"Of course," he nodded seriously, trying to hide the slight stab of disappointment. "I quite understand." He fumbled for some way to prolong their conversation. "Steam, I believe, is beneficial for the throat."

"Is that so, my lord?" Her eyes widened in what must be pretend fascination. "I begin to suspect that you too are a master of the singing arts."

She was playing with him. And to his complete surprise, he was more than willing to go along with it.

He raised his chin to meet her gaze and inclined his head to the side in a show of modesty. "Not a master, I assure you."

"A scholar then." Her eyes ducked down once again to the rushes on the floor, and he sensed her withdrawal. Mayhap she was as aware of the frisson that had sprung up between them as he was? A frisson that should never exist between servant and master. But the connection he felt was real, sincere, uncaring of position. And if he allowed their conversation to falter for another moment, this unanticipated joviality would become nothing more than a memory.

"A scholar. I would grant you that." He sprang to his feet in sudden eagerness to extend the game they had unwittingly entered into. But he hadn't reckoned on the effect which her singular, untouched loveliness would have on him. A beat passed as he took in her intelligent face, which was alight with mirth and daring. "I recognise beauty when I see it." His voice was rough, his words rushed.

She took half a step backwards. "You are too kind," she stuttered, alarm flickering across her previously composed features.

He'd frightened her. He must put it right.

"Would you like me to sing for you now?" he offered wildly. Anything to take the look of fear from her eyes.

It worked. Her mouth once again twitched, showing her efforts to conceal a smile.

"Very much, my lord."

He pressed his lips together. He knew no songs. "Perhaps a duet?"

She inclined her head. "Very well."

She launched once again into her uncertain tune, and this

time he raised his voice along with hers, following her discordant notes up and down and to all beats in-between. Within seconds their mouths had stretched into smiles which were now impossible to deny. Moments later Kitty erupted into a peal of laughter, and he followed suit, holding onto the fireplace as his shoulders shook with merriment.

Kitty regained her composure first. "When did you hear me sing?" she asked, with such upfront honesty that Guy was taken aback.

"Here, in my solar," he answered promptly. "A few nights since."

She acknowledged the truth of it with a faint grimace. "Forgive me, my lord."

"There is nothing to forgive. The sound of your voice made me forget my troubles for a moment." There he was again, spilling the private truth of his heart to a woman he hardly knew.

She smiled but her eyes slid away from his. She was preparing to withdraw from him again. He could feel it in the air. Yet she hesitated for long enough to give proper consideration to his rash words. "My mother always said that was the power of singing. Of music."

A beat passed. "I believe your mother to be correct," he said quietly.

This was madness. To what end was he trying to prolong their conversation? She was his serving maid. He should dismiss her back below stairs. But once she had gone, he would be alone once again. Just him and his demons.

She swallowed, as if she too were aware of the rare closeness this moment had provided for them. "If my singing brought some respite from the pain of your injury, then I am glad of it."

He nodded curtly, reluctant even now to acknowledge that moment of vulnerability. She had seen him wracked with pain, barely able to stand. He had heard her sing. In this, they had shown one another glimpses of their true selves.

"Will you sing for me again?" he asked quickly, before he

could think better of it. "With your true voice."

A glimmer of uncertainty passed over her green eyes. "Is that all you want from me?"

Another upfront question which startled him anew.

"Of course." He gave the assurance readily. He was not his uncle. He wouldn't impose himself on a servant, no matter how drawn he felt to this particular maid. He only wanted to sit for a moment and enjoy the unparalleled beauty of her singing.

True to his inner musings he withdrew from the fireplace and sat back in the chair.

She watched him quietly for a moment, as if gathering her thoughts, then she settled her cap more securely, lifted her chin and began to sing.

At once he was seized by the richness of the melody. Kitty's voice soared through the quiet room, a force of pure, unfiltered beauty and power. He was unfamiliar with the words, yet some jumped out at him, pulling him into those recesses of memory he was most fearful of exploring. She sang of hope and loss and love, and Guy found himself forced to remember his little brother. The joy of his laughter and the bitterness of his unnecessary passing. He was taken back to nights spent in the chilling cold of the battlefield, scanning the faces of the dead for friends. And simultaneously, to sources of unexpected happiness. The rosy dawn of a sunrise. Birdsong over a babbling brook. The warming glow of comradery.

When she finished, he found his eyes were wet with unshed tears. Tears he hastily blinked back. Kitty's song had left his emotions exposed. He longed for contact from another human soul. For the first time, he felt an urge to unburden himself. To vocalise his loneliness, his pain and his fears that he may never make it back to the service of the king.

His eyes met hers across the short distance of the room. He saw a faint flush rising to her porcelain cheeks and her chest rise and fall with a heightened heartbeat. Her womanly curves drew his attention. Such a generous bosom narrowing to a waist he could surely span with his hands.

Her lips parted. Lips that he could imagine pressing to his own. Confusion clouded her brow.

"Did my song not please you, my lord?"

How could he answer? Her song had wrung the life from him.

"It was very pleasant," he answered hoarsely. And he kicked himself for the anxiety coursing through her beautiful eyes. She had expected approval and he had provided none. She was still young enough to feel the sting of rejection.

He rubbed at his temple. She was young. And she was under his employ.

And he was not his uncle.

"Thank you, Kitty."

"You are most welcome, my lord."

As she bobbed into another small obeisance, he almost waved his hand and told her not to bother.

This woman, whoever she was, was no servant.

She went about the castle like a chambermaid yet she sang like an angel and spoke like a noblewoman. She was an enigma still. More so now than ever.

He rubbed at his temples again, weary with this ceaseless internal debate. How wonderful it would be to trust without first searching beneath the surface of things.

"Is there anything else, my lord?"

He glanced up to meet her level gaze. How could he question the motives of one so modest and lovely, with a voice surely gifted from above?

"Nothing else, Kitty. You may retire for the evening."

Did disappointment flash across her even features? Disappointment which he found mirrored in his own heart. Their stolen evening of irreverent gaiety was at an end.

She walked towards the doorway. In another moment she would be gone.

"Will you sing for me again? Tomorrow?" His voice rang

through the solar. Too loud. Too eager.

She turned, unable to hide the pleasure in her eyes. She too must feel this connection between them. A connection he should sever at once, or else risk obtaining as grievous a reputation as the previous Earl of Rossfarne.

"I should be pleased to," she said simply.

At once his worries vanished. Kitty was no slattern. She wouldn't tell false tales of impropriety down in the servants' quarters. She would sing, and he would listen. For a short time, he would be released from the incessant weight of his burdens. What business was this of anyone else?

"Good night, Kitty."

She inclined her head. "Good night, my lord."

She took the life and buoyancy from the room with her. Guy sat for a moment and allowed the silence to wash over him. It had been a strange evening. Not what he had anticipated. But better. A thousand times more delightful.

Thomas had brought him a jug of fine mead some time earlier. Guy had imagined he might need it, but the mead had sat forgotten on a side table. Kitty's presence had been intoxicating enough. Now he poured himself a goblet and drank it down quickly. The taste was surprisingly good. He poured another, then stayed his hand. He must not drown his troubles in drink. He'd seen many a good knight wander down the road to ruin that way.

Far better to listen to a maid singing than to seek solace in a bottle.

He could think up a thousand arguments in its favour, but deep down he knew his request was wrong. It was wrong because he was drawn to Kitty. Heat traversed his loins at the sight of her. When she sang, it was as if he was gripped by a fever. She was a curious mix of young and wise, slender and curvaceous, modest and knowing. In another life he might have run his fingers through her rippling mane of fiery hair. Might have pressed his lips to hers and let his hand roam free over her long limbs.

Seeking to bring her pleasure. Seeking to find his own.

He slammed the goblet onto the tray and wiped his lips. Was he becoming infected by his uncle's salacious spirit?

Kitty was a servant in his employ. Therefore, their union was an impossible dream. Guy would not become a man who preyed upon his household. It would be an abuse of power, and the very idea turned his stomach.

He would keep his distance, but her presence was vital to ensure his sanity in this claustrophobic space. Not for long, however. His wound was healing. The first stirrings of strength were returning to his left hand. He would oversee the necessary repairs to make the castle safe for the long winter months, then he would leave.

And the long summer nights ahead of him would be lightened by Kitty's sweet singing voice. Nothing more.

At last, a plan. His lively mind began to run through the necessary steps. He must find a stonemason to repair the gatehouse. But before that, he needed to establish exactly how low his uncle had allowed the coin chests to become. Distrust of the household, mixed with a fear of further bad news, had made him reluctant to investigate when he first arrived in Rossfarne, but now he knew the servants better. It was unlikely the stout cook would mount a heist against him. And as for bad news, it was better to know the worst than to live in fear and uncertainty.

The coin chests were secreted inside the well in the great hall, that much he knew. He would have Thomas bring them out tomorrow, together with any jewellery that had survived the reign of the old earl. Although Guy strongly suspected the old man would have squandered any pieces of value and lost the rest on loose women and gambling.

Guy left the solar and started ascending the stone stairs to his bedchamber, holding a candle in his good right hand to illuminate the way. The castle's silence was absolute. Most inhabitants were already asleep. But despite his intentions to go quietly, Guy cursed aloud at the thought of jewels and gambling.

He had forgotten the cloth bag of jewels taken from Owain the Drunkard. Jewels which he must return to the man's daughters.

He should never have taken them. Only misplaced pride and a determination to prove himself physically dominant, despite his injury, had carried him to the neglected manor to retrieve his ill-gotten winnings. That and ale. Too much of it. He had been twisted up with bitterness absorbed from his past, spiked with frustration following the theft of his own coin.

He must tread a different path if he didn't want to finish up the same way as his forefathers, despised by all who knew them.

But Shoreston Manor had seemed deserted when he rode over there the next day and he had no wish to waste another journey. Maybe one of the servants knew of Owain and his daughters?

He shouldered open the door to his bedchamber and placed the flickering candle on an oak chest. The castle servants kept themselves to themselves, rarely mingling with folk from the town of Rossfarne. But Kitty had travelled through the town recently, she may have heard something.

He would ask her tomorrow, he resolved, when she came to his solar.

Chapter Nine

T HE EARL OF Rossfarne leaned back in his chair and regarded
her steadily. His chiselled features were illuminated by the
dancing flames of the fire, but it was impossible for her to
decipher the expression in his dark eyes.

It was hot in the solar. So very hot. A trickle of perspiration
ran down her spine, beneath her plain woollen dress. Kitty
wished she was wearing something lighter, less restrictive. She
had summoned depths of passion and channelled them into her
song, but now that it was over, those fierce emotions rampaged
through her body with nowhere to go. Heat suffused her,
bringing a flush to her chest and neck. Her hand went unwittingly
to the buttons of her bodice. If she could only have a little air.

Something changed in the earl's expression as her fingers
found the first button. He leaned forwards, gazing at her raptly
and, as her eyes fixed upon his, Kitty's pulse sped up. They gazed
at one another, across the narrow width of the room and a new,
unfamiliar tension uncoiled inside her core.

Air, all she wanted was air. She remembered the low-cut
dresses concealed within the chest and suddenly they didn't seem
indecent anymore. As if her fingers had a life of their own, they
undid the top button of her bodice, and it opened a fraction.

She felt some relief but not enough, not nearly enough. The
heat of the room had found a home deep inside her and now it
demanded release. She opened a second button, then a third.
Now her dress was open in a deep V shape and her breasts

strained at the remaining fabric.

The earl spoke up softly. His voice was as rich as velvet. "Don't stop."

She wouldn't stop. This was what she wanted. His eyes on her. Mayhap even his hands on her. They had sung together and laughed together. In that, he'd revealed his true soul and now she couldn't look at his finely carved, muscular body without a hot flush of desire shooting through her.

She undid the fourth button, such a tiny thing to have such significance, and her dress fell away from her shoulders, the bodice pooling around her waist. The earl sprang to his feet in a heartbeat, arms outstretched ready to gather her towards him. She closed her eyes in delicious anticipation of his touch...

Kitty sat up in horror. Her body was flushed and damp with sweat. Darkness surrounded her and it took a moment for her to realise that she was alone in her small, narrow bedchamber.

Alone, mercifully alone.

Her breath came hard and fast. What kind of madness had infected her sleep?

She put a hand to her neck, weak with relief to find her cotton chemise still in place. It had only been a dream. But what a dream. Her mind still raced. Her body still pulsed. If only she had slept just a little longer and experienced the joy of his warm hands upon her exposed flesh...

What was she thinking?

Kitty had never expected to experience passion or desire in her life. Such emotions were for other people, not for her. She'd long closed her mind to thoughts of romance, or even companionship with any man.

Especially a man so darkly handsome as the Earl of Rossfarne.

Kitty covered her face, embarrassed by her own thoughts and the sudden spirals of her cravings. Thank goodness she'd been allocated a single servant's room and there was no one present to witness her delirium.

She got out of bed and walked to the window, shunting open

the shutters to let some fresh, sea air into the narrow chamber. She scooped up her long hair and held it away from her neck, enjoying the sudden rush of coolness. That was better. She had grown too hot in bed. Maybe that was the cause of her strange dream? That and the bewildering events of the night before.

Kitty squeezed her eyes shut. She didn't want to remember that sudden rush of happiness when their voices had joined in unison. Nor the leap of merriment in his dark eyes or how it had felt to abandon propriety and laugh together. Those feelings had been heady, sharp and unanticipated. For a moment, she'd almost forgotten her place as a servant. It had been like bygone times at Shoreston, giggling with Rosalind over some shared nonsense, secure as part of a tight-knit duo. Except her deep affection for her sister sprang from a different place entirely to this disturbing attraction for the earl.

Enough. She clenched her hands into tight fists, exhausted by her errant thoughts, only to find a far more painful memory creeping to the fore.

Her throat constricted as she recalled the closed expression on his chiselled face when she finally sang for him properly. She'd expected praise. Nay, she'd expected something more. Hoped, even, that the man sitting before her might experience the same tumult of emotions as she. But no. He'd all but dismissed her out of hand.

Her singing hadn't pleased him. She had the limited experience of a girl born and raised in a small fishing village, but Kitty had always been able to read people. Her skill had, to some degree, protected herself and Rosalind from the worst excesses of their father's drinking. The Earl of Rossfarne was in some way disappointed with her. Yet he had asked for her to sing for him again. What did that mean?

She fingered the buttons of her chemise, flushing once more to think of her wanton dream-self who had undressed under his scorching gaze. She was becoming as bad as the women of ill-repute who had acquiesced to the old earl's commands, only to be gossiped over and condemned come the next market day.

She clung to the windowsill and lowered her head to the incoming breeze, feeling once more the coolness of his appraisal.

"It was very pleasant," he'd said. Polite and disinterested when she had given him everything.

She remembered the revealing, low-cut dresses folded away in his solar. Imagined the women who had sung for him in the past. Beautiful women, delighted to be entertaining a knight of the realm. How had she ever imagined such a man would find pleasure in a plain, domesticated creature such as she?

Why did she care so much anyway? Her only duty at Rossfarne Castle was to recover her family jewels.

Nausea churned in Kitty's stomach. She had let herself and her sister down, revealing her lineage through her ill-advised singing. No low-born servant would know the song she had regaled him with last night. It was one she had learned from her music tutor. If the earl only put two and two together, he would surely begin to see through her falsehoods.

Nay, Kitty corrected herself. He already had. That was why he questioned her about her training. That was why he had requested her presence a second time. To confront her with the truth.

To claim her as his own.

"You belong to the Earl of Rossfarne."

Her body began to shake so violently she feared her legs might give way beneath her. She was scared, but fear was just one of many emotions coursing through her.

Could it be that a tiny part of her wanted to be claimed?

Swallowing hard, she gripped the windowsill and wrestled away her impure thoughts. This was no good. If she couldn't work in the castle unnoticed then she must leave. At first light. Before her subterfuge was uncovered.

Because everything had changed.

Until now, although she'd feared for her physical safety, she'd had faith in her wits and quick thinking. But if her mind were to become muddled with dark desires, who knew what traps she may walk into? Even willingly…

It was all becoming too dangerous.

For the rest of the night, she paced the wooden floor of her restrictive chamber, watching for the first rays of sunlight to penetrate the dark blanket of night. Weariness stole through her limbs, but she refused to give in to the ache of exhaustion, not when there was every possibility of her falling once more into such troubling dreams.

Would the earl look into her eyes and see the sinful thoughts spiralling around her mind? Would he know that she had unbuttoned her bodice and arched her body for his touch? The prospect was enough to make her stomach churn. How could she stand before him now?

She couldn't. She must leave. Again and again, she arrived at the same conclusion.

They would have to live without the jewels. So be it. If the rumours were true and the earl was impoverished, there was every chance he had already sold them. She turned this idea around in her mind and found it strangely pleasing. It released her from any obligation. She had tried her best, but had failed through no fault of her own.

There was no harm done. Not if she left today.

Kitty was a fisherman's daughter, and the rhythms of the tides were as familiar to her as the rise and fall of the sun. She knew the tide would be out just after dawn, leaving the causeway free. If she left now, she would be back at Shoreston Manor before Rosalind came down for breakfast. Her sister's pleasure at her unexpected return would outshine any disappointment over the jewels. Kitty knew this in her bones.

She dressed hurriedly in the simple gown she'd worn to come to Rossfarne Castle. She placed Lizzie's straw hat upon her head and breathed in the familiar fragrance of lavender from the dried sprigs their servant kept hung in her closet. It was the scent of home, so different to the sea salt and ancient stone which permeated the austere rooms of the castle. Kitty wondered how she had stayed away for so long.

Her stockinged feet would make no noise on the stone stairs. She slipped downwards through the blessedly quiet servants' quarters, holding her wooden pattens in her hand. No one had yet risen, though Kitty knew that Cook would soon be stumbling through the cavernous kitchen and beginning her daily chores.

She would miss Cook. In other circumstances she might try to say goodbye, but how could she explain her hasty departure?

No. It was best to leave unnoticed. To slip away, as if Kitty the chambermaid had never been.

She would be Miss Katherine again, to Alfred, Lizzie, and the occasional caller. At least, until the inevitable happened and they were compelled to leave Shoreston. But now she had experience to draw upon that would hold her in good stead for finding work elsewhere.

Lost in thought, she stumbled into the great hall and was brought up short by the sight of Thomas disappearing down the well. Kitty put a hand to her racing heart. Was she hallucinating? She stepped closer and peered down. No, without a doubt, that was Thomas's balding head she could see, making steady progress down the dark shaft of the well.

What was he doing?

On her arrival at the castle, Agnes had told her that this well had been positioned in the Great Hall in case they were ever under siege. Happily, such an event had never yet taken place and they drew all their water from the large well in the outer courtyard.

Was Thomas checking to see if this second water source had dried up?

Were they preparing for battle?

Kitty recalled the earl's summary of the castle's inhabitants. "No guards, no musicians, no entertainers." They had but the marshal and a few meagre stable hands to protect them. And the earl himself, a trained knight. But still, the odds seemed stacked against them withstanding any attack.

Her mind racing, Kitty stared into the depths of the well and jumped in surprise when Thomas's head and shoulders once again appeared. He was facing away from her towards the empty fireplace and she instinctively ran to hide behind a stone pillar.

Thomas heaved himself out of the well and placed his hands on his knees to recover his breath. His clothes were bone dry, but nonetheless he exuded an air of a man pleased with his findings. Kitty watched as he leaned back over the perimeter wall and brought up a coil of rope which he began to haul upon.

Whatever was on the end of the rope was far heavier than a mere bucket, for the man strained and moaned with effort. Eventually he tied the rope to an iron handle, braced himself and hauled up a great chest, so heavy he staggered under the weight of it.

Kitty's skin grew hot. This was a coin chest, much like the ones they kept in the cellar at Shoreston. Was it empty, as Agnes had foretold? Given the weight of it, she suspected not.

Thomas leaned down again and fetched up a second chest, then a third. By now, Kitty was regretting the impulse to hide. She couldn't cross the hall without drawing attention to herself, but if she didn't leave soon, the tides would be against her.

With four stout chests in a semi-circle around him, Thomas rubbed his hands together with glee. He glanced from left to right, checking his privacy, then squatted down and unlatched the nearest chest. The lid opened with a creak and Kitty couldn't help a gasp of surprise at the glittering array of jewels contained within. Thomas chuckled excitedly, reaching out to run his gnarled fingers over the sparkling gemstones.

She could almost believe there was treasure here fit for King Edward himself.

Kitty leaned against the pillar for support. Agnes had been wrong. The earl was rich beyond her wildest imaginings.

Thomas opened the next chest. This was filled with silver coin. Enough to pay an army of guards. Enough to fill Rossfarne

Castle with music and dancing and lavish furnishings.

The earl was a miser then, like his uncle. Those glimmers of humanity she had seen were fake after all. He had taken her family's fortune without a second thought while all the time he had this wealth hidden down a well.

Her stomach churned as if she might be sick, and Kitty moaned as the pillar seemed to give way against her.

Thomas whipped his head round and spied her.

"You," he snarled. "I might have guessed."

He stalked across the stone-flagged floor towards her, his cruel face screwed up with a mixture of victory and displeasure.

Kitty tried her best to straighten up as the cold of the pillar brought her back to her senses. "I have done nothing wrong," she declared calmly.

"Oh no," he sneered. "You hide here and watch me reveal the whereabouts of his lordship's coin chests and then plead innocence?"

"I am not hiding. I am merely on my way to the kitchen." Kitty wasn't wearing her servant's garb, but she trusted Thomas would not notice. Thank goodness she had left her other belongings upstairs in her chamber. "You, however, were rifling through possessions that do not belong to you."

He flinched and she saw her wild aim had hit its mark. "You are an impudent chit," he stated. "I should have you flogged."

"Why not put that to the earl?" Her voice was brave and strong though inside she quailed. "And I shall tell him that I saw you opening a chest and examining its contents. Mayhap looking for something small that would not be missed."

Thomas visibly bristled, his small eyes flickering from left to right as he sought a defence. "You shall do no such thing."

"Nor shall you," she declared. "I suggest we both get on with our days. I, for one, have work to be doing."

Holding her head high, Kitty left the support of the pillar and walked towards the kitchen. She was conscious of Lizzie's straw hat, suddenly heavy on her head. How had Thomas not questioned her? It was too late now for her to leave the castle with the morning tides. She must stay at least until luncheon, which meant she must return to her bedchamber and change her clothes. But now she had set her course towards the lower floor and she couldn't alter it until Thomas had left the Great Hall.

By the time Kitty reached the kitchen, she was cold with indecision. The morning had lasted more than a day in terms of what she had witnessed. Her head still spun with surprise over the earl's unsuspected wealth. She wasn't prepared for the figure of Cook, already busily kneading the bread. Nor for the sound of a bell ringing outside.

"Kitty, thank goodness you're down early. Answer the door for me, please."

Kitty nodded her assent and pulled back the heavy bolts from the back door. Outside, bathed in fresh morning light, was a young delivery boy. Kitty blinked in surprise. Deliveries usually came to the castle by boat, but this child had obviously run across the causeway. Worry for his wellbeing clouded her already shattered mind. He must return soon or else risk being cut off.

He thrust a letter towards her. "Take this, please miss."

She found her voice. "I will," she said. "You must hurry back."

But the boy was already running as if a hound were after him, his blond curls bobbing on the back of his tunic. Though small, his legs ate up the ground easily. He would make it, she decided.

What a risk to take for a mere letter. She looked down at the folded paper for a name, but nothing was inscribed. She turned it over in her hands, noting the red candlewax and a seal as familiar to her as her own name.

Her mother's seal. The letter was from Shoreston. They hadn't addressed it to her. They'd just hoped she would recognise the seal. And thank goodness she had.

Hands trembling, Kitty ripped open the seal and unfolded the letter. It was from Rosalind. She would know her sister's careful hand anywhere.

Kitty's breath caught in her throat. She couldn't read it here. There was no one about, but that wouldn't be the case for long.

Kitty walked quickly across the yard and slipped into the old buttery, leaving the door open for light. The room was cold and full of cobwebs, for it had not been in use for many years. She shuddered to think of the rats and other creatures lurking in the corners, but her desire to read Rosalind's words eclipsed any squeamishness.

My darling sister,

I write in perverse hope that this missive shall somehow find you. We know not even what name you are living under and beg of you to send word that you are at least safe.

Are you safe, dear Kitty? I cannot think that you are. Not in that dark and cold castle. Not with the Earl of Rossfarne as your lord and master.

I must tell you that he came here just as you left us. A great temper hung around him and Lizzie and I hid in the pantry until we heard him ride off. What he wanted with us we dare not dwell upon, for it seems likely that he came to Shoreston in search of you.

Kitty, my heart threatens to jump out of my chest with worry. You must return to us. I have no need of mother's jewels so long as my dear sister is with me.

You will be pleased to learn that I have learned new skills in your absence. Lizzie has declared my loaves to be almost as well-risen as your own. You see, I am not some pampered miss with only a dowry to secure her future. I am resourceful and strong, just like you.

Without Father here to drain what is left of our coffers, we are doing well in Shoreston. It is only worry for you that keeps us from being truly happy. Do you remember the Erkines? They slaughtered a pig to celebrate their son coming home and were left with more ham and bacon than they could possibly store. They begged us to take some, merely to prevent the meat from going to waste. And so, we are well-fed and rested, waiting only

for your safe return.
  Please send word. Soon.

Your loving sister, Rosalind.

Kitty pressed the letter to her heart, wishing she could hold her younger sister so close.

She had spent less than seven nights in Rossfarne Castle, yet the time away from home had dimmed the light of her responsibilities. Rosalind's words had brought them back into sharp focus.

She didn't want her younger sister learning to bake bread. She didn't want the hard-working Erkines to provide them with food. Rosalind may have been taken in with their false tales, but Kitty recognised the gift of bacon for what it really was.

Charity.

Charity which she didn't want. Didn't need. She was here in Rossfarne Castle with an earl who was far richer than she had ever imagined. She must recover her family jewels, take them home and put all of this to rights.

Whatever it took.

The confusion and worry of the morning had cleared away. Kitty was calm and resolute.

She returned to the kitchen, to the enquiring gaze of Cook.

"Who was at the door?"

It took Kitty a moment to frame an answer. She couldn't tell of her letter from home. She'd allowed her fellow servants to believe she had no family. It was easier that way.

"A tinker," she mumbled at last. "He had wares to sell but they were poor."

Cook tutted as she slammed shut the kitchen door. "I hope you sent him on his way. We don't want his sort around here."

"I did."

Agnes paused in sweeping the floor and looked at her curiously. "Why are you dressed like that?"

Kitty's hands flew to her straw hat. "I'm sorry. I meant to go for a walk but I lost track of time. I'll go and change."

"Don't rush about so, you'll do yourself an injury."

Cook's warning followed her up the narrow stairs, but Kitty was too preoccupied to heed it. She glanced about the great hall, pleased to see no sign of Thomas, and flung herself up the curving stone steps to the servant's chambers.

It seemed an age since she had crept from this room, intending to run away back to Shoreston. She should have known better. Problems were never solved by running away. Her mother had taught her that.

Kitty placed Lizzie's straw hat safely in her closet and shook out her servant's dress. Its drab modesty irked her, though she had never noticed before. Now she contemplated that her voice may have pleased the earl, but her appearance most likely did not.

But did she want him to take pleasure in her appearance?

Her head was spinning. If only she had someone to talk to. Or the merest hint of experience with the opposite sex. For many years, her only thoughts of men and marriage had focused on Rosalind and how she might make a good match for her sister.

Kitty tugged the fabric down over her chemise. It fit snugly over her hips and bosom. She'd never paid attention to her curves, but now she wondered if they might, somehow, work in her favour. If only she could draw his eye towards them.

Her cheeks grew hot at the very idea.

And then what? she demanded of herself. *Will you flutter your eyelashes and suggest that he hands over the jewels?*

She sank down onto her hard bed, suddenly dispirited. She'd looked everywhere for the jewels. There was only one room they could be in. The earl's bedchamber.

Just like in her dream, her fingers rose to the top button of her bodice, and she undid it. Her heart pounded just beneath her hand.

Could she do whatever she needed to recover Rosalind's chance of a future?

Chapter Ten

FOUR ORNATE COIN chests were positioned on the floor next to his bed. Coin chests which were large, heavy and full to bursting. Such riches he had never seen the like of, not even while travelling with the king. Guy could scarcely believe the evidence of his own eyes. Why had his uncle lived such a meagre, joyless existence when he could have purchased anything he wanted?

Guy suppressed a shudder as his mind found the answer to his unspoken question. With his heavily bolted tower room and infamous reputation, the old Earl of Rossfarne had openly enjoyed a life of base, indolent pleasures. To most people, the cold state rooms, shabby furnishings and sparse household hinted at poverty, but his uncle had found his thrills elsewhere.

"There's rubies and pearls in this next one." Thomas all but licked his lips in anticipation.

Guy looked coldly at his manservant, small and dark against the thin shafts of light shining through his unopened shutters. "How do you know that?"

Thomas blanched. The chests were closed. His indiscretion was apparent.

"I wanted to check that I had brought up the right chests, my lord."

Guy bit back an enquiry as to how many chests could be hidden inside one narrow well. There was nothing to be gained as Thomas would never acknowledge any lapse on his part. But equally, Guy would not forget this. He filed the incident away in his mind.

Still, he had no wish to explore the chests under Thomas's watchful gaze. Not now the spark of distrust had been lighted between them.

"My horse is unsettled," he addressed him levelly. "Kindly go to the stables and enquire after him."

Thomas rose to his feet. His face showed displeasure.

"Ensure the stableboys are feeding him well," Guy added. "They are accustomed only to cart horses."

He suspected this faint praise would bring Thomas back on side. Although he was growing to dislike the man and his mean ways, Guy knew the benefits of having a long-standing servant here at Rossfarne. Without Thomas, he would be surrounded by strangers.

Thomas nodded, colour returning to his cheeks. "I'll see to it now, my lord."

"If you could reassure me that he has had his fill of oats, I would go easier about my morning," Guy added for good measure. He wanted Thomas out of his way so that he could properly document the contents of the chests.

Thomas left the chamber, his footsteps heavy as he descended the stone steps, and Guy sighed with relief. He had not expected his manservant to be so hasty in carrying out last night's instructions. Thomas had laboriously carried up the coin chests before Guy had even woken. Now he juggled his desires to explore them with a rumbling stomach, for he had not yet broken his fast.

But food would have to wait. He had never anticipated finding wealth such as this. Wealth which would not only finance repairs to the castle and pay his tithes but wealth which could transform life in Rossfarne Castle.

But he did not intend to stay, he reminded himself. What use were extra servants and welcoming fires if the master of the house was sleeping elsewhere, beneath the flag of the king?

He must arrange better security, that was apparent. None but

Thomas had seen the riches in the well, but still, they could not remain there. And he must hire guards, right away.

Alight with purpose, for the first time in months, Guy stepped lightly over the nearest chest and reached down to heave open another. At once, a sharp stabbing pain overtook him. He must take things slowly. Now was not the time to set back his recovery.

He straightened up, taking a step backwards and falling clumsily over the open chest. A new wave of throbbing agony clutched his left side as he landed awkwardly, banging his head on the floor.

"Damnation," he cursed, curling himself up into a ball and waiting for the pain to lessen its cruel grip. But his movement didn't aid him, instead a ripping sensation unfurled along his ribs, bringing fresh, stinging pain and a sensation of wetness.

Had his wound reopened?

Guy could curse his stupidity. He could shout and wail and beat his hands upon the floor, but none of this would help. He needed to get upright and assess the scale of the damage. But his strength had drained away from him. And the positioning of the coin chests meant he couldn't roll over and push himself onto his good arm. He would have to shout for help.

How long was it since he sent Thomas to the stables? Mayhap his servant had dallied on the stairs. He might still be within hearing distance.

Guy closed his eyes, hating this moment of weakness. What wouldn't he give to be healed and well again? But his recklessness in throwing himself in front of an opponent's blade had saved the life of a friend's young squire, and he couldn't regret that.

"Thomas," he croaked, aware even as he said the name that he would have to shout louder than that. His choices were clear. He could broadcast his current position, or else stay here, perhaps for hours, until Thomas returned.

His good hand gripped the edge of his tunic. "Help me," he roared.

A scurry of light footsteps announced his plea had been heard. Who would enter his chamber and see him so enfeebled? He grimaced as he realised this person would also spy the heavy coin chests. Another would witness the extent of his newfound wealth. Who could he trust with such knowledge?

It was not in his gift to decide. He was in the hands of fate.

A knock sounded on his chamber door. He winced with the inevitability of summoning them inside and all that would mean. Still, he had no choice.

"Enter," he commanded. His voice at least still carried authority.

"I heard shouting, my lord," came a voice, high and musical. A voice that had permeated his dreams.

Would he have wished for her to come? *No.* She was the last person he would want to see him like this.

"Oh." With one short exclamation, she communicated all her surprise.

"Help me up," he ordered.

"Are you hurt?" She was beside him in an instant, bringing with her a faint and surprising scent of lavender. His eyes opened to rest upon an unexpected expanse of creamy flesh. Had she come to his aid before she had a chance to finish dressing?

"I'm not," he lied, hating to be so enfeebled. "But I cannot stand without assistance. These trunks are in my way."

She turned her attention to the wooden chests and leaned down to try and shunt one away from him, delivering him a wondrous view of the sloping rise of her bosom. His throat dried up and his heart beat hollowly against his ribs, but he couldn't force himself to tear his gaze away.

She was an innocent. She knew not how she was affecting him.

"It's too heavy," she panted. "I can't move it."

"No matter." He closed his eyes, although not through pain. "If you can allow me to put my weight against you, I will be able to stand."

Would she bear his weight? She was but a slender young girl.

But Kitty nodded without a second thought and bent beside him, placing her scarcely concealed breasts inches away from his face. "Put your arm around my shoulder," she instructed.

Were it not for the searing pain in his side, Guy would have ordered her from the room. Her dishevelled presence threatened to usurp the thin veil of self-control he had managed to assert last night in the solar. It took an iron will to clamp down on his unworthy thoughts, but the nagging ache he felt all across his body claimed precedence over his baser desires, and when Kitty levelled herself against him to better distribute his weight, all he could think of was the need to protect his wound.

"You're bleeding," she exclaimed, as they staggered together towards his bed.

He gritted his teeth. His worst fears were realised. "I will be better once I am laying down."

She manoeuvred him onto the bed and then lifted his legs onto the covers. He opened his mouth to stop her and then closed it again. He may hate to admit it, but right now he needed her help.

"Let me see." Without waiting for permission, she leaned over him and lifted his shirt, biting her lip in concern when she saw his angry, snaking wound.

A wound not seen by anyone but himself, the doctor and Thomas.

Guy fixed his eyes on the faded tapestry hanging above his bed. Now that Kitty had helped him into bed and seen the extent of his injuries, there was nothing to be gained by sending her away.

"How bad is it?" He forced out the question.

Her gaze was focussed on his bare chest, and he could not read her expression. "I need to see more." Again, without asking for his leave, Kitty unbuttoned his shirt with slim, dextrous fingers and then pulled it to one side. He was naked from the waist up, exposed to her gaze.

He exhaled sharply. Despite his pain and her innocence, he was unable to ignore the frisson he felt.

She swallowed, and he wondered if she too sensed the magnetic pull between them. Her fingers dropped to his chest, and he flinched at her featherlight touch, torn between pleasure and agony.

"It is not as bad as I feared, though I must bathe away the blood." Her voice was calm and practical, shaming him for his wandering thoughts.

"There is water in the basin," he said.

He felt her absence when she stood to fetch the basin and relaxed when she returned. Her touch was soft and welcome, even though the water was cold. She bathed his wound with the tender care of an experienced nurse, and he remembered how she had told him about tending to another, long ago.

His flash of envy for the unknown man was shockingly strong.

"That's better," she said at last.

He opened his eyes to find her perched above him. She sat on the side of his bed, yet had angled her body towards him to better reach his left side. Her chest rose and fell with her breathing. Breathing that was surely faster than usual? Breathing that matched his own.

Her bodice was unbuttoned, not indecently so, but enough for the call of her exposed flesh to be impossible to ignore. His eyes were drawn relentlessly towards the soft swell of her breasts. At first, he tried to avert his gaze, but when Kitty stayed still and silent, he allowed himself to glance once more at the creamy softness of her neck.

How he longed to reach up and trace a hand over the hollow of her clavicle.

Wanton thoughts. But the maid didn't attempt to cover herself, despite the intensity of his admiration. She must be aware of it, for a red flush had swamped her usually pale cheeks.

A new thought invaded his mind. Could she want him, despite his disfigurement? Just like he wanted her? The answer to one of those questions was quite obvious. His want was real and solid, beginning to strain at the part of him that was still clothed.

Her want was harder to gauge. But he took some encouragement from the fact that she had come to his chamber with her dress unfastened, like an offering.

An offering he should deny, but he was but flesh and blood. A mere man filled with urges and desires he'd repressed for too long.

Hardly daring to breathe, Guy raised his right hand and placed it gently against the curve of her cheek. She leaned into it, surprising him again with her willingness.

She was beautiful.

He'd noticed before, of course, but now with her loose hair billowing around and her breathing grown deep and tremulous, her loveliness floored him. He wanted to touch more of her. His hand moved to the softness of her hair and he coiled it up behind her head before letting it spill out, like a breeze of autumn leaves.

"Kitty," he breathed, just to say her name out loud.

She jolted, as if the sound of it had woken her from a slumber. She looked down at her unbuttoned bodice and back up again, uncertainty clouding her green eyes. The spell between them was broken.

"I'm sorry," she stuttered.

"For what?" He shifted his position, gathering his composure.

"I shouldn't have sat…" She paused and swallowed awkwardly. "I was bathing your wound." Her eyes darted down to his chest and then sideways to the floor.

"For which, I thank you."

She got to her feet, fastening the top of her dress with shaking fingers.

"I offer further thanks for coming to my aid so quickly," he offered, wanting to ease her discomfort. Wanting her to stay. Wanting her.

She lowered her head meekly. "I shall leave you now, my

lord."

Damnation. He didn't want her to go. He wouldn't allow it.

"You told me once that you had nursed a man who was cut by an axe," he said, his mind racing with the effort of remembering her tale.

She paused, indecision flickering across her face. "I did."

"What say you to nursing me back to full health?" He smiled, pretending he cared little for her response.

A beat passed. She would refuse him. He had shocked her with his impropriety. What madness had caused him to caress her cheek?

"I should be pleased to do so." Her answer, when it came, made his flesh tingle with relief.

"I must return to the service of the king," he continued, wanting to remind himself of this fact in the face of his sudden, overwhelming desire for Kitty. "As soon as possible."

Her face was impassive, but her voice showed concern. "You must rest, a while at least." She pushed her hair back behind her ears as if suddenly keen to hide it.

"Yes." He twisted impatiently. "But once strength and ease of movement return to my left hand, arrangements will be made."

She hovered closer, her traitorous hair fanning out like a waterfall. "May I see?"

The damage to his hand was on the inside but he still held it out towards her.

Kitty frowned. "It is too dark in here."

"I like it that way."

"If I am to nurse you, I must be able to see my patient." She folded her arms across the plain wool of her dress.

Her calm reasoning made him feel like a petulant child. "I prefer the shadows."

Kitty regarded him steadily for a moment. "I do not believe your place is in the shadows, my lord. No knight of the realm should linger there for long."

His breath caught in his throat. *Had she any idea how poignant those words were?*

Kitty walked regally over to his high arched windows and threw open the heavy shutters. He blinked as light streamed into the room, illuminating all he had plunged into darkness.

He readied himself to accuse her of impudence. To demand she return the room to his preferred state. But a shaft of golden light hit the granite wall over the fireplace and he found himself mesmerised by it. Kitty herself was haloed with light, like an angel. She took a step closer to the window and looked out.

"It's a beautiful morning," she said lightly.

"And you have brought some of that beauty in here." His throat was dry.

She turned to face him. "The light won't come in unless you let it."

She could see him properly now. The extent of his ruined body would be visible, even the childhood scar on his clavicle. She would see all he was, on the outside at least.

He shifted his gaze away from her, not ready to see the flash of pity in her eyes.

In a moment she was beside him again, her light fingers probing his wrist and hand.

"Can you make a fist?"

"Not one that would serve me in battle," he quipped.

Why had he asked this maid to nurse him? He should have known that in doing so, he would be obliged to demonstrate his physical frailties. It had been desire, pure and simple, and he cursed his baser instincts for bringing him here.

Though it hadn't been lust that prompted his request. More a desire for Kitty's presence. An urge to spend more time with her. He had not sunk to his uncle's depths of depravity.

"Why have you not asked for help before?" she asked, puzzled. "Surely that would have aided your recovery."

He couldn't deny the truth of it.

"I don't like to ask for help," he answered, through gritted teeth.

He expected a soft reprimand, but Kitty's face showed sudden comprehension.

"Nor I."

She smiled and he returned it. The tension between them had been replaced by something deeper. An understanding that surpassed sensual desire.

"You do not think me foolish then?" he asked lightly. "To suffer alone rather than communicate my needs?"

She paused in her exploration of his ruined hand. "I would do almost anything rather than ask for help from another."

There it was again. That flash of intrigue. What was her background? Her true background? No servant would know how to sing with such measured control. Nor were they likely to be familiar with the haunting words of the final ballad she had sung for him.

Perhaps she was the daughter of a minstrel? For all her efficiency as a servant, Guy did not believe this was the life she had been born to. But she had not asked him about the knotted scar on his clavicle. She hadn't pried into the presence of the coin chests. He would respect her privacy, just as she had his.

"I would like to try something, if I may?" Her questioning expression broke into his thoughts.

"Go ahead."

"Close your eyes," she whispered.

His instinct was to refuse. To lay in pain was one thing. But to remove one of his senses, quite another. Especially when they were surrounded by coin and jewels.

This enigmatic maid, who had lied to him at least once, could lift a handful of silver and be gone down the stairs before he realised. She could do almost anything, and in his current weakened state, he couldn't hope to stop her.

He gazed into her face and saw the calm kindness he had first identified down on the causeway. The sincerity and patience that had quietened his frightened horse.

He closed his eyes.

Her quick footsteps crossed his chamber. He heard rustlings, as if she reached for something, and then she returned and fell quiet.

His remaining senses flinched with suspense. He could hear nothing save the ever-present roar of the sea. Feel nothing, bar an unfamiliar warmth stealing over his legs as the morning sun rose higher in the sky. Then there was the lightest touch on his left hand. Less than a touch. A feather stroke. His fingers flickered in response.

Kitty spoke up. "Did you feel that?"

"I did."

It came again. A feathery sensation which was almost unbearably light ran down his arm from his elbow to his wrist. His weakened muscles pulsated in response, but the resulting pain stemmed from the ache of healing.

His lips curled into a smile. "What are you doing?"

"An experiment."

The feathery sensation ran over his knuckles and for the first time since his accident, Guy's hand clenched into an instinctive fist.

Kitty laughed in delight. "An experiment which seems to be working."

He opened his eyes to see her kneeling beside his bed, brandishing the feather quill from his writing desk. Morning sunlight danced across her beautiful hair.

"Clever idea," he acknowledged, unable to dampen down his rush of excitement at this new development.

She nodded thoughtfully. "If we can start to rebuild your muscles, your recovery will be all the quicker."

It was all he had wanted since taking up residence in Rossfarne Castle. "Thank you."

She stood up, suddenly a dutiful servant once again. "Shall I come again tomorrow?"

"No." He resisted the urge to reach up and touch her arm. "Tonight. Come and sing for me, tonight."

She dipped her head. "Very good."

He watched her walk carefully around the scattered coin chests. She hadn't so much as mentioned their presence, even though one was evidently bursting with silver. Was this the act of a circumspect servant, or a refined lady?

Would her gaze have been drawn by the jewels which Thomas proclaimed rested in the second chest?

He remembered now the decision he'd made late last night.

"Kitty," he called.

She paused at his doorway and turned with a smile. "Yes, my lord?"

"When you came here, did you pass through the village of Rossfarne?"

Had her expression hardened? It was difficult to tell in the haze of light surrounding her.

"I believe so."

He struggled upright. "Tell me, did you find any commotion in the village? Any gossip?"

She looked away from him and down to the floor. "I came straight to the castle."

"I see." He slumped back onto his bed. Never mind. He would have to ask someone else.

"May I ask why, my lord?" Her voice was more tremulous than he'd ever heard it.

He rubbed at his temples, weary now with pain. "Because I am seeking the daughter of a man named Owain."

Chapter Eleven

HIS WORDS SICKENED her, literally. Her stomach heaved and her vision blurred. It took all her strength to remain standing in the doorway of that cursed room. She blinked rapidly to disperse her nausea and recover her wits.

"Owain?" she repeated, to give herself time.

"He lives in a manor just outside Rossfarne."

The earl shrugged his muscular shoulders. She had sat on his bed and allowed him to caress her. Nay, she had enjoyed his touch and yearned for more. And all the time he had been playing with her.

But if he intended to claim her, would he not have done so by now? Despite his injuries, he could have overpowered her at any moment. Instead, he had shown restraint. His touch had been gentle. He had confessed his own weakness.

That could only mean one thing. He had not worked out who she really was.

The realisation made her heart pound afresh, for at any moment he could place her. Her hair, which she had intended to keep covered, was loose around her shoulders. Moments earlier he had run his fingers through it. And her hair was the distinctive feature that linked her to her father.

He lifted his head from the pillow to see her better, a question flashing through dark eyes which she had seen grow luminous with feeling. She had believed their time together meant something. She had started to believe in him, the wounded knight who wanted only to hear her sing. Trust had knocked at her door and she had stood back to let him in.

And all the time, the earl searched for Owain's daughter.

"Kitty?" He frowned. "Are you well?"

He pushed himself up on his right elbow as if he would come over to her. She raised her hands to ward him off.

"Just thinking, my lord," she answered. "I know of no one with that name."

"I see." He relaxed back onto the pillows. "I shall enquire elsewhere."

His words were a punching blow to her stomach. Of course, he would do so. It was only a matter of time before her true identity was discovered.

But how galling to leave now, when she had secured admittance not only to the earl's solar but also his bedchamber. This new opportunity had fallen into her lap, though she would not now be able to exploit it.

The coin chests she had seen Thomas haul from the well were all around the room. She cared not for their contents, however lavish and sparkling they may be. She was no thief. She wanted only what was hers. The bag of jewels which must be secreted somewhere in the room.

Sunlight streamed through the window, illuminating every corner. Why had she wasted her time ministering to the earl when she should have been searching for her family's fortune?

Kitty bit down on her lower lip to control her trembling. The chance to look for the jewels was still within her reach. She must stay in the room, even though her instincts screamed at her to run.

"You are lost in thought," he observed. A smile transformed his face as he watched her.

She wanted to shake her head and accuse him of treachery. How could he lay there and smile at her, looking for all the world like an honourable man? A man she had wanted to know better? He was as cunning as a fox—sleek and beautiful on the outside, yet selfish and manipulative on the inside.

And she was the foolish maid who had fallen into his trap. Well, she wouldn't stay there for long.

Kitty drew deeply on her strength. "I am thinking anew," she lied. "The name, Owain, it is familiar although I struggle to place it. What business do you have with him?"

Her question was forward for a servant. Yet she was a servant who sang to order, bathed his wounds and allowed him to cup a hand to her cheek. A blush warmed her face and neck as she recalled how his fingers had brushed against her flesh. Tension twisted deep inside her at the memory, and she walked quickly to the window to appease it.

Their relationship had already strayed beyond what convention allowed. Why shouldn't she try to discover his plans?

Outside, the morning sunshine dappled the rough grass and brought a rosy hue to the unforgiving castle walls. Just minutes earlier, she had thought herself almost happy, content at least. She should have known better.

He hadn't answered her question. And every second she spent in his presence increased the likelihood that he would realise her true identity.

She twisted around to face him, expecting confrontation of some kind. She would run if she had to. How quickly she had been brought to fear, when earlier she had known a willing surrender to his touch.

The earl's eyes were closed, and a pulse jumped in his cheek. At once her emotions turned again to sympathy. He was a brave knight who had fallen in battle and wanted only to return to the service of his king.

Nay. He was a cruel overlord who had entered into a wager with a drunkard, with a living soul as the stake.

She put her hands to her face in distress. If only she could find the jewels and be gone, put all this confusion behind her.

The earl cleared his throat and Kitty straightened up. Had he witnessed her moment of weakness?

"My business with Owain is unfinished," he said, his voice expressionless.

She took a deep breath. "And with his daughter?"

Now his surprise showed on his face. "I have had no dealings with his daughter. I know nothing of her, save the unfortunate fact of her parentage."

It was not what she had been expecting. She turned again to the window so he shouldn't see the bewilderment in her eyes. The gate to the inner courtyard banged shut, and the unmistakable figure of Thomas strode into view. She gripped her hands into fists with frustration. He would be on his way here, which meant she had only minutes at her disposal.

She whirled around, her eyes frantically scanning the room. It was furnished sparsely with merely a canopied bed, a lone closet and a colourless tapestry on the wall. The coin chests, she ignored. She'd witnessed them being hauled from the well that day and knew they were unlikely to conceal what she sought.

Beside her was the washstand, from where she had fetched the basin. Her gaze flickered down and confirmed what she already knew. The only other items it contained were a rather jagged comb and a chipped jug.

What parsimony from a man as rich as he.

"What ails you, Kitty?" he asked her directly.

"I am thinking that these chests should be moved, my lord. Else you may fall once more."

It was the wrong thing to say. A look of great irritation passed over his handsome face.

"I am not in the habit of tripping. Do you think me a child who has not yet learned to walk?"

She thought quickly. "No, my lord. Merely that they are positioned so inconveniently."

"I will have Thomas see to it."

That was her cue to leave. Her time was up. Her gaze raked once more over the room and landed on the small writing desk. It was in the far corner of the room, too distant to warrant a casual stroll towards it, but she had plucked the feather quill from its stand on the desk earlier. She knew it was bare save a sheaf of papers and an abandoned saddlebag.

Her heart rate picked up. The saddlebag. She'd thought at the time that it was an odd shape. Something bulged within it. Something that could so easily be her cloth bag of jewels.

What pretence could she have for striding across his chamber once more? The feather quill she had laid carefully on a small bedside chest, and it would be most strange for her to return to it. Her mind went blank under his watchful gaze. Did he know what thoughts were racing around her head? Was he even now wondering where he had previously seen such a blaze of colourful hair?

"May I get you anything further, before I leave?"

He swung his legs off the bed and stood up slowly. She had forgotten about his height and obvious strength. Bare-chested as he was, she could see each clearly-defined muscle rippling beneath his bronzed skin. Even the angry, snaking scar could do nothing to diminish his physicality.

The delicious tension she'd felt earlier pulsed once again, deep inside her.

"You can fetch me a fresh shirt."

She walked quickly over to his closet, glad of the clearly de-fined task. Hope jumped inside her that her jewels may be somewhere inside, but one quick look confirmed otherwise.

The saddlebag on the writing desk. They were hidden there. She knew it in her bones.

She pulled out a clean shirt and tentatively held it out towards him. Would he expect her to put it on him? She had never dressed a man. Her arms shook at the idea of once again coming close to him.

But he merely took the shirt from her and nodded his thanks.

She must leave. There was no good reason to extend her stay, and at any moment Thomas would appear. All was not lost, not when the earl wanted her to sing for him in his solar and tend further to his injuries tomorrow.

She thought quickly. "I will find herbs to better aid your recovery, my lord."

He looked pleased. "Good. You can bring them for me tomorrow."

"Of course." That was her plan.

With the shirt still dangling from his fingers and the sunlight dancing across his chest, the earl lowered his eyes to meet hers. "Don't forget to come for me, this evening," he paused. "To sing."

She inclined her head. How could she forget?

THE WEATHER WAS unseasonably hot. Not a cloud could be seen in the deep blue sky and the relentless afternoon sun, combined with the steam and heat of the kitchen, made them all irritable. Not even Cook had a kind word to say as she bandied around orders for the evening meal.

The earl, it seemed, was in a mood for celebration. On a whim he had demanded a new menu for tonight. One that required roasted pheasant and a platter of sweet pastries. Agnes made barbed comments about the earl's impending bankruptcy, and Kitty kept her lips pressed closed together. Sweat trickled down the back of her woollen dress and she longed to escape outside. To pull off her stockings, walk on the beach and let the waves run over her feet. Her longing for a breeze eclipsed even her thoughts of recovering the jewels.

At last, her kitchen duties were complete, and she could wearily climb the stairs to her room, not to rest but to prepare to meet the earl.

A smell of cooking meat and stale perspiration hung about her. She couldn't meet him like this. Again, the lure of the sea came upon her. She could walk into the waves and lower her hot, aching body into the sparkling water. It would be bliss.

It was but a pipe dream. Children were encouraged to play in the waves on a hot day. Servants were not. Even as Miss Katherine of Shoreston, Kitty hadn't enjoyed the sensation of floating in the shallows for many years. Only when Alfred had cut his arm and the village healer had advised saltwater bathing, had she come anywhere close. But even then, she had stood back from the waves and watched enviously.

She gripped the hem of her dress and yanked it up over her head, pulling the heavy material where it clung to her damp skin. The relief of evening air against her body was recompense for the struggle. She allowed herself a moment of rest, standing in her chamber clad in nothing but her thin chemise.

A chemise which also carried a whiff of the kitchen. With a surge of irritation, Kitty wriggled her shoulders out of the straps, stepped out of it and kicked it into a corner. She had a half day coming up and would—by necessity, it seemed—spend it in the laundry.

Naked from top to toe, she sponged herself down with cold water from the basin, then made herself decent again in a fresh chemise and her one remaining servant's dress. She resented the restrictive weight of it. Such clothing was not designed for a climate like this. She'd be better off wearing the scanty, fanciful fabrics hidden in the earl's solar.

No sooner had the thought entered her head than her body flushed with tingling shame at the memory of her dream.

A dream which she had all but re-enacted in his lordship's bedchamber.

She bade herself to be calm as she fastened her hair securely beneath her cap. She was ready to descend to the solar.

She knocked on the closed wooden door and tentatively pushed it open. The first thing she noticed was the shock of the light. She had grown accustomed to gloom and shadows at Rossfarne Castle, but the earl had opened the shutters in here too.

"Come in, come in," he beckoned. His voice was relaxed and

jovial, so unlike his usual fierceness and caution.

"My lord." She lowered her head in greeting.

The earl swivelled around on the armchair to look at her properly. A flagon of wine sat beside him.

"Let us dispense with all of that, shall we?" He smiled up at her. "No titles. No bowing. For tonight, you shall be Kitty and I shall be Guy."

Guy. She turned the name around in her head and found she liked it. But nevertheless, she wouldn't dare address the earl by his first name. She swallowed hard. What other intimacies did he have in mind?

"You sing to me like one of the king's own musicians," he added softly, as if alert to her worries. "And the king's musicians know me by my true name."

He had been drinking, she knew the signs. His words were not slurred, but they ran together freely. He would not address her this way if he were sober. Her instinct was to recoil, knowing all too well what dangers wine and mead could bring upon her. She shifted uncomfortably, forcing down haunting memories of her father's drunken behaviour; the nights she had spent with her body shielding Rosalind behind a flimsy locked door, covering her sister's ears so she should not hear his ribald cursing and threats of violence. And then there was the final, harshest indignity. Her father had gambled her away whilst under the influence of drink, and if she lived for a hundred years, she would never escape the shame of it.

But the earl, Guy, was not her father. His goblets of wine had made him relaxed and at ease, not foolish and aggressive.

She ventured closer. "Are you celebrating?" She bit back 'my lord.'

She expected a denial, but he nodded without pause. "Today, I discovered myself to be a wealthy man, Kitty." His eyes met hers and she knew him to be sensible and alert despite the liquor. "As you know, from seeing the coin chests in my chamber."

She couldn't deny it. "My concern was with your injury."

"Nonetheless." He raised his eyebrows. "You are a woman of intelligence. You know what you saw."

"I saw enough silver for you to hire musicians of your own," she quipped, unable to resist.

"Indeed. And to employ a great number of servants."

"To bring comfort and cheer to the castle," she dared to venture.

He raised his goblet in a toast. "Exactly that." He drank deeply. "My uncle chose to spend his days in the gloom, but now I see different options before me."

He had never referenced his uncle's reputation before. A reputation which had tarnished her view of the current earl before she had even spoken to him. "Many tales were told about the old Earl of Rossfarne," she almost whispered.

Guy leaned his head back against his chair. "I know the unsavoury dealings he had with the folk of the town of Rossfarne, yet I had not realised his infamy stretched as far as Belford."

She bit down on her lip at her stupidity. Had he caught her out in her deception?

"Shall I sing for you?" She walked in readiness over to the empty fireplace, eager to change the subject.

He looked across at her, not as an earl to his servant but as a man to a woman. The sincerity in his face made her pulse pound.

"I believe I would prefer to talk," he said, surprising her. "Pray, come and sit beside me." He patted the chair which was pulled alongside his own.

Kitty swallowed down her fears and did as she was bid, resettling her skirts around her ankles.

"Would you care for some wine?"

"No thank you, my lord." She shook her head quickly.

He tutted. "Guy, my name is Guy. I do not hear it often enough, these days. Please, do me the favour of using it."

Her heart was beating like a hollow drum on a battlefield. "Very well."

"Say it," he insisted, pouring himself another goblet of wine.

"Guy," she said. The word brought a new flush to her hot cheeks.

"Thank you." His finely carved lips curled upwards into a contagious smile and Kitty felt some of her anxieties lifting away from her.

"It is a fine name," she ventured.

His expression grew colder. "My mother chose it." He gazed into the empty grate for a moment and then turned towards her again. "I try not to think of my family. Not my parents, nor my uncle. Indeed, I had not seen my cousin Otto for many years before his last visit here.

She would rather not remember the lecherous old man, Otto's father, who'd had such clear designs on her virtue. But her curiosity was piqued. "Do you have no other relatives?"

"Very little," he declared, running his right hand through his thick, dark hair. "I had a brother," he allowed, "but he is dead."

For a moment the pain this caused him showed in his face, and Kitty looked away out of respect. "My mother is dead," she found herself admitting.

"And was she a kind woman?"

"The kindest."

"Then you know something of loss."

They sat in silence for a moment. It was on the tip of her tongue to tell him about her sister, but Kitty stayed quiet. It was best if he knew nothing more about her real life.

"Tell me," he said, visibly rousing himself. "What tales have you heard about my uncle?"

The question startled her. "It is difficult to say." Her tongue wetted her dry lips.

"Come now, don't be shy. I know what kind of a man he was." He looked at her consideringly. "Did word spread about the tower room?"

Her toes wriggled with discomfort. "Yes."

"Ah." He took another long drink of wine. "And what was said about that cursed place?"

She couldn't bring herself to say what she knew. "I did not understand the stories, sir."

"Not 'sir.'" He wagged a finger in her face.

A new thought occurred to her. The tower room would be the perfect place to hide something away from prying eyes. No one ever went in there. She had been convinced her jewels were in Guy's bedchamber, but was she naïve to dismiss this option so quickly?

"Guy," she tried again. "What happened in there?"

"In the tower room?" He pursed his lips as if reluctant to say.

"I should like to know," she bravely went on, despite a trembling in her knees. She folded her hands tightly in her lap, her fingernails digging into her palms.

"Well now, I hardly know how to answer." A laugh bubbled up inside him. "I didn't expect that sort of question from you, Kitty."

She was blushing furiously now. "Do you ever go in there?"

"I have been inside once," he confessed. "And what I saw made my cheeks almost as red as your own."

Horrified, she placed her head in her hands, but he gently pulled them away.

"I'm sorry for teasing you," he whispered, his breath warm against the top of her head. "I believe that you know not what you ask."

"The ways of men such as the old earl are entirely unknown to me," she stated boldly.

"I expected nothing else."

He was so close. She could smell his masculine scent of leather and sea salt. He hadn't let go of her wrist and the warmth of his encircling fingers travelled up her arm. Slowly, almost imperceptibly, he traced a small circle over her pulse point with his thumb.

"I am not like those women," she said weakly, to herself as much as to him.

He sighed and released her hand, making her immediately bereft.

"Forgive me. I am drawn to you Kitty, not only to your voice, but to you. Believe me though, I mean you no harm." He swallowed. "I am not like my uncle."

"I know that," she blurted back, reaching over for his hands in her haste to reassure him. He linked his fingers with hers, looking at her with open surprise. "I'm drawn to you, too," she said. The admission was unplanned, but it was the truth. A truth she had barely even acknowledged to herself. She fixed her eyes on her hands. Hands which she'd always thought of as large and ungainly, but now they appeared small, swamped as they were inside his. How had she dared to touch him?

What should she do now?

Even if she wanted to pull her hands away, she couldn't. It was as if they belonged to someone else. Her body yearned to move closer to him.

"Kitty," he paused. "My intentions towards you are honourable. I invited you to my solar only to hear you sing. But you should know, your presence and your proximity risk making me forget myself."

She wanted him to forget himself. But at the same time, she trembled with uncertainty.

He squeezed her fingers gently, released them and placed his hands softly upon her forearms, his strong fingers bunching the cheap fabric of her sleeves.

"You should leave now," he said hoarsely.

"I don't want to leave."

The sultry heat and strangeness of the day had placed her under some sort of spell. Rational thought deserted her. She wanted only to feel his touch and prolong this wondrous time. She didn't even care about recovering her family jewels, not at this moment.

"Then I must kiss you," he stated, his eyes boring straight down to her soul.

Her heart pounded against her ribs and that coil of tension once again flickered in her core. She had never been kissed, not properly. She had never desired it, but now it was all she could think of. His lips on hers. The rasp of stubble against her cheeks. But would a kiss lead to something more? Strength and vigour radiated from him. She recalled the rippling muscles in his chest and shoulders. Once he took hold of her, she would never be able to escape.

No matter. He had offered his kiss and she wanted it.

He stood up suddenly. "I will say goodnight." His voice was harsh and abrupt.

"No," she protested. "I want you to kiss me."

In less than a heartbeat his strong arms had encircled her and lifted her to her feet as if she weighed no more than a feather. His good hand stroked the length of her spine, coming to rest at the small of her back.

"Are you sure?"

"I'm sure." She tilted her face up towards his, unable to wait any longer.

His lips settled upon hers, gently at first, in a kiss so sweet and gentle it unfurled something inside her. Kitty reached up and cupped each side of his face, delighting in the raspy feel of his stubble and the warmth of his body against her. He inched his face away and his eyes gazed down at her. Dark eyes, full of feeling, which she could get lost in.

His hand caressed her spine, sending jolts of anticipation through her. He kissed her again, more firmly this time. She arched into him, parting her lips in surprise at the wave of pleasure he was unleashing. Guy moaned slightly and pulled her towards him, claiming her mouth with his own. She gasped at the magnetic thrill of his tongue touching hers. Such intimacy she had never imagined. She could taste him, and he could taste her. The coil of tension deep inside her clenched with wanting.

He pulled away from their kiss. Breathing hard, he rested his forehead against hers.

"That did nothing to satiate my longing for you," he said, his left hand roaming her back and making her press herself more firmly against him.

"I didn't want you to stop."

He gave a low chuckle. "Nor I, believe me."

But he had stopped, all the same. Did something about her displease him?

Had she done it wrong?

All the fire and certainty of the previous moment deserted her. Kitty felt only flushed and embarrassed.

"I want you, Kitty," he said, easing her fears. "But I shall not permit myself to have you. I am not the type of man to bed a servant."

His words were a slap in the face. Of course, she was nothing to him but a servant. If he knew the truth of her birth, would he want her more?

Her mother was Isabella of Answick. But her father was a drunkard who had gambled her away. How had Kitty ever imagined that a man like this would choose a woman like her?

Keeping her eyes fixed firmly on the floor, Kitty backed away from the warmth of his arms.

"I will leave you, my lord."

He put a hand to her chin and lifted it. "I am sorry for my lapse of control," he said, a range of emotions flickering across his face.

At once, she longed again to move into his strong embrace. But there was no comfort for her there. Not when she was living a lie.

If she revealed who she was and why she had come to the castle, would he understand her deception? Return her family heirlooms?

Every day under his roof she had feared him finding out. Feared that he might claim her, ravish her. But now that she had kissed him, she knew she would always be safe in his arms. The Earl of Rossfarne had no streak of cruelty to him. He was an honourable man. A knight.

So how could she admit to him that she was the unfortunate

daughter of Owain?

"You have no need to apologise," she said firmly. "The lapse was my own."

She bobbed her head politely and left the room, before he should see the tears prickling at the corner of her eyes.

Chapter Twelve

GUY HAD ACQUIESCED to letting in the light, but now there was too much of it. Days of cloudless heat had settled over the town and castle of Rossfarne, making farmers fret over the wilting harvest and fishermen long for a breeze to fill their sails. Sunlight flooded the castle, shining a bright, relentless beam into long-forgotten chambers.

He had opened himself up to Kitty. She'd broken through the high barriers he'd erected to keep everyone at a distance, and she'd glimpsed the real Guy, the one he preferred to keep hidden. He could no more barricade his defences against her now, than he could command the skies to darken.

Each day she came to his chamber and calmly, quietly, ministered to his wound. On the first morning, she brought with her leaves from a strange green plant, which he couldn't help eying suspiciously.

"Comfrey," she said, in answer to his look. "I found it growing in the small meadow behind the castle and dried it in the pantry overnight. Packed into your bandages, it will reduce the swelling."

He'd baulked at the return to bandages, hating the way they swathed his body and restricted his movement, but was touched by her thoughtfulness. Kitty had braved the relentless, smothering heat to go out and gather herbs for his sake.

He would have liked to show her how much he cared. He longed to catch hold of her hand and bring her fingertips to his lips. To caress away the worry lines at her temple. He would do all that and more. But after their moment of weakness in the solar, the kiss that had swamped him with passion and temporarily stolen his sanity, he promised himself that he would never again act with impropriety towards her.

He no longer asked her to sing for him. As pure and beautiful as her voice was, his mind would turn to lust the moment she entered his solar. She was an innocent maid. He was an earl. It mattered not how he burned for her. To kiss her again would take what they had and turn it into something sordid.

She had exclaimed with surprise upon unwinding that first lot of bandages. "See how it has helped?"

He'd looked down, expecting an angry red scar, but found instead something smaller, thinner. A mark which was already fading into his bronzed skin.

"The herb you brought?"

"Comfrey." She gathered up the shrivelled leaves from the bandages. "Our village healer prescribed it for Alfred, our servant, the one who was cut by an axe."

It was only afterwards that he'd wondered at her words. Had she really said 'our servant'? What could that mean?

He watched her closely as she went about her days. Her work was meticulous as ever, but something about her bearing had never rung entirely true with the idea that she had come from the servant class. Could it be that Kitty's family had once enjoyed some degree of privilege but latterly had fallen on hard times? Or was it wishful thinking on his part to imagine her as more highborn, more suitable as a match for someone of his standing? Either way, she remained a servant in his employ. The exact circumstances of her birth mattered little besides that.

As his body healed, his movement and sense of freedom began to return, though the oppressive heat made riding or even walking outside difficult. Kitty was to come again to him this morning, but in the face of his impressive recovery, he knew she would announce any day that her ministrations were no longer necessary.

What then? He would be bereft without her.

Her light footsteps sounded on the stairs, then came the knock. Three times in quick succession. It was the sound he now lived for.

"Enter," he called. He longed each day to see her. And each day he worked hard to hide his longing.

He waited for her by the washstand, where the light streaming through the large window was at its brightest. This had become their custom. Her quick fingers would remove the bandages, skimming over his flesh and bringing goosebumps to his skin. Her eyes, however, remained fixed studiously on his injuries. Did she know how she affected him? He couldn't tell. Her touch, her movement, her pronouncements were all strictly professional.

This morning, she paused in her task. Her gentle hand stayed against his chest while she crouched lower and put her head closer to his wound. At once her sweet breath hit his shoulder blades and he felt the traitorous twitch of desire deep inside him.

"It is fully healed," she announced, and for the first time in several days she raised her beautiful green eyes to his.

His need to see the proof wrestled with his wanting to stay held in her gaze. His heart beat heavily. It was the news he'd sought mixed with the inevitable consequence he'd been dreading.

"See for yourself." She stood tall and backed away from him, folding her hands demurely in front of her apron.

He glanced down at the thin line which had replaced the searing red stripe of agony he'd feared would never leave him.

"You have worked miracles," he said. His voice was calm though his emotions raged.

His words brought a flickering smile to her lips, but she still did not look at him.

"Not I, my lord. It was God's grace, along with the healing power of nature."

What now? He should thank her, dismiss her and get on with his day. He had letters to write. He must see about hiring castle guards and ordering repairs to the gatehouse. But once Kitty had left his chamber, he would be reduced to chance meetings on the stairs, perhaps a shared look over a meal served in the great hall. His mind reached for a reason she should stay.

Kitty sighed, as if she had come to a decision. "Though the wound itself is healed, the muscles surrounding it will need some time to adjust."

He held his breath. Was Kitty herself offering him a solution?

"What would you suggest?"

She pursed her lips and directed her gaze towards the window, away from him. "There is a kind of curative massage which may help."

"Curative massage? I have not heard of such a thing."

She looked as if she regretted speaking up. "I watched the healer perform it with Alfred."

"And do you think you could do it?" The idea of her hands upon him sent his pulse pounding, but would he be able to retain his thin veil of self-control?

She worried at her lower lip. "I'm not sure it would be proper."

Nor was he. But he couldn't let her go, not while the chance to prolong their time together was so tantalisingly close.

"It is merely a continuation of the nursing care you have already provided."

She nodded her agreement. Her composure was absolute, bar the quick rise and fall of her bodice, denoting a heart rate just as fast as his own.

Was this madness? He had kept his promise to act with propriety until now, but each day it became harder to resist her. And now, with the baking heat lending a shimmer of unreality to their surroundings, it would be all too easy to give in to temptation.

He shook the notion away. He was a knight of the realm, not some base fool living at the mercy of his sexual urges.

"Where would you like me?" he asked.

His question brought a flash of colour to her cheeks, and he regretted his choice of words.

"You will need to be sitting, as otherwise I will not be able to reach." Her hands lifted to emphasise the distance his shoulders stood above her.

He remembered how it had felt to circle his fingers around her delicate wrists.

"On the bed then. Shall I put my shirt back on?" He was determined to be practical, to banish the tension that had sprung up between them.

"No, leave it off." Her voice was small.

He strode over to the bed and lowered himself onto the corner of it. He loosened his shoulders and widened the stance of his legs, to better distribute his weight.

She was behind him. He could sense her even though he couldn't see her. He closed his eyes, tense and ready for her touch.

Her fingers were soft and warm. They dipped over the wall of muscle in his shoulder, gripping and pulling to release knots he never even knew were there. Guy found his head lolling forwards and a great sense of relaxation descending over him. Her palms pushed against his upper back and then ran down the sides of his arms, bringing pinpricks of excitement to his bare flesh. Despite his good intentions, desire was uncoiling within him with every sure, controlled movement of Kitty's hands. Now she was concentrating on his left side. On the shoulder he had thought of as ruined. But her gentle kneading brought him no pain, only pleasure.

Pleasure that was building inside him. Pleasure he craved and tried to deny at the same time. Her breath hit the back of his neck. If he reached behind him, he would find her soft, womanly curves. Heat pulsated through him as he gripped down hard on his self-control. It was no good. In another moment his need would overtake his rational thoughts.

Kitty darted away from him as if he had spoken the warning aloud. Bereft of her touch, he breathed deeply to calm his passion.

"What is it?" he asked, his voice came out hoarse and deep. He turned to look behind him to find a most curious expression flickering across her face.

"I was gathering my thoughts, my lord."

He raised his eyebrows. "Are they gathered now?"

She worried at her lower lip, but resolution shone in her eyes. "I believe so."

Part of him throbbed for her still. He dared not move lest he scare her away.

"Are we to continue?"

"Most certainly."

She stepped up behind him once again. This time, when her hands ran up his bare arms, her touch was slow and steady, almost as if she had calculated the most precise way to stimulate his desires. Her fingers spanned out against his backbone and then stroked the length of his spine, spread to his sides and travelled up his body to settle on his shoulder blades.

He exhaled sharply. Her touch was weaving magic, putting him under a spell. The sultry heat of the room mixed with her seductive gestures, intentional or not, would surely prove to be his undoing. His mind flashed with images. He could turn in less than a heartbeat, gather her up into his arms and lay her down on the bed. He imagined his own hands being free to explore her soft curves. He would unbutton her bodice and lower his lips to her breasts.

Enough. He could stand no more. He launched himself away from the bed and stalked over to the window where the brightness hurt his eyes.

"Have I displeased you, my lord?"

"Only in that your touch is driving me wild," he shot back.

He expected his confession to shock her, but when he glanced over his shoulder, he saw her standing as bold and resolute as before.

"It is overly warm in here," she stated. "Perchance you're in need of fresh air?"

If only. His gaze raked over the still courtyard and the parched earth. "The only fresh air in this whole cursed place can be found out there." He motioned beyond the far tower to where the sparkling sea lapped gently at the sun-drenched cove.

She was beside him, standing too close for his comfort. She smelled of meadow grass and something citrussy. Her soft lips parted as she raised herself on tiptoe to see where he was pointing.

"The sea?"

The fabric of her sleeve brushed against his chest and the sensation was enough to tip him over the edge, where self-restraint was no longer a burden.

"The sea." He couldn't help himself. He placed his hands upon her narrow waist and spanned his fingers outwards.

She didn't flinch away. If anything, she moved imperceptibly nearer. "I believe saltwater bathing can be highly beneficial for healing."

Bathing in the sea. He hadn't done so since he was a child. But as tempting as the notion was, it couldn't compete with the beautiful young woman who was almost in his arms.

"I can think of other ways to exercise," he growled, inching her closer. His thumbs skimmed upwards until he could feel the press of her lower ribs through her dress.

She swallowed but didn't pull away. A battle was being fought behind her eyes. Indecision washed over her face, but he saw no sense of fear.

She reached up to touch his face and he closed his eyes as her fingers brushed lightly against his skin. She was soft and tender; he was hard with passion, like a tightly coiled spring.

Not like this. He must regain his self-control.

"Saltwater bathing is an interesting idea." He forced the words out while his eyes remained closed. Immersing himself in the cool, clear water would chase the heat of passion from his body.

He heard her sharp intake of breath. "I believe it has enormous benefits." She shifted slightly, coming dangerously close to the part of him still straining with desire. "If it pleases you, my lord, I will bring down a change of clothing for you."

Her practical mindset shamed him afresh. He must leave her, before he spoiled her virtue further.

"It pleases me," he stated.

She nodded her capped head. "Then I shall meet you in the cove."

Chapter Thirteen

HE WALKED QUICKLY out of the chamber, his wooden-soled shoes clattering down the stone steps in his haste. Kitty stood in the centre of the room, weak with relief and awkward with shame.

Her ruse had worked. Guy had left her alone, which meant she could take possession of her jewels. At last, she had found a way.

But at what cost?

Masquerading as a servant was one thing. Today, her duplicity had reached new heights. Little had she realised what influence she wielded over the earl. He was powerful and wealthy, while she stood before him with chapped fingers and a maid's apron. But then his body had yielded to her soothing hands. Suddenly he was pliant and biddable. As his customary alertness was replaced by clumsy, smouldering passion, she had spied the saddlebag and known, instinctively, that she must press this unforeseen advantage. Even though the territory was unexplored. Even though with every breath she took, she longed to give herself over to the fantasy she was spinning between them. A man and a woman, free to be together, wanting only each other.

Though Guy's mention of the sea had been a stroke of luck.

Kitty bit down on her lip. She was deceitful, dishonest, all the things she hated. But if she didn't move soon, it would have all been for naught.

Far below her, an outer door banged shut. Was it Guy leaving for the cove, or Thomas returning? Kitty couldn't dally a moment longer. She ran over to the writing desk and turned over the saddlebag in her hands. The leather was soft and supple, but the buckle was stiff. It would be easier to take the whole thing, but the saddlebag belonged to Guy and Kitty only wanted what was hers. Plus, if the saddlebag remained where it was, the jewels may not be so quickly missed. Her fingers shook with anxiety. Finally, the buckle opened, and she tipped out the contents.

There they were, the Answick jewels. Still in the familiar cloth bag which carried the faint scent of Shoreston.

Kitty's heart pounded. This was the moment she'd been hoping for, ever since father handed the jewels over to the strange man in the carriage. But now the man wasn't strange to her—he was kind and respectful. He had demons but he also had integrity. The sound of his voice made her heart leap. And she was on the cusp of betraying him.

Would he have returned the jewels to her if she had confessed her true identity? Mayhap he would. Now that she knew him better, she could almost believe it. But if she took them now, she would never know.

Her stomach churned with indecision. To give him this opportunity, she must tell him the truth. She was the daughter of Owain the drunkard. Her own father had gambled her away.

No. It couldn't be done. She couldn't bear to see the pity shining from his dark eyes. Once he knew who she was, he would never again look at her with respect, let alone desire.

She dropped the jewels into her apron pocket as unshed tears burned at the corners of her eyes.

HE HAD KICKED off his shoes and his feet were bare like his muscular chest. He stood in the shallows with the waves rushing up over his toes, his breeches rolled up above his knees. A smile played across his handsome face and the sun shone down on him like a blessing.

He had never been so attractive, nor so unobtainable.

Kitty crept along the beach, shame pulsating through her. She was a petty thief. A common criminal. She had been in his employ under false pretences all along, but now there was no turning back. She had hidden the jewels inside her closet, knowing as she fastened the door that this must be her final day at Rossfarne Castle. She had a half day this afternoon and low tide was expected at sunset, meaning the causeway would be passable. Her fate was sealed.

She should be full of joy, for she had done what she set out to achieve. Rosalind's future was once again bright with possibility. But a small voice had started up in her ear and it would not be silenced.

"What about your own future?" it whispered. "What about Guy?"

But Guy had no place in her future. He had never been hers, and now he never would be.

He turned towards her, breaking through her thoughts with a smile as warm as the day. "You have come, at last."

"It took a while for me to gather a change of clothes."

Her arms were full of his things. A soft blue shirt and long breeches which she'd hurriedly grasped on her flight from his chamber. The masculine scent of him was impressed upon them; she'd been breathing him in since leaving the outer walls.

"No matter." He gestured impatiently. "Come and enjoy the water. It is very refreshing."

She looked around for somewhere to keep his dry clothes and spotted a long, flat stone which would suffice. She folded them neatly and placed them down, painfully aware that this could be the final service she would perform for him.

She had nursed his strong body back to health. Felt his muscular arms closing around her. And now she was planning to sneak away from his castle.

It would be improper to go and stand with him, as if they were equals, friends, or even something more. Yesterday she would have refused, citing work in the kitchen or perhaps a headache. But she had abandoned propriety when she deliberately ran her hands down the length of his spine, delighting in his response.

And she might never get another chance to stand at his side.

She kicked off her pattens and her stockinged feet sank into the soft sand. It was difficult to walk, but she crossed the beach with as much dignity as she could muster, hovering just behind him when her courage failed.

He didn't turn to face her, but he was aware of her presence, she could tell by the set of his shoulders.

"Have you removed your stockings?"

She blushed, even though he was looking away from her. "No, my lord."

"You should. I can't imagine how dreadful it would be to paddle in stockings."

Her pulse began to pound. Her body became as warm within as the parts exposed to the bright sun. "I was not intending to paddle."

"That's a shame, on a day like this." Now he turned, and the impish smile on his face chased away her prim concerns. "After all, there's only the two of us here."

She shouldn't do it. But she was going to. The sun was hot and relentless. Her dress was clinging and restrictive. What harm could it do to allow herself the slightest breeze?

"Don't look," she cautioned.

He swung his gaze back to the waves. "I will not."

She wobbled with the effort of pulling off her first stocking. When it eventually came away, she fell into the soft sand with a small grunt, but Guy kept his promise and didn't turn. She stayed where she was to remove the second, forsaking etiquette in a sudden urge to be free.

The sand felt glorious beneath her toes. Warm, but wonderful. She strode out to the shallows and squealed with surprise as the cold water rushed over her feet, soaking the hem of her dress.

"It's good, isn't it?" He looked at her sideways.

"Very good." The tide drew back, leaving her feet firmly planted in the sodden sand. She half closed her eyes, giving herself over to the moment. "I haven't set foot in the sea since I was a child."

"Me neither. But today, that changes."

Without further warning, Guy lunged forwards and dived into a coming wave, surfacing moments later with rivulets of saltwater cascading down his muscular torso. Her lips parted at the vision. She should look away, but her eyes were drawn to him like a moth to a flame. He laughed and shook the spray from his shock of hair before jumping in once more and gliding beneath the surface of the sparkling sea.

It was as if she had stepped into a different world, where the usual rules didn't apply. There was only the bright, searing sunlight, the crashing of the waves and the distant call of the gulls. Only Guy, uninhibited from pain and unbound from decorum. Splashing in the water like a young man without a care.

"Kitty, it's glorious." He rose from the waves like some mighty deity, all rippling muscles and bronzed flesh. "Come join me."

She laughed aloud at the absurdity of the idea. "You know I cannot."

He walked steadily towards her, his fingertips cresting the waves. "I know of no such stipulation."

Her mouth went dry with sudden longing. She wanted to tell him to stop. To come no nearer. With every step, he unleashed a sort of tension deep inside her core.

He reached out for her hand, and at the touch of his fingers she knew she was lost to propriety.

"My dress will be ruined," she tried one last time.

He pulled her gently towards him, into the shallows. "Have you no other?"

She had but one other, and she should know better. But it was already too late. Her skirts grew heavy with water and then floated up around her. The cold rushed up her calves, making her gasp with surprise and delight. Suddenly, the urge to lower herself into the revitalising waves was overwhelming. She bent her knees, marvelled at the sensation of water rising around her thighs, and allowed herself to fall back. She straightened her legs and leaned back on her hands, delighting in the ebb and flow of the foam. Luxuriating in the release from oppressive heat. Her skirts swam up and around her, but she didn't care. She shaded her eyes from the sun and found Guy gazing back at her with steady approval.

"You should come in further."

"I cannot swim." She worried briefly that her casual confession might have given away the circumstances of her upbringing since it was considered ill bred for a lady to know how to swim…but even the low-born daughter of the cordwainer—a girl the same age as Kitty—had stood in the shallows and watched her brothers splashing in the sea during the hot summers of their childhood. Mayhap it was something few daughters were allowed to enjoy, regardless of their birth.

"Then I shall come to you."

He splashed towards her, his soaked breeches clinging to every bulging muscle. She allowed her eyes to rest on the flat plane of his stomach and felt again that fluttering tension wriggle inside her. Her breath shortened and her heart beat faster against her ribs. She grew conscious of her ridiculous, water-laden skirts, her flushed cheeks and the cap which had moulded to her head with sea water.

Newly emboldened, she pulled it off and flung it behind her in the direction of Guy's folded clothes, not bothering to look to check where it landed. The rush of release as the faint breeze stirred through her hair was as liberating as the saltwater rushing about her bare legs. She ran her wet fingers through her long curls, uncaring that Guy was watching her.

She would give him this and more.

If he placed her now as Owain's daughter, then so much the better. At least that would give her the opportunity to be honest.

"You should always wear your hair loose."

She pushed a long tendril back over her shoulder. "I doubt Cook would approve."

"Then it is lucky for us both that we are not in view of the castle."

His words sank through her like a stone. She swallowed hard as rational thought rose up to quell her spiralling passions. She had already burned one bridge when she took the jewels from Guy's bedchamber. Would she so willingly burn more by giving up her virtue? With a man who did not know her real name?

"Kitty," he breathed, as if to prove her wrong. "In a moment, I'm going to kiss you. If you don't want me to do so, you must speak up."

Here was her final chance then, to return to her family a pure maid.

But what benefit would purity bring her, when she never hoped to marry? Never *wanted* to marry?

She couldn't imagine ever wanting another man. There was only Guy. This would be her last chance to know what it was to be loved.

She surrendered her purity readily, cupping her cold hands around his warm cheeks and drawing him towards her.

"I want you to kiss me," she said. A surging wave ran up her bodice, urging her on.

His face lowered to hers. She knew instantly that this would be no chaste, exploratory meeting of lips. Not sweet. Not hesitant. His mouth claimed hers with an urgency that took her breath away. She sank against him, grateful for his muscular arm snaking around her back, giving her strength she could lean against.

His tongue moved against her lips, and she parted them eagerly, gasping at the thrill as his tongue found hers. He pulled her closer as a wave crashed over them both, soaking them through. Drenching salt water cascaded down her kirtle, like a fast-flowing river. Guy laughed and brushed back her dishevelled hair.

"I think we should move out of the water," he said, his voice low and rough.

She tried to stand but her heavy skirts pulled her back down into the slippery, soft sands. Instantly his strong hands were beneath her, lifting her to safety. She balanced herself against him as the waves crashed against their legs and once again his warm lips found hers. His arms gripped her tightly and before she knew what was happening, he had scooped her up and was carrying her up the beach.

"Your arm," she protested.

"Hush," he growled in reply. But he shifted her in his grasp so that his left arm was merely beneath her knees with his other arm bearing most of her weight. She let her head fall against his salt-flecked shoulders, tasted the sea upon his sun-baked flesh. He stifled a groan as her tongue moved against the hollows in his neck. "You drive me wild with longing."

Good. She had no experience of such things, but she implicitly wanted to give him pleasure.

He carried her to where the rearing cliffs cast some welcome shade onto the hot sand, sank to his knees and lowered her gently down. "Are you sure this is what you want?" he whispered, gazing into her eyes.

In answer she rose up on her elbows and kissed him deeply. He groaned out loud as he wrapped his arms around her, and she allowed her hands to travel across the muscular expanse of his chest. Kitty had always been tall, but crushed in his embrace, she felt dainty and feminine.

He pushed himself to the side, keeping one hand securely in the small of her back and with the other, he began to carefully unlace her kirtle. She wriggled at his slow pace, wanting to feel the warmth of his hands on her flesh, but he chuckled softly and spoke against her mouth.

"All in good time, my sweet girl."

At last, the clinging material loosened away from her. He parted the gown and ran his hands over her shoulder blades, skimming his fingers beneath the straps of her chemise. A coil of tension grew tighter in her core.

"Guy," she whispered, twisting her fingers in his thick, water-logged hair.

He lowered his face to her breasts, only the thin fabric of her chemise coming between his hot breath and her untouched flesh. Then he rose up, leaving her momentarily bereft, and reached out to fully open her kirtle, moving all the time with unhurried, sensual slowness. His eyes travelled hungrily down the length of her body, lingering over her breasts and the darkness between her thighs. She followed his eyeline and flinched when she realised her chemise had grown transparent with seawater.

"You are beautiful," he said. Then he dipped his head and took the rosy nub of her breast inside his warm mouth, sucking and pulling, exploring all he could. Kitty writhed with new longing, arching her back against him and closing her eyes in ecstasy. His hand travelled down her body, over the swell of her hips and the concave dip of her belly, to rest just above where the new cravings of her body told her she most wanted him.

She wriggled in the sand, needing to tip his fingers lower, but with his other hand he caressed her left breast, stroking with his fingers and tickling her with his tongue. Her breath came in hot, jagged bursts when he once again took her tender nipple inside his mouth.

Now, at last, his lower hand was moving, slipping down-wards between her legs. The salty wetness of her chemise chafed at her thighs, and as if divining that this would be no good, Guy reached down and hitched up her underskirt. She sighed with deep relief as his gentle probing finally found her curls. A delicious tension was spreading out inside her, suffusing her limbs with heavy passion. His lips lowered to hers for the briefest kiss and then suddenly, his fingers were inside her.

She gasped with surprise and understanding. This was what she had wanted. How did he know how to touch her in such a precise way? It was as if she'd been made with the curve of his fingers in mind. Tension mounted in her core and for a moment, she couldn't hear the waves or the gulls, she forgot about her wet dress and the cool sand, all she could feel was Guy's touch and her urgent need for him. Waves of pleasure rippled over her as her body raced towards a destination she didn't understand. But oh, when she arrived, the release was sudden and startling and all-consuming. He stilled his fingers but stayed inside her as she clenched tightly around him, her lips parting in surprise.

"Beautiful, beautiful," he murmured, skimming his lips across her clavicle and then laying his head down beside hers.

Kitty blinked, struggling to catch her breath. Her heart pounded as the world steadied around her.

Guy gently removed his hand, stroking her body as he brought it back up to her shoulders and pulled her towards him.

"Is all well, Kitty?" he asked.

She had no words and no voice to say them with. She could only move closer into his embrace, fitting her head beneath his shoulder blades where it seemed to belong.

"Talk to me," he urged, lifting her chin and gazing into her eyes.

Did he expect to see regret in her gaze? He could look forever without finding it, for she had none. She had made her choice when they stood together in the waves, nay, earlier, when she ran her fingers along his muscled shoulders and felt him quiver at her touch. But she had never anticipated the execution of that choice to be so…wonderful.

This handsome man had touched the secret parts of her. She had given herself to him. He'd taken her to heights of pleasure she'd never dreamed of, and now he asked if she was well.

She pressed her lips to his. "I never thought it could be like that."

His hand moved into her hair. "It isn't always. Only when

two people really," he paused, "want to be together."

She traced circles on his chest, enjoying the way he responded to her touch and shocked by her own daring. Her hand moved lower, towards the flat plane of his stomach, and she heard his breath catch in his throat.

"I want to be with you," she whispered. "And I want to give you pleasure, like you just did for me."

He groaned, but reached out to still her exploratory touch.

"I would like that very much," he chuckled, interlacing his fingers with hers and flattening her palm against his ribs. "Believe me."

"Then why do you stop me?" She pushed herself onto her elbows and looked down upon him, at the curve of his lips, the strong arch of his cheekbones and his dark eyes, flashing with desire.

"To give you a chance to reconsider." He sat up, drawing her against him. "What we have done so far…" He pursed his lips. "Kitty, you are still a maid. Still intact for your wedding night." He dropped a light kiss on her mouth to stop her protest.

"I will never marry," she protested. It was on the tip of her tongue to tell him everything. "It matters not. I only want you."

"And I you," he spoke against her shoulder. "And I will be unable to resist you for much longer." He pulled away from her and glanced down towards his breeches. "Do you not see the effect you have on me?"

She followed his gaze to where a significant bulge strained at the wet fabric. Acting purely on impulse, she reached out her hand and stroked it with her fingers. At once, Guy groaned. A deep, guttural sound.

Emboldened, she spanned out her hand and ran it down the length of him, delighting in his clenched muscles, his thinly held restraint.

"Stop, I beg you," he whispered. "I would not ravish you here, where the midday sun threatens to scorch your flesh."

He was right. The small amount of shade they had enjoyed

was disappearing rapidly as the sun rose higher in the sky.

"Where then?" she breathed.

His eyes bored into hers and she held his gaze, proving her intentions. She would not stop now, for all his fine words.

"There is only one place in the castle where we are guaranteed privacy."

"The tower room," she guessed, uncaring, so long as she might show him how much he meant to her. Before she left him, forever.

He paced over to the pile of clothes, sunlight dancing on his toned flesh. "You should put this on." He held out the shirt she had brought for him. "I do not believe the dress is salvageable."

It was a sodden mess of sand and saltwater, pulled all out of shape and heavy in her hands.

"But what about you?"

He smiled, lighting her desires afresh. "I am the Earl of Rossfarne. If I fancy a dip in the sea and return to the castle half clothed afterward, who is to stop me?"

She bit down on her lip. "I have no such freedoms."

He helped her on with the shirt, buttoning it securely to cover her decency. She breathed in the scent of him. If only she might keep it, always.

He cleared his throat. "There is a separate door. If you reach the castle from the cove and head straight for the north tower, you will see it." His grip tightened on her shoulder. "But no one will see you."

Her heart thudded inside her. This would have been where the old earl took his wanton women—as well as scared girls from the village, compelled to comply with his enforcement of Prima Nocta. And now she was preparing to follow in their footsteps.

"I will go in the usual way. And I will meet you at the tower room," he paused. "Unless you change your mind."

Chapter Fourteen

Guy's heart beat louder than his footsteps as he paced through the Great Hall and ran up the tower stairs. One thought pulsated through his mind, beating like a great resounding drum.

Will she come? Will she come?

He couldn't blame her if she chose to stay away. After all, he had placed the decision in her hands and with it, the seed of doubt in her head. Needs must. Her choice must be made with a rational mind.

Not that his mind was in any way clear. Not when the feel of her was imprinted on his skin, the taste of her in his mouth.

He paused as he passed the entrance to his bedchamber, noting with some small part of his brain that the door had been left unlocked. Such had been his haste to get to the beach earlier. His hands went automatically to his breeches, but the pockets were empty. The keys must still be in the room.

So be it. He hadn't the patience to search for them now. Not while his whole being burned for her. Kitty. The enigmatic maid who had somehow calmed both his horse and his own frenzied demons. She had shown him kindness. Broken through his barriers. And all the while, her green eyes captured him in a spell of her own making. One powerful enough to chase away the darkness, even before she ran her palms over the bare skin of his back.

He slowed to a walk on the final flight of steps. Here the

stone treads were narrow and slippery. But he was no longer afraid of injury. He slowed only to prolong this moment of not knowing.

If she wasn't there, he would not pursue her.

He emerged onto the half-landing and his eyes adjusted to the gloom. The sight of her made him warm with relief.

"You came."

She looked him straight in the eye and he wondered why he had doubted her. She had given him her word, and she was not one to do so lightly.

"Of course."

Her voice was steady, but her arms trembled beneath the folds of his shirt. He put a reassuring hand to her slender shoulder as he reached into a crevice for the iron key he had found some weeks ago. The key was long and rusted with age, but when he slid it into the lock, it turned smoothly.

He should have brought candles. The tower room was small, circular and dark. Just two slit windows to relieve the gloom. Once inside, even the relentless crashing of the waves faded away.

Kitty crossed her arms over her chest, shivering in the sudden chill.

"The walls are so thick, the heat doesn't penetrate," he said.

"It must be freezing in winter."

"Indeed." He wanted to keep her talking of such mundanities. Anything to stop her eyes wandering around the infamous room he deeply regretted bringing her to.

What was he thinking? To bring an innocent maid to a place where such vile acts had taken place?

He closed the door behind them and then wished he hadn't. Gloomy as it was, the stairwell had cast a shaft of light into the room. Now they were plunged into near total darkness. He could just about make out Kitty's pale face.

"There must be candles," she suggested, practical as ever.

"There must," he agreed. He put out his hands and felt for

the wall, remembering some wooden shelves on the far side.

This was madness. He should apologise. Let her leave.

"Here. I've found something."

There was a rustling sound, then the spark of a tinderbox followed by the flickering flame and sour smell of a tallow candle.

His eyes found her. She stood with her back to him, holding the candle high to survey the room. Her beautiful hair rippled down to her waist. But what expression showed in her eyes, he dared not guess.

The newly lit candle cast dim light on a circular room hung with velvet drapes. Affixed to the stone walls were a dozen wooden cabinets. A cursory glance on his last visit had told him they stored a variety of objects, in themselves harmless. Though if the stories of the old earl were to be believed, the uses they were once put to would have been unsavoury at best. He should have emptied the room and burned the lot, including those antique chests in the solar. But he hadn't deemed it important. Rossfarne Castle had been a place to convalesce. What care did he have for the props of the previous occupant?

But he'd never imagined he would be bringing a young woman here. Much less one so innocent, for whom he cared so deeply.

Clarity of thought gripped him anew. He cleared his throat. "Kitty, a girl like you shouldn't be in a sordid place like this. I never should have suggested it."

Her face was impassive. He imagined she was thinking of a way to concur, with grace of course. But when she finally spoke it was to issue an order.

"Lay down."

"Pardon me?"

"On the bed." She smiled suddenly, sunshine after rain. "I'm not letting you talk me out of this for a second time."

Mercifully he had instructed the servants to strip the bed when he first arrived. "Are you sure?"

She nodded firmly. "Those are your orders."

"I hear and obey, my lady." He held his hands up in surrender, unable to resist a burst of laughter. Desire pricked him once again and he walked over to the bed willingly, even though he had only ever followed orders from the king.

She sat down beside him and placed her palm on his chest to lower him down.

"You must help me," she said, her breathlessness betraying her nerves. "I'm not sure what should happen next."

Longing surged through him and his need for her hardened as she lowered her sweet lips to the planes of his stomach. Her breath was warm, and her kisses were light, chasing all notions of restraint from his mind.

"I assume I should divest you of these?" She raised her head to meet his eyes, her hand hovering over the fastening of his breeches.

He suppressed a moan of pleasure. "You assume correctly."

She untied them with deft fingers, showing no hint of surprise when the male part of him burst free. He closed his eyes, focusing his energies on keeping control when his loins surged towards release. Warm fingers danced along his sensitive skin. Warm breath invited him to arch towards the source. When he felt her take him in her mouth, just the tip, just ever so tentatively, he knew he would be lost.

Quivering with effort, he sat up.

"Am I doing it wrong?" she asked him directly, worrying at the lip that had been caressing him to distraction.

He struggled to speak, such were the emotions swirling within him. "No, Kitty," he said, when he finally found his voice. "Not at all. But it isn't right for me to lay back and allow you to do all the work."

Her lips formed an O of protest, but he silenced her with a long, deep kiss. She was warm and heavy in his arms. So close, so very close. But he would show her again what pleasures her body was capable of.

He unbuttoned the shirt and let it fall from her slender shoulders. Kitty herself gripped her chemise and pulled it over her head, her tumbling autumn-coloured hair glinting with gold in the candlelight. She was more than he had dreamed. Creamy skin, soft, generous curves and a waist so narrow he could span it with his hands.

"Your turn to lay down," he breathed, raining kisses down her neck. She complied, giving in to the urges of her body as his mouth traced a line over her high, firm breasts. He moved lower and kissed her curls, exulting in her sharp moan of surprise. Then he gently parted her thighs and tasted her fully as she writhed with pleasure. He was gentle and exploratory, following her signals as to what pleased her, wanting only to take her to the edge, not teeter on the brink.

He rose over her, linking his fingers with hers, moving with deliberate slowness. As much as he longed to bury himself inside her, he must ensure she was ready. Their union should bring her only pleasure, no pain.

He nudged himself in, just slightly, and her eyes flew open. "Oh, Guy."

He felt the effort of restraint in his whole body, but he stilled for her. Her palms ran over his back and down over his buttocks.

It was all the invitation he needed. He sank into her and was immediately lost. She wrapped her arms around his shoulders, bringing his weight down on top of her and kissing him deeply as he moved inside her. Their hearts beat as one and their bodies moved together, slowly at first but soon rising to a rhythmic crescendo of mutual pleasure.

Waves of tension built inside him with dizzying speed. It was too much to bear. Just in time, he mentally pulled himself back, taking a moment to gaze down at her rapt face and to drop a featherlight kiss onto her parted lips. His breath caught in his throat as she tightened around him, her hips rising to meet his thrusts. He felt the moment she tipped over the edge, and he instantly felt himself come undone in turn, rational control giving way to sensual pleasure as he roared towards release.

He fell down beside her and pulled her into his arms. Cradling her spent body as he caught his breath and waited for his heartrate to slow. A glow of pleasure was still upon her. He traced delicate circles on her soft skin, marvelling at what had passed between them.

He looked into his heart for regret and found none. Yes, he had been overcome with desire, but it felt right to hold Kitty in his arms. She accessed a part of him he'd locked away from all others. She'd brought in the light and shown him how to trust again.

He would take care of her. They would be together. He would find a way.

A shudder ran through her and he lifted her chin to find her face wet with tears.

"Don't be sad." He kissed them away fervently, thinking how best to reassure her. "Our coming together means a great deal to me."

"To me, too." Her voice shook with emotion.

"When I met you, I was a broken man. Not just my body, but inside."

"No," she interrupted, but he ploughed on.

"No one but Thomas knows of this, but shortly after I was injured, my bag of coin was stolen. It contained my earnings for the year. Enough silver to bring warmth even to my uncle's castle."

She stilled, listening hard. He could feel her heart beating against his chest even though the dim light cast by the one candle made her expression impossible to read.

Guy swallowed, unsure where this urge to unburden himself had sprung from, but not wishing to stop. With every word he spoke, a dam inside him shifted apart.

"As it turned out, I didn't need the coin anyway. You saw yourself how full the castle coin chests are?" He glanced down at her, and Kitty gave a small nod in response. "But it was never about the amount of money that had been stolen. It was the fact of the theft. Someone took advantage of my weakness. They saw me, laying injured in my hospital bed, and they ascertained that I was a man who could be crossed." He clenched his fist in momentary anger, but then calmed himself when he breathed in the citrus scent of her hair. "I promised myself, long ago, that I would never be that sort of man."

Images of his younger brother assaulted him once more. Angus had died because he was too small to defend himself. Memories of that terrible day had been buried so deeply inside him that even Kitty's presence couldn't shine a light upon them. All he would allow himself to recall was the cold, undeniable fact that Guy, as the older brother, had failed young Angus. He had known, from that day, that for the rest of his life he would have to be bigger, stronger and fiercer than any other opponent.

She wrapped her hand around his clenched fist and dropped her head onto his shoulder.

"I'm sorry," she whispered.

"You have no need to be sorry." He looked down at her in amazement. "You are the one who showed me there is goodness to be found, in people, even here in this castle which was full of darkness before you came."

She shook her head. "No, you've got it wrong."

"Yes," he insisted, kissing her hard. "And I would have you here always, to show me the way to the light." To illustrate his words, he leaned over the side of the bed and brought the flickering candle closer to them.

She opened her sea-green eyes and gazed frankly into his. Painful indecision passed over her face and he knew she must be thinking of the unlikelihood of their union. An earl could never marry a servant. But resolution tightened within him. Guy was not a man to bow to the dictates of convention.

"I want to be with you, Kitty." The words were wrenched from him. A declaration of feeling from someone who professed to having none.

And his words found their mark. He saw the moment the

clouds shifted from her eyes and she smiled, alight with new possibility. "And I you."

"Then it shall be." He dropped a kiss onto her pert nose as the belltower tolled for midday, the dull echoes reverberating around the bare walls of the tower room. Guy was startled to realise the whole morning had passed without him attending to any business, although nothing seemed as significant as the beautiful woman in his arms.

Kitty put a hand to her heart, seeming to share his concerns. "The midday bell."

"Is there some place you need to be?"

"Many places, my lord. I mean, Guy." A blush found its way to her cheeks as she struggled to navigate this new path.

Guy caught at her hand. "Not 'my lord,' not anymore. I will find a way forwards for us, I promise."

"I believe you." She took a breath. "It may in fact prove easier than we fear."

That was exactly as he hoped. He dropped a kiss onto her palm, but saw how she wrestled with the need to be elsewhere. He stood and stretched his arms overhead, marvelling afresh at the ease of his movements. Life fanned out before him, brimming with possibilities.

Their love-making had banished the gloom of the tower-room. He could have new windows put in and turn this into a study, or a day-room. The views would be magnificent.

He reached for the blue shirt and passed it back to Kitty. "You cannot pass through the castle wearing this."

She caught at her lower lip. "The servants will be eating in the great hall."

His mind raced, searching for a plan.

"Then the kitchens will be almost empty. If you leave through the tower door and come in through the back, scarcely anyone will see you."

Her eyes widened. "One would be too many."

"Come down to my bedchamber first. I will find you a travelling cloak. You can simply say you were gathering more herbs and wore it to ward off the sun."

At that moment, a distant crack of thunder rolled over the sky ahead. Kitty put her head to one side. "The weather is breaking."

"At last." He pulled on his breeches and helped her with the shirt. "The noise of the storm may provide some distraction for us."

Hand in hand, they slipped down the spiral staircase, waiting at each bend to ensure no one was present. They reached Guy's bedchamber without incident, and he closed the door behind them, sliding shut the bolts to guarantee another few moments of privacy.

"The storm clouds are gathering." Kitty stood at his window, gazing out at the castle grounds. The bright, searing sunshine had been replaced by a sky as grey as the granite walls of the tower room. She jumped at another crack of thunder.

He pulled a dark green cloak from his closet and folded it around her shoulders. It was far too large, but it would certainly cover her modesty.

"Do you know where you're going?" He didn't want her to leave his side, not even for an afternoon.

"Back the way I came." She smiled, momentarily transformed. He was struck anew by her grace and bearing. "Guy, may I tell you something?"

He smoothed the cloak over her arms. "Anything."

She lifted her chin to look him in the eye. "My name is not really Kitty. It is Katherine."

"Katherine." He liked the way it rolled from his tongue. "Why do you not use such a beautiful name?"

"I did once." Her eyes darted to the side. "I believe I may do so again."

"You should." He dropped a kiss onto the top of her head. His cloak swamped her. She needed a hand to hold it closed and another to prevent herself falling over its folds. It would never do, not for climbing down the tower steps. Surely, there was a pin somewhere that Thomas used on such occasions?

He walked over to his washstand but found nothing. He scratched his head, aware that time was passing. His desk then. Maybe he could fashion something from there. Or else Kitty could make use of one of the Answick jewels?

He smiled at his fancy, but the smile froze on his lips when his fingers encountered the saddle bag. It was empty. The Answick jewels were gone.

Someone had stolen from him, again.

Chapter Fifteen

KITTY SAT ON the lumpy mattress in her narrow bedchamber, bidding her hands to not shake as she listened to the panicked sounds echoing through the castle beneath her. Rushing footsteps sounded on the stairs, accompanied by the banging of doors and the occasional shouted warning. It took her back to that terrible night when she and Rosalind had hidden in the pantry at Shoreston, listening to Owain tear the house apart in his search for the very same jewels.

These gems must be cursed, to have wreaked such havoc on her life. Especially today, when happiness had briefly seemed within her grasp.

Tears brimmed in her eyes and Kitty dashed them away impatiently. Clarity of vision had never been more vital. At any moment, Thomas may bang on the door and demand her room be searched. She would have no choice but to comply.

She needed but another minute. Her needle flew through the woollen gown she had brought from home. Her sewing was untidy, if anyone looked closely, they would notice the uneven hem and the strange bulges within it. But why should anyone look closely at the dress of a serving maid?

Her fingers trembled with emotion and the needle slipped, plunging directly into her thumb. She winced with pain and a bloom of blood flowered on her skin. Blood as red as the rubies which were secreted into her dress.

If only she had confessed the truth before Guy realised the

jewels had been taken. The words had hovered upon her lips, she waited only for the courage to say them aloud. Courage which fled from her when she saw the dark rage which descended upon him. Anger transformed his face, turning him from someone she trusted into a man she feared; the infamous Earl of Rossfarne. Her knees had trembled, and her mouth had clammed tightly shut. Even then, she could have made her confession.

"I am Owain's daughter. The jewels belong to me."

Simple words, which might have made all the difference.

Tears came properly now, streaming down her face with no chance of being checked. Upstairs in the tower room, she had vowed to return the jewels at the first opportunity. Once they were safely back in the saddle bag, she could finally tell Guy the truth about who she really was.

But she hadn't been braced to admit to theft as well as deceit.

Guy's fist had crashed down onto the writing desk, sending his quill and a raft of papers drifting to the floor.

"I will not be made a fool of twice," he roared. "The castle shall be searched. Whoever stole from me will be flogged."

Kitty couldn't remember how she had fled up to her own bare room. All she knew was that her fate was sealed. No relationship could succeed when it had begun in darkness and deception.

Thomas flung open her door, his cruel mouth twisted up into a smile. The man was in his element.

"Stand aside," he ordered. "I have orders to search this room."

Her legs shook like jelly, but Kitty managed to move herself to the back wall. She leaned against the cold stones, needing support. Thomas crossed to her small closet, bringing with him a waft of stale ale. She closed her eyes as he rifled through her meagre possessions, tossing Lizzie's straw hat onto the floor and taking obscene delight in running his gnarled fingers through her stockings.

"What's this then?" he exclaimed, as his eyes alighted on

Guy's travelling cloak, which she'd flung onto her bed. He fingered the heavy brocade. "Unless I'm very much mistaken, this belongs to his lordship." The manservant crossed his arms, enjoying his moment. "Do you care to explain how it comes to be in your chamber?"

Kitty met his stare levelly. "As you can see, Thomas, I am in the process of mending it." She indicated her needle and sewing kit.

He narrowed his eyes. "I know of no tear in that cloak. It hasn't been worn since winter."

She shrugged her shoulders, showing how little she cared for his prior knowledge. She was sore inside, from what she and Guy had done just hours earlier. She had felt so close to him then. Safe and protected, maybe even cherished. But now, scarcely hours later, she was being interrogated by his manservant.

She straightened her back, ignoring the burn at the top of her thighs. "You may examine it, if you wish. Even do me the favour of returning it to his lordship. My work on it is finished."

He scoffed at her suggestion. "I am not here to fetch and carry for a chambermaid."

Their eyes clashed in an unspoken battle of wills.

"Then may I help you with something else?"

His gaze flickered over her crumpled woollen dress and she held her breath as he loomed over it.

"More mending, I presume?"

"It is my half-day and the weather is inclement." A splatter of rain hit the shutters, emphasising her words. "I am keeping myself busy as best I can."

He shot her a look of dislike. "Return the cloak at your first opportunity."

He stalked from the room and she sagged against the wall with relief. One hurdle had been passed. Now she must wait until nightfall to put the rest of her plan into action, and leave Rossfarne Castle, forever.

"SAINTS PRESERVE US, Kitty, you're never going outside in this storm?" Cook gasped in horror, as Kitty crossed the kitchen and wrestled with the heavy outer door which had been bolted shut against the storm.

"I want only a breath of air," Kitty reassured her, hating her lie. Wind whistled around the castle and rain fell against the granite walls like arrows from an invading army.

"It will be the death of you," Cook protested, half rising from the rocking chair she'd pulled away from the window.

Kitty rammed her straw hat onto her head, aware of the futility of the gesture even as she did so. Her mind raced for a reason why she might want to go outside at such a moment, when the skies had darkened and the rain fell in torrents, but only a madwoman would do so.

Or a woman driven mad by love and her own lies.

"It has been a trying day. Especially coming after the heat. I am suffocating inside these walls."

"True enough." Cook settled back down in her chair. "That Thomas took great pleasure in turning my store cupboard upside down. I'd have minded less if he cleared up afterwards." She held a warning hand out to Kitty. "You don't be long though, mind, or I'll send a search party after you. And stay away from the ramparts. The waves come right over on a night like this." The old woman sat up straighter as if suddenly remembering something. "And the gatehouse, of course. It was struck by lightning not many months since."

Kitty nodded to reassure her, her gaze swinging past the darkened window. It was not yet nightfall, but clouds had blackened the sky since late afternoon. They had lost all sense of time; the search for the stolen jewels taking precedence over the daily rituals of castle life. Guy had not been seen at all. He'd sent orders to cancel his meals. Any chance Kitty may have had for one last exchange, however veiled, had vanished.

Part of her was glad of it. How could she have looked him in the eye after this?

Cook, though, was a different matter. "Thank you for your kindness to me," Kitty declared boldly. She couldn't say a proper goodbye, but she could at least express her gratitude before she left.

Cook looked up in surprise. "Well now, that's nice to hear. You're welcome, pet. I say we all have to look after one another, being so apart from the mainland."

Kitty swallowed a lump in her throat as she finally managed to wrestle open the door. More lies. More deceit. To someone else who didn't deserve it.

Walking outside was like stepping into a different world. The storm was fully upon them and in the swirling winds, Kitty struggled to orient herself. Within seconds, the driving rain had soaked through her woollen dress. Lizzie's hat flew from her head, evaded her grasping fingers and bowled off in the direction of the choppy sea. Strands of her long hair broke free from her hasty plait and whipped her face, but she had no choice but to continue. Once she reached the causeway, she would run. In less than an hour she'd be back on the mainland, perhaps able to spy the chimneys of Shoreston peeping above the trees.

Arming herself with thoughts of home, Kitty ploughed on, her feet sliding on the wet cobbles. The storm was like a personal attack; all her inner turmoil had been manifested into this force of wind and rain which now set itself against her. Thunder rolled overhead with an elemental rumble. She put her hands to her beating heart and squeezed her eyes shut until the fearful sound faded away.

She must get to the causeway. Kitty put one foot in front of the other, tears now streaming down her face to mix freely with the rain. Only a thief or a fool would be out on a night like this. She was both.

As she turned the corner to the cove, lightning forked

through the dark skies and illuminated the crashing waves. Yes, the causeway was clear, but it was far from safe to cross. She had never seen the sea as high as this. The storm drove a relentless succession of white-tipped, angry waves towards the mainland, drenching the causeway even though the tide was still out. If she attempted to cross, she'd be washed out to sea within seconds.

Kitty's wobbling legs came to a halt. Her plans had come to naught. Hot tears stung her eyes. It was no more than she deserved.

She couldn't return to the castle, not when leaving had been so hard, but neither could she stay outside.

The stables. She could shelter there until morning and leave at first light.

Kitty caught at her wind-lashed hair with one hand and lifted her dripping skirts with the other. Progress towards the outbuildings was against the wind and even harder than before. She leaned for a moment against the crumbling walls of the gatehouse, before remembering how lightning had torn through this building in a previous storm. Sobbing with fear, she plunged back into the rain. By the time she reached the safety of the stables, she was weak with exhaustion.

Rain beat down on the roof, but inside all was calm. Horses looked up from munching their hay to examine the curious, bedraggled creature who disturbed their evening routine. Kitty staggered forwards, relieved to be out of the disorienting winds. Her skirts dragged against the floor, heavy with rain as well as the jewels sewn into the hem. Her heart pounded beneath her bodice, but here was safety.

She tried to speak, to reassure the watchful horses, but no sound came out of her mouth. She inched forwards and a great trembling came over her body. She was chilled to the bone, with no means of getting warm.

Maybe there was a blanket somewhere that she could use? Kitty pushed a strand of wet hair away from her face. It all seemed very difficult. The pathway through the stables, to where she was sure the stableboys kept their store, suddenly morphed into an upwards slope. She staggered forwards, blinking to refocus her eyes.

All she needed was something to rest against, just for a moment. But the gates of the stalls were too far away. She was going to fall. The nearest horse looked at her with surprise as she teetered towards it. Footsteps sounded on the cobbles. Footsteps from someone with a long, swift stride. As if from a great distance, she heard her name being called. Strong arms gripped her shoulders and pulled her up towards a broad, muscular chest she could lean upon. Gentle hands cupped her cheeks.

"Kitty, what are you doing in here?"

She rested her head against Guy's broad shoulders, conscious only of the warmth and solidity he represented.

"You're soaked through. Come, let me find a rug to dry you."

He walked her up the rearing slope. Kitty's flesh burned and her legs trembled. All the strength had left her limbs, leaving her with no choice but to submit to his care.

"Why are you outside of the castle, on a night like this?"

How could she answer? Only with the truth. She parted her lips to say the words but all that came out was a wail of sorrow.

He shushed her with a warm kiss on the top of her head. "Don't speak. Just sit."

They had entered the grooms' store. Guy guided her towards a short three-legged stool, and she sank onto it gratefully. In another moment, he covered her in a rough woollen blanket, rubbing at her arms to bring feeling back to them.

"It's no good," he said. "Not with your dress clinging to your skin so."

There was nothing for it but to let him unbutton her bodice and peel the sodden material from her chilled body. She put up many a weak hand to help him, but her fingers were chilled and useless, and Guy's movements brisk and efficient. There was none of the fiery chemistry from earlier, only her need to be warm and Guy's instinct to take care of her.

When she was clad only in her chemise. Guy once again wrapped the coarse blanket around her shoulders and this time she took comfort in the weight of it. She reached up to hold the folds together and for the first time, vocalised her thanks.

"When you've had a chance to recover, I will demand an explanation for how you came to put yourself in such jeopardy." He smiled down at her. "It's a wonder I was here to find you."

He had found a rough cloth from somewhere and was now tenderly drying her hair. She closed her eyes as a tingling warmth gradually stole over her body.

"How come you are here yourself?" she asked at last.

"To check on my horse. He's full of nerves, even without the storm. I didn't want him to do himself an injury. The stablemaster is unused to horses bred for battle."

She couldn't allow anyone else to see her like this. Kitty's eyes flew open. "Where is he? The stablemaster, I mean."

"I dismissed him and the stableboys for the night." Guy shrugged. His handsome face, creased with concern, loomed in and out of focus. "To tell you the truth, I wanted to be alone."

"I'm sorry," she cried out. A phrase to cover more than he knew.

His hand settled on her shoulder. How she longed to grasp hold of it. "Drink this," he said, handing her a silver hip flask.

The burning liquid scalded her throat. She coughed and her eyes watered, but it brought a welcome warmth to the insides of her stomach.

"Thank you," she mumbled.

He walked over to the half open doorway at the other side of the stables, just as forked lightning tore through the sky. The thunderclap was so loud that Kitty closed her eyes and wrapped her fingers around the edges of the stool, holding on until the fearful rumbling finally ceased. When she opened her eyes, it was to see Guy's tall, muscular figure shining golden in the lamplight.

"The storm shows no sign of abating," he said, turning to face her with a furrowed brow. "I think we must stay here for now, else we'll risk another soaking."

She had no wish to go back out in the storm, but the stool was wobbling beneath her tired limbs.

Guy picked up a pitchfork and dug it into a stack of hay. The fresh, grassy fragrance washed over her as he spread the hay evenly over the stone cobbles.

"Here," he said, when he had built up a thick layer. "You can lay down and rest."

Unease must have shown in her face, for he laughed lightly. "Kitty, after all that has passed between us, you must know that you are safe with me."

She had no hope of expressing her true emotions. Instead, she bit down on her lip until she tasted blood. "The stableboys," she said at last. "They can't find me here."

"They will not." He reassured her. "I will wake you at first light. But for now, you must rest."

He helped her onto the thick, sweet-smelling hay and covered her tenderly with the rug.

"Rest," he repeated, dropping a chaste kiss onto her forehead. "And I will make sure you are not disturbed."

"Guy." She reached up to catch hold of his fingers. "Thank you."

There were so many things she needed to say, but weariness overwhelmed her and her eyes were closing of their own accord. She stretched out beneath the blanket and permitted her frenzied thoughts to settle.

She would explain it all in the morning. She would find the right words; words that would make everything okay again.

As she drifted off to sleep, she heard Guy whispering against her ear.

"Thank you, Kitty," he said, "for showing me that there are still some people in this world who can be trusted."

Chapter Sixteen

H E DIDN'T SLEEP a wink. How could he when such thoughts chased around his mind, tormenting his every moment?

For a while he stood and watched Kitty sleep. Her face looked so young and untroubled. He would have stretched out beside her, enjoying the feel of her strong, warm body against his, but he hated the prospect of disturbing her. She had been so distressed; through exposure to the storm…and something more. Was it their previous intimacy that had caused her such anxiety?

He rubbed at his tired eyes, forcing himself to think back to the events that had taken place only that morning. Kitty had wanted his touch as much as he wanted hers, he was sure of it. He had not forced her. He ground his teeth at the very idea.

What then, had happened? Why had she turned from a confident young woman into someone so clearly distressed?

His eyes once again rested on her sleeping face. Had someone struck her? Been unkind to her? He knew Thomas had searched her room. Guy had been unable to think of a reason he should not, and to warn his manservant out of one specific chamber when orders had been given to search the entire castle would only cause suspicion.

He rubbed at the stubble on his cheeks and tried to settle on the three-legged stool where Kitty had perched earlier, but it was far too small for his long limbs.

He'd wanted to shield Kitty from gossip and suspicion. Even when the black rage had descended upon him, one thought had been clear and true in his mind: Protect Kitty. Ensure no one discovered what they had done. And once the matter of the stolen jewels was dealt with, he'd have returned to the more pressing task of finding a way for them to be together.

He jumped up from the stool, frustration swelling within him.

He shouldn't have become so fixated on the theft of the jewels. Should have kept his focus on Kitty. Instead, he'd become a frenzied fool, obsessed with enacting revenge. And why did revenge matter?

It didn't. Not when he had a good woman by his side. A castle to call home. Coin chests that were full to bursting.

"Never lower your guard," his father had said. It was the motto he'd been raised by. To sense hostility long before it arrived. To trust no one.

But his father had lived a lonely, angry life. What if he was wrong?

His hand clenched into a fist. Kitty had shown him the joy that could be found by letting in the light, but the darkness lived inside him, was as elemental to his life as the oxygen he breathed. And he didn't want to live in darkness, not anymore.

The first, pink rays of morning light were casting a tentative, rosy glow through the half-door of the stables. Guy had promised to wake Kitty at sunrise, but they had a short while left to them still. She looked so peaceful. He didn't want to wake her, not just yet.

By waking her, he risked losing her all over again.

He must find the right words to explain himself. To promise that never again would he allow a dark rage to consume him.

Could he make such a promise? No, but he could promise to turn over a new leaf. To be more humble, more trusting, less inclined to look for the worst in people.

Seized by a surge of energy, he walked out into the dawn, alive with hope for a future he'd never dared to believe could be his. One filled with, dare he think it, love?

Could it be true that a woman as lovely as Kitty might feel the same way about him?

Guy strode into the outer courtyard. The early morning air had been washed clean by the storm. Everything smelled fresh and newly alive. His boots splashed through puddles of rainwater as his eyes roamed automatically over the castle ramparts, looking for damage. He stopped, hands on his hips, and swivelled around. The walls were high and unbroken, despite the ceaseless assault from both the skies and the waves. He pursed his lips, unable to believe in such good fortune.

Maybe his luck was finally changing?

The first musical notes of birdsong floated high overhead and Guy felt his lips stretch into a smile. New life, new hope, was all around him.

He must wake Kitty now. Wake her up and profess his true feelings for her.

He spun around, ready to stride back towards the stable yard, when his attention was caught by something on the ground. A white body, splashed with red. He looked closer and grimaced when he realised he was looking at a gull with a broken neck. It must have become caught up in the storm and dashed against the ramparts by the strong winds.

He reached out with the toe of his boot and gently prodded the creature, checking for any signs of life, but it didn't stir. He'd have one of the stableboys remove it.

A muscle twitched in his jaw. He must wake Kitty and talk to her properly before they arrived.

She was still sleeping when he returned. Once more, he felt reluctant to disturb such peaceful repose, but she would be mortified if anyone discovered her.

He cleared his throat. "Kitty," he whispered, shaking her shoulder very gently.

She opened her eyes, blinked and sat up in a rush when she realised where she was. The blanket fell away, revealing a chemise so sheer that the pink of her skin showed through the thin fabric.

Guy averted his gaze politely. "I'm sorry to wake you, but it is sunrise," he addressed a nearby horse.

Kitty pulled the blanket more securely over her shoulders. "Thank you, my lord."

Her words sent a chill through him. "Not 'my lord,'" he corrected her. "Please, don't address me as such, Kitty. We know each other better than that." Her cheeks flamed red, and he regretted his choice of words. "Allow me to fetch your dress," he muttered.

He had hung it over a stable door to dry last night. The fabric was still damp, but it would suffice to wear back to the keep. He gripped the woollen garment tightly, breathing in the scent of lavender. He couldn't let her dress now. If he turned his back, the moment would be lost.

"May I speak with you?" The words came out more forcefully than he'd intended. She took half a step backwards. Where had this fearful reserve sprung from?

From his own actions. His shouting. His anger at being stolen from once again.

He shook his head to dislodge the remorse. He couldn't undo yesterday's rage. He could only hope to tread a new path, today.

"As you wish." She hung her head so her beautiful auburn hair fell forwards, obscuring her face.

He would like to look into her sea-green eyes when he told her how he felt. Instead, he gripped his hands together and shuffled his feet like an anxious youth.

"Katherine," He tried out her true name, liking the way it rolled off his tongue and wishing to conjure the warmth and connection they had shared just yesterday. But then he faltered. How could he proceed? "I am falling in love with you," he blurted out. He clamped his lips together, unaccustomed to the sudden vulnerability which accosted him. But despite the tingle of nerves which made his pulse pound and his breath catch in his throat, he didn't regret telling her the truth.

He expected her to look up, to show some surprise. But Kitty shrank further back into the shadows of the store room as if his declaration had filled her with dread.

"What is it?" he demanded. "What's wrong?"

She put shaking hands to the sides of her head, swaying as if at any moment she might fall. "Nothing is wrong, my lord. How could it be? It is only that a girl like me doesn't deserve the regard of an earl."

"Nonsense." Anger surged in his veins. Anger which, just moments ago, he had vowed to leave behind him. "Haven't I shown you already how high my regard is for you?"

"In so many ways," she sobbed.

"It is I who am not worthy of you." The realisation seeped through him. Kitty was beautiful, wise and strong. She would have many suitors. Mayhap she was even fleeing one when she came here. He was older than her and scarred to boot. Had he been naïve to imagine that one so young and lovely could care for a body so battered and bruised as his?

"No," she shook her head staunchly. "Not that."

He was right. The truth was written all over her. He had made a fool of himself.

"Here." He flung the dress towards her. "I will detain you no longer."

But instead of travelling through the air towards Kitty, the gown slumped to the floor and clattered on the cobblestones. Kitty gasped and held herself rigid, her eyes half closed in new despair.

What was this?

He snatched the dress from the floor. It was heavy in his hands, too heavy. How had he not observed this before?

"Don't." Her eyes were fixed on his now, wide open and pleading. "Please."

"Don't what?" He was confused, embarrassed, but far beyond him shimmered a truth that he wasn't yet ready to accept. "What's inside the dress, Kitty?"

Let it be nothing. Let her explain it away, he prayed silently.

She shook her head. "It isn't what you think."

Why then was she acting so strangely? Afraid of him, like a thief about to be found out.

His hands wrestled with the dress, encountering hard objects sewn into the lining. He looked more closely at the uneven hem, fingering the bulges inside it. Something sharp pricked against his finger.

"Damnation, Kitty." His voice was low, his spirit broken. "Tell me it is not you who stole from me."

She stood straighter now, her green eyes burning with conviction. "It was not *I* who stole," she shot back. "'Twas *you* who accepted something that did not belong to you."

With trembling hands, he ripped open the hem. Out fell the Answick jewels, sparkling with rich, vibrant colours against the dull grey of the cobbles. They both looked silently down upon them. At their undeniable reality.

"It was you." He said the words, but he still didn't believe them. A shiver of shock pulsated through his veins, and he folded his arms against the sudden chill. Time slowed down as he tried to fit this new detail into the complex tapestry of their burgeoning relationship.

She put a hand to her face and he saw, distantly, that tears were flowing down her cheeks. "I didn't want you to find out like this," she sobbed. "I was going to tell you."

His hand clenched her torn dress so hard his knuckles turned white. "Was this your plan all along then?"

She looked him in the eye. "Yes."

Her answer sliced him through like a knife. "Why?" he floundered. "What wrong did I ever do you, for you to repay me so?"

She hugged her arms around her chest. The blanket had long since dropped to the floor but neither of them cared. It lay on the stone cobbles next to the jewels. "It was not like that," she said hesitantly. "Once I got to know you, everything changed."

"Yet still, you stole." Anger burned through his disbelief. He remembered his thoughts upon encountering her for the first time on the causeway. How Kitty conducted herself like a lady, not a servant. "Are you some bastard child of my uncle's, come here to claim your inheritance?" Revulsion swirled in his stomach.

"No." She shook her head vehemently. "Please, Guy, I can explain." She took a step forwards, then retreated again when she saw the anger in his eyes.

Anger which he should rein in. But his loss was too great. Everything he had started to believe in had been built on lies. Everything he'd been daring to reach for, was but a mirage.

"You told me once that you were seeking the daughter of a man named Owain." She clutched at her stomach as if her confession was causing her actual pain. For a moment, he wrestled with the urge to offer her comfort, but he chased it away.

You have been made a fool of already.

He ran a hand through his dishevelled hair, trying to keep his temper in check. "I was."

"I am that daughter." She stared at the floor, not at the jewels, but at a patch of hay. "I am the woman you were looking for."

Her words made no sense to him. "Then why did you not say?"

She looked up in shock. "Is that not obvious? How could I stand the shame?"

"You lied to me about your past. I asked you several times."

"Because I could not admit the truth." She hung back in the shadows. "My own father gambled me away."

It was a shock to hear her say the words out loud. So she had known of the sordid details of their wager all along? Just hours earlier, this realization would have rocked him, but now it changed nothing.

"We do not carry the sins of our fathers," Guy growled. "We forge our own paths. And yours was forged with deceit."

Something like anger blazed in her eyes. "That is easy enough for a man to say. Less so for a woman, who can be passed around like a mule." She clasped her hands together. "Every day I longed to tell you the truth. But the jewels, you see, are truly mine." Her voice shook with undeniable sincerity, but her words were like fine rain on the surface of a deep lake. They did not permeate.

"If you wanted jewels, I would have given you jewels." Guy forced the words out, though the truth of it sickened him. He would have given her everything, all that he had and more besides.

"They are not for me, they are for my sister," she cried.

Guy motioned her protests away. "At any point, you could have told me who you really were." He spoke slowly, thinking aloud. "I would have handed over the Answick jewels in a heartbeat. I didn't even want them. I tried to return them twice."

She blanched at his words and her eyes flared with understanding. "*That's* why you went to Shoreston? I heard of your visit. No one dared to open the door to you."

"Because of who I am?" Shame crawled up his insides as he remembered that dreadful night at the grubby alehouse.

"They don't know you." Her face crumpled with grief. "They only know your uncle, and your family's reputation."

"And they could not see past that." He paused to take a deep, ragged breath. "Nor could you. Not even after yesterday and all that passed between us."

His knees felt weak, as if his legs might give way at any moment. He had dared to believe that what he and Kitty had was real, something solid to be built upon.

"I was wrong." She ventured closer towards him. "Believe me, I know that now."

"But it is too late."

"It isn't." She put her hands to her heart. "Please don't say that."

He looked at her as if for the first time. "You aren't even a serving girl. You are from a titled family, descended from the

Duke of Answick."

She stood her ground. "I have worked hard every day since my mother passed away. See?" She showed him her reddened hands.

He took hold of her fingers, holding her flesh against his for one last time. "One truth, amidst so many lies."

"I wanted only to provide a better future for my sister," she whispered.

Her defence was reaching him, slowly. He could well understand that urge to protect a younger sibling.

"I would have given your sister anything you wanted," he said, honestly.

"I couldn't be sure."

Something snapped inside him. Kitty's protective instincts for her family were admirable, and he could not begrudge them. But nor could he hope for a life with her, when she lived her life for another. Not when the bond of trust between them, so newly formed, was irreparably shattered.

Without trust, their relationship had no foundation.

"Do you always put her first?"

She nodded, slightly but emphatically.

He released her hand. "Take the jewels," he said. "They are rightfully yours. They always were."

Her eyes dropped to the floor and then shot back up towards him. Would she fight for him? Would she push through his defences once again, like she had so many times before?

Yet, for all the time he'd known her, she'd wanted only to get her hands on the jewels, for her sister.

He turned away, unable to look at her.

"Guy?"

He stood with his back to her, gazing out unseeingly at the sunrise.

"Low tide is upon us," he stated. "You can cross safely back to the mainland. Take a horse if you wish. Take anything. But please, don't ever return."

Chapter Seventeen

"I 'VE BROUGHT YOU some chicken broth."

Rosalind's pretty face peeked around the edge of the door. Kitty sat up in bed, allowing the blankets to fall away from her as she blinked her way to wakefulness.

"How long have I slept?" Her whole body felt heavy and leaden.

"So many hours," Rosalind giggled as she edged into the room carrying a heavily laden tray. "Lizzie said you must have kept fine company up at the castle to be so weary."

Kitty blanched. She had done that and more. But no one at Shoreston must ever find out about it.

"You shouldn't be waiting on me." She swung her legs out of the bed, wincing when her feet made contact with the bare wooden floor. "I shall get dressed." She had no enthusiasm for the day ahead but was determined to pull her weight as usual.

"Stay right where you are." Rosalind's voice carried the authority of the lady of the house, despite the fact of her clean white apron. She placed the bowl of broth upon a side table and straightened Kitty's blankets. "You need to rest," she fussed, "and I'm here to make sure you do exactly that. Shall I open the shutters?"

Kitty shook her head. "No. The sunlight hurts my eyes." Her heart beat hollowly as she heard the echo of previous conversations with Guy.

Rosalind pulled a face. "It's very dark in here. I'll just open them a fraction."

Kitty submitted wearily to her ministrations, turning her mind from the man who still haunted her thoughts. "I didn't recover mother's jewels just so you could fetch and carry." She motioned towards Rosalind's apron. "They are your dowry; with them you can make a good marriage, but not if you insist on acting like a maid of all work."

"Never mind that." Rosalind batted away her hands and perched on the side of her bed. "I still can't believe you managed it. However did you fool the earl?" Her young face was alight with curiosity.

Kitty took a sip of broth. It was very good, seasoned to perfection by Lizzie no doubt, but she wasn't hungry. She wasn't sure she would ever be hungry again. Still, eating would buy her time against Rosalind's questions. She made a careful show of dipping the spoon into the bowl and swirling it around.

"Is he as fearsome as his uncle was?" her sister persisted.

Kitty sighed and put down her spoon. "Not at all." Sorrow darted through her and she bit her lip to stop the tears from forming.

"He's hiring new guards, did you know? Alfred told us there's been a great commotion down in the village."

Kitty swallowed hard. Her vision blurred, but Rosalind chatted on regardless.

"Lizzie said he must be wanting new guards since he discovered the jewels were stolen. He's guessed his castle was infiltrated, but he'll never work out who by." Her voice rose with pride.

"The earl has plenty of jewels and riches. He has no need of ours." Kitty forced her words to be level and calm.

"Still, though." Rosalind leaned closer, a smile dancing over her lips. "Men like that don't like to be stolen from."

How true. Kitty didn't trust herself to reply. She gazed down at the creamy broth and felt her stomach turn.

"But my clever sister got the better of him." Rosalind stood up and the thin mattress lurched. Kitty clutched her bowl to stop it from spilling. "I'm so proud of you."

Kitty's throat constricted. She hadn't been clever. She'd been foolish in the extreme.

"It's over now," she said, her fingers gripping the bowl so tightly the whites of her knuckles showed through. "We must put the whole thing behind us and look to the future."

Even though her future stretched out bleak and empty without Guy.

Rosalind's eyes widened and she bit down on her lower lip, a habit she'd had since childhood. "It's funny you should say that." She put a hand to her neckline, fingering a simple silver chain. "I have something to tell you." She paused and took a breath. "But Lizzie says I should wait until you're up and about." She folded her arms and wandered over to the shuttered window with a show of nonchalance. One slender hand played with the slats of the blind while the other tugged restlessly at her long braid of golden hair.

Despite the dull ache of her heart, Kitty was intrigued. "No, tell me now." She raised her eyes to her sister's, longing for any news that might distract her.

Rosalind shook her head. "Eat and get dressed," she insisted. "Come downstairs when you're ready. We have such a surprise for you." She smiled gleefully, unable to contain her excitement and Kitty felt a slight lessening of her own sorrows. It was a gift to see her younger sister so carefree.

But as Rosalind's light footsteps echoed down the wooden staircase, Kitty placed the bowl of broth down on the floor and put her head into her hands, sinking into the now-familiar sensations of loss and regret that she'd been working to keep at bay ever since she arrived back at Shoreston.

They had been so pleased to see her. Pleased and effusive with gratitude. She'd borne it as best she could, accepting the praise she didn't deserve. *You must have been so brave,* they'd told her. *So clever, to trick the earl.* None of it was true. She hadn't needed bravery or wit or cunning to recover her family fortune.

All she'd needed was honesty. But she'd realised it too late.

"You must have had a terrible time," Lizzie had fussed over her, tutting at her ruined dress and tired eyes.

Kitty had pressed her lips together and nodded mutely, unable to confess the truth. She'd known both great despair and deep joy with the Earl of Rossfarne.

Alfred had said little, but the clumsy affection of his hand on her elbow, together with the relief shining in from his face, had told her all she needed to know.

Wordlessly, she'd tipped the jewels onto the scrubbed kitchen table and for a moment they had all gazed upon them in silent reverence.

Rosalind put her head back and shrieked with pleasure. "You did it."

"Mercy upon us." Lizzie clutched her crucifix. "I never thought I'd see those jewels again. Nor you, dear Kitty. I feared we had lost you to that terrible man." She blinked back tears.

Kitty bit back her instinctive defence of Guy. What could she say?

"It was easy, in the end. They were there for the taking."

"We can repair the roof," Rosalind enthused, "and hire new help. You won't have to work so hard now, Kitty. You've earned the right to a rest."

"No," Kitty protested. "The jewels are for your dowry."

Rosalind and Lizzie exchanged a look which she was too tired to try and decipher.

"Let's say no more of that now," Lizzie said firmly. "This is a day to celebrate. The roof can wait. It can all wait."

Such an air of gaiety hadn't been known at Shoreston for many years. Alfred fetched out his old penny whistle and Rosalind danced around the kitchen, occasionally swinging a mildly protesting Lizzie into her arms along with her. They all cajoled Kitty to sing, but she rebuffed the calls as lightly as she could. Singing would always remind her of that time in the solar with Guy. When they had laughed together and happiness had been truly within her reach, if only she'd known. Now, sadness had lodged itself deep within her heart and she felt as if she might never sing again.

It was a relief when Lizzie noticed her yawns and sent her off to bed. Kitty had believed she would lay awake restless, remembering all she had lost, but weariness had overcome her.

She straightened her back, tuning into the familiar sounds of Shoreston. Snatches of conversation floated up from the parlour below. Outside, the steady clip clop of horse's hooves announced a passerby or a visitor.

Glory be, she'd hoped she would be spared visitors for some time yet. Kitty sighed. As much as she longed to hide in the half-light of her bedchamber, she would have to face them all at some point.

Gritting her teeth, she pushed herself up from the bed and reached for her stockings.

A BUNCH OF freshly-picked wildflowers had been abandoned to wilt on a hall table. Kitty picked them up and inhaled deeply. At Rossfarne Castle, every sense had been tinged with sea salt and bracing winds, but here at Shoreston, the smells were homely and comforting: newly baked bread and dried lavender. The fresh fragrance of cornflowers and honeysuckle.

She must put the flowers into water. But who had brought them?

She glanced around. The hallway was empty, the house apparently deserted. She walked through to the sun-filled kitchen.

"Hello?" she called, but there was no response.

She poured water from a jug into a small vase and positioned the flowers so the smallest were at the front. They brought a splash of summer colour to the bare windowsill and plastered walls.

Kitty rubbed her arms. This kitchen had once been as familiar to her as her own hands, but now it felt quiet and strange. She missed the constant bustle and steam of the castle kitchen. The fussing of Cook and even the muted complaining of Agnes.

Where was everyone?

"Lizzie?" she tried.

They must be out of earshot. She left the kitchen and headed for the parlour, pushing away memories of how she and Rosalind had hidden behind the heavy drapes, surrounded by the wreckage of the room just a few weeks earlier. Tentatively, she pushed at the heavy door, bracing herself for unwelcome reminders of that fateful night. But the room had been put in good order. Mother's cabinet had been mended, by Alfred no doubt. And the candlesticks looked to have been recently polished. More surprisingly, the room bore the air of recent celebration.

Kitty put her hands on her hips and looked around. A pewter jug and four goblets stood on a silver tray on the centre of the table. She stepped closer and sniffed. The jug still carried the scent of mead. But neither Lizzie nor Alfred were fond of intoxicating drink. And Rosalind most certainly wasn't.

A stifled giggle came through the window. Kitty paced over and flung back the drapes, but there was no one there, only the swinging of the wooden gate disturbed a glorious summer afternoon.

"Rosalind?" she called. The giggle had a girlish quality, which could only be her sister's.

From the other end of the house, the back door banged shut. Kitty raced back through to the kitchen, to find Rosalind smoothing down her skirts. She'd thankfully removed her apron and was dressed in a pretty pale blue gown with wide sleeves and a demure neckline.

"What's going on?" Kitty demanded.

"Nothing, why?" Rosalind asked innocently, but a pink flush warmed her cheeks and her hair had partially come unbraided.

"Where have you been?"

"Just outside, in the garden." Rosalind twisted a strand of golden hair between her fingers.

"Alone?"

Her sister bit down on her lip, a telling trait. "Not exactly."

Kitty folded her arms and rested against the doorway, weariness battling her intrigue. "Are you going to tell me what's happening? Why have people been drinking mead in the parlour?"

Rosalind's gaze went behind Kitty, who turned to find Lizzie standing in the kitchen doorway.

"Can I tell her now?" beseeched Rosalind.

"Go on then." Lizzie wiped her hands on her long apron, a smile lighting up her face. "Miss Katherine, it's such good news."

"We were celebrating." Rosalind folded her hands behind her back. "Although it wasn't the happiest of celebrations, dear Kitty, because you weren't there."

"You mean, this was before yesterday?" Kitty tried to make sense of it.

Rosalind nodded. "It has been a most wonderful week."

Kitty sat down on a hard kitchen chair and crossed her ankles, waiting to hear more. Lizzie bustled forwards.

"Can I get you a glass of water? You look ever so pale, Miss Katherine."

"I'm fine." Kitty waved her attentions away clumsily. She had grown unaccustomed to such niceties.

Rosalind perched on the edge of a seat and then stood up again, too excited to be still.

"I can't keep it from you a moment longer. Kitty, I'm engaged to be married." Her face was alight with joy.

The words made no sense to her. Kitty repeated them, looking for some hidden meaning. "Engaged to be married? To whom?"

Rosalind nodded happily. "To Richard Erkine."

Kitty rubbed at her temples, trying to understand. The Erkines owned farmlands at the other side of the river and usually sat behind herself and Rosalind at chapel. Mrs Erkine was a stout woman with a kind smile, her husband was polite and well-presented.

"He's been learning his lessons with a cousin in Dun Holme. He came back to Rossfarne while you were away," Rosalind explained, eager for a reaction.

Of course. Mrs Erkine had been a regular caller to Shoreston when Mother was alive. Kitty cast her mind back to that golden-hued time and recalled a plump-cheeked young boy, just a couple of years older than Rosalind.

Richard Erkine.

The last time she saw Richard Erkine, he'd been playing hide and seek in the stable yard with her sister. The two of them had been good friends when they were young, she remembered now. Lizzie would bake honey cakes especially for his visits, then make a great show of chasing the pair of them out of the kitchen.

"But Rosalind, you're too young to be married," she exclaimed, her mind struggling to adjust to this new information.

Her sister pressed her lips together. "Kitty, you mustn't be so disapproving. Of course, we won't be married right away. But Richard and I have known one another all our lives. And anyway, you don't know the best news yet."

"The best news is that Miss Rosalind is happy," Lizzie said, with a pointed look in Kitty's direction.

"I'm very happy, but I also know how my sister frets," Rosalind declared. "The best news is that the Erkines have offered to buy some of our land."

Kitty frowned. How could so much have happened in her absence? "But are they offering a decent price?"

"Why should they not? And anyway, the land is just going to waste. We haven't had anyone to work the fields for years."

Kitty couldn't deny it. The fields of Shoreston had once yielded a decent crop, but years of neglect had left the land barren. She placed her elbows on the kitchen table, trying to make sense of it. "Why would the Erkines show us such kindness?" She bit back the word "charity."

Rosalind leaned forward and took hold of her hands. "Because their son is in love with me?" she offered, blushing despite the ease of her words. "Because they are decent people. Because they actually do want the land for themselves." She paused. "People do nice things, sometimes, Kitty."

Kitty put a hand to her head, struggling to keep up. She'd been so consumed with the need to build a better life for her sister, that she'd never imagined it could happen without her willing self-sacrifice. "What does all this mean?"

Rosalind gave a bubbling laugh. "It means that, even before you brought back the jewels, our financial worries were over. But now we have the jewels as well." She shrugged, brimming over with good fortune.

"We will have to offer them to the Erkines as a dowry," Kitty thought aloud, unable to let go of her natural instincts to worry. For so long she'd seen the Answick jewels as key to Rosalind's happiness.

"You will do no such thing," Lizzie interrupted. "It's all arranged now, with no need for a dowry. That family is lucky enough to have Miss Rosalind joining them."

"Don't you see, Kitty?" Rosalind leaned forward, her eyes alight with excitement. "We're rich. Our troubles are over. You can keep the jewels for yourself."

The happiness shining from her sister's face was enough to convince Kitty that she really had found love and the promise of a joyful future with Richard Erkine. Rosalind would be cared for and content, which was all Kitty had ever wanted for her. So why did she feel so much despair?

"I don't want the jewels." Kitty's throat closed over the words.

Rosalind sat back. Disappointment flashed through her eyes, but only for a moment. "Then we will sell them and use the money to make much-needed repairs to the house. Shoreston will be a grand residence once again. You shall live here in the style that Mother intended, no longer beating rugs or baking pies. And I shall come to see you often." She smiled beatifically. "It's all going to be wonderful."

An icy numbness spread across Kitty's chest. The future Rosalind described was everything she had once hoped for. But now she'd met Guy and known the possibility of love and happiness for herself. Now everything had changed. Now she wanted more. His touch, his kiss. The feel of his muscular arms drawing her close. His smile, his laugh. His strong body, which she had nursed back to health.

She put a hand to her mouth to keep this whirlwind of emotion inside her. Her eyes fluttered closed. In another moment she would regain her composure. Such bittersweet reminders of their fleeting time together might assault her often, but she would learn to put them aside. That part of her life was over.

"She's overcome," Lizzie remarked. "It's no surprise, not after all the poor girl's been through."

"You're safe now, Kitty. You never have to leave Shoreston again." Rosalind squeezed her shoulder.

Kitty forced her eyes to open and summoned a smile. "And I never shall," she stated, forcing her true feelings deep down and locking them away. "I'm so happy for you. For all of us."

Chapter Eighteen

GUY READ THE message one more time and then placed the slip of parchment neatly on his writing desk and folded his hands together. He must pen a reply to the king, but first he needed a moment to gather his thoughts.

He turned in his chair to the solar window and gazed out at the sparkling sea, but he didn't see the white-tipped waves and soaring seagulls, he saw a tall young woman with tumbling auburn hair, enticing curves and a wide smile. She had worked here for no more than a month, yet every foot of Rossfarne Castle was permeated with Kitty's memory. He couldn't so much as eat a meal without thinking of her and missing her. This room, which had once been his sanctuary, had grown almost unbearable. She had sung for him by the fireplace. They had shared their first kiss while standing on that very rug.

It would be easier to put her behind him once he returned to the service of the king. He flexed his fingers. His body was healed. His mind ready for a fresh challenge. He hadn't been expecting a summons so soon, but now he saw that the timing could not have been better. Tomorrow, he would join King Edward on the tumultuous borderlands, where they would prepare for battle.

He must get ready. There was much to do. He had no time to wallow over a girl who had lied to him, stolen from him, cheated him. Not even when the memory of how they had come together still lit a fire inside him. She had been so responsive to his touch, and his body had sung for her. But it could never be again.

He would find other avenues for pleasure. Ones that did not stave open his heart and leave him vulnerable.

A knock sounded on the wooden door.

"You sent for me, my lord?"

Guy beckoned for the marshal to enter. The man was clad in a smart but plain tunic, his dark hair neatly combed away from his sun-tanned face.

"I am leaving tomorrow," Guy announced, without preamble.

The marshal looked surprised. "So soon? We were not anticipating your departure."

Guy drummed his fingers on the desk, unwilling and unaccustomed to sharing details of his personal life. "The situation has changed. In my absence, you will once again assume charge of the castle. I trust this is to your liking?"

"Happy to serve, my lord." The marshal dipped his head.

"Ensure the repair work continues on the gatehouse. It must be weather tight by winter."

The marshal nodded. "And the extra guards? Shall we stand them down?"

Guy thought for a moment. "No. I want the castle to be secure. I may be gone for some time." A question flickered behind the marshal's eyes, but he was too well-trained to voice it. The man, however, had served him willingly and without question; mayhap he deserved more of an explanation. Guy sighed resignedly. "There is little to bring me back here." He raised his eyebrows to check he understood. "I will remain with the king for as long as he needs me."

"We shall be ready to welcome you home, whenever that may be," the marshal said, stiffly. He cleared his throat. "May I speak freely, my lord?"

Guy motioned with his arms and pulled his face into a neutral expression, even as his heart sank. "Of course."

The marshal hesitated, glancing around the room to ensure they were alone. "It has not always been easy to find men willing to work at Rossfarne Castle, not locally anyway." He dampened his lips with his tongue.

Guy felt a surge of impatience. "You mean, because of the old earl? Speak freely, man."

A tremor passed through the marshal's features, but he stood his ground. "Very good, my lord. Yes, because of the old earl. He was not well-liked, hereabouts."

"I should say that's the least of it," Guy interjected, folding his arms and leaning back in his chair.

The marshal nodded again. "But I believe the situation is beginning to change. Slowly. At least, with one exception." He ground to a halt and the silence grew heavy between them, broken only by the mournful crying of gulls outside.

Guy took a deep breath, willing himself to remain calm. He wanted to provide steady employment for those who had served him reliably. Therefore, he must listen to their concerns.

"Are you going to tell me what this one exception is?"

"The villagers speak of a young woman." He shifted uncomfortably and fixed his gaze on the window behind Guy. "A Miss Katherine Alden."

Kitty. It could only be Kitty. Guy gripped the arms of his chair to steady himself.

"I have never heard that name," he said truthfully, though a memory tore at his heart. Kitty, enfolded in his travelling cloak, the folds of fabric swamping her, lifting her chin to meet his eye with steady composure. *"My name is not really Kitty. It is Katherine."*

"No, my lord." The marshal's words brought him back to the solar.

"Who is she?" Guy demanded, more harshly than he'd intended.

The marshal looked hot and uncomfortable, though he stood with a straight back and his arms smartly by his sides. "Her mother was a noblewoman. Her father, less well born. But the family is well known hereabouts, and various rumours are circulating."

Guy raised an eyebrow as a chill of apprehension twisted in his stomach. "Rumours?" His voice was icy.

"They say that Miss Katherine is here." The marshal looked embarrassed.

Guy steadied himself. He must dissipate this speculation, for Kitty's sake more than his own. Heaven knows, he had no desire to see her reputation spoiled.

"I do not believe I have ever been introduced to a Miss Katherine Alden," he said slowly, gathering his thoughts. "But I may know where these rumours have sprung from. Did I perhaps meet the young lady's father in the alehouse?"

The marshal looked faint with nerves. "That is what I have heard."

Guy waved his hand, aiming for nonchalance. "A most unfortunate encounter. But one which, thankfully, held no repercussions. The man was a drunkard. A scoundrel no less."

"Oh, yes, my lord," the marshal interrupted in his eagerness to agree. "He has now been chased out of Rossfarne."

"Is that so?" Guy took a breath. *Did that leave Kitty without a protector?* The idea brought him up short, before he came to the realisation that Owain could hardly have been described as such. No doubt Kitty was better off without him. And hadn't she proved that she could look after herself well enough? He shook away his concerns. Kitty's reputation had rested briefly in his hands, but her future wellbeing was not his responsibility. "Both the family's jewels and the family's daughter are safe and well in the family home." He cleared his throat. "To the best of my knowledge."

The marshal heaved a sigh of relief and widened his stance. "That will make recruiting the new men easier, my lord."

"I am glad to hear it." Guy tightened his lips. What would these new men say if they knew the truth, that Miss Katherine Alden had gained entry to his castle and his heart through dishonest means?

That he was the victim here?

The marshal bowed his farewell. Guy waited until his footsteps had faded from the great hall before allowing his anger to surface.

"Damn it all," he swore, bringing his fist down heavily onto his desk and making the ink splatter onto the king's summons.

Never lower your guard.

It pained him to think it, but his father had been right all along. He would batten down the hatches. Bolt all the doors. Shore up his heart in the way that Rossfarne Castle would soon be closed to intruders. No one allowed in. Nothing allowed out.

He rose to his feet, too frustrated to sit still at a desk. His whole being coursed with impatience. He had lingered too long in Rossfarne, allowing the sunlight to shine into all the cracks and crevices he usually kept hidden. It was time to be gone.

His riding boots rang out against the stone flags of the great hall. When he stepped outside, a slight summer breeze rifled through his hair. The sky was powder blue; the air warm and welcoming. It was a beautiful day, but Guy cared nothing for it. He strode towards the stables, looking neither left nor right, scattering stable hands in his path.

"My lord." The groom nodded politely.

Guy put his hands on his hips. "Is my horse well rested?"

"He is, my lord. I've never seen him so settled."

Guy didn't believe it, but when he paced over to the stall, his horse was peacefully munching hay. His head was lowered, his eyes liquid calm. Guy stroked his silken neck and the horse breathed softly into his hands.

"We are returning to the life we know," Guy told him.

His horse was bred for battle. No wonder he had struggled with the dull tedium of civilian life. But after several weeks, he had adjusted to the quiet rhythms of the castle.

Just like his master.

Guy lifted his eyes to the spot he had last seen Kitty. It was achingly benign. Straw-strewn cobbles. A low wooden beam.

Horse blankets, neatly folded on a cracked chest. He had declared his true feelings moments before discovering her dishonesty. The memory still twisted like a dagger in his gut.

He leaned his head against the horse's powerful shoulder and breathed deeply, quelling a rising tide of emotion.

Have I been too harsh with her?

As if hearing the question spoken out loud, the horse snorted and pushed his nose against Guy's belly.

"You think so?" He pulled the creature's ears, unwittingly replaying their final conversation as he had so many times before.

"I wanted only to provide a better future for my sister," she'd said.

An admirable motivation, for anything but theft and deceit. Deceit against *him*. When he had only ever shown her kindness.

A groan swelled inside him and he bit down on his lip lest the sound come out and the stable boys hear his anguish. The metallic tang of blood filled his mouth.

Would he have been driven to such extremes to provide a better future for Angus, were he ever given the chance?

Yes, the answer came from deep within him. He would have, in a heartbeat. But not if it meant lying to Kitty. She was the one person he would prioritise above all others. Even his younger brother.

This time he couldn't push back the torrent of memories. He closed his eyes and nausea swirled in his stomach as images from that fateful day in his youth cascaded through his mind.

"Take your brother out riding," his father had demanded. "Go beyond the estate, onto the cliffs. I'm putting you in charge. Make a man of him."

Fifteen-year-old Guy had murmured a protest. "Angus is no natural horseman. He's happier riding here in the paddocks. What need is there to frighten him on the cliffs?"

His father's brow had darkened further. "Who are you to question me, boy?"

Guy had complied, leading a reluctant Argus out onto the Forbisher cliffs on a wild, blustery day, when gusts of wind spooked the horses even more than the crashing white-tipped waves below them.

"Don't communicate your fear to the horse," Guy had instructed his grey-faced brother, who had only just celebrated his tenth birthday.

But both horses were in a state of terror, snorting and prancing and refusing to go beyond a natural bend in the coastline. Moments later, as his mare reared up beneath him, Guy discovered why. A group of wild boars, grunting and growling their intent, came out of the trees. Angus cried out as his horse bucked in distress.

"Hold on," Guy shouted. He reached into his belt for the dagger he always carried, gripping with his thighs as his mare shied to the side.

Two small boars came into view and Guy's fingers stilled on the handle of the dagger. The boars were only protecting their young.

"Steady, girl," he said to his mare. "Turn back," he said to Angus. "They won't follow us."

He lowered his weapon, took his eyes from his target.

Disobeyed his father's golden rule. *Never lower your guard.*

Decades later, Guy could still hear Angus's last words as his horse bolted towards the edge of the cliffs, chased by the angry boar.

"Guy, help me," he'd screamed.

The squeal of terror as the horse plunged to its death, taking Angus with it, was a sound that punctuated his nightmares.

His mother blamed him, absolutely, for the death of her youngest son. And his father hadn't wasted any time in laying his own guilt and responsibility firmly at Guy's feet.

"You were in charge," he roared, full of the black rage that tainted their lives.

Then he took aim at Guy with a dagger of his own, to show him how it should be done. The dagger landed squarely above his clavicle. Not threatening his life, but leaving a permanent knot of memory too painful to bear.

Standing by his horse in the stables of Rossfarne Castle, Guy drew on his steely reserves of strength, barricading his defences against the onslaught of feelings which he'd spent most of his life holding in check.

He wouldn't crumble. Not today. Not ever.

Any regret he harboured over Kitty, paled into insignificance given the burden he already carried.

He cleared his throat and issued a command to the groom.

"Prepare my horse. We leave tomorrow."

Chapter Nineteen

ALFRED CAME INTO the kitchen, staggering under the weight of the wood he carried. He nodded to Kitty and Lizzie, who were busily rolling out pastry on the scrubbed pine table, and tipped the chopped logs into the basket by the fire.

"You'll never guess what I've heard," he declared, putting his hands to the small of his back and stretching.

"The king himself is coming for tea?" quipped Lizzie. "I could believe almost anything after the time we've had."

Alfred guffawed. "Not quite, but not far off."

"Mercy on us." Lizzie put a floury hand to her bosom. "He's jesting, surely?" she appealed to Kitty.

Kitty longed only for peace and quiet, but she turned a practised smile onto Alfred. "Tell us, please."

"His lordship is returning to the king's service." Alfred nodded in the direction of Rossfarne Castle. "Our Earl of Rossfarne happens to be a knight of the realm. Not a scoundrel, like his uncle before him. And that's not all."

Kitty lowered her face until her hair hung forwards and obscured the blush that rose to her cheeks at the mention of Guy. Her heart pounded as if he was standing in the room beside her.

"Alfred, finish your tale before we grow weary of it." Lizzie flapped her hands at her fellow servant.

"He's shutting up the castle." Alfred helped himself to a slice of fruit pie, newly brought from the oven. "He'll be gone for months, years perhaps."

His words reached Kitty as if through a haze of fog. She half rose from her chair, panic sending pinpricks of heat to her arms and legs.

"Years?" she repeated.

Alfred shrugged, oblivious to her turmoil. "He's leaving the marshal in charge," he said, through a mouthful of pie.

Kitty stood up and her chair clattered to the stone floor behind her.

"Mercy, what is it now?" demanded Lizzie. "The good Lord knows my nerves can't stand any more surprises."

Kitty couldn't find any words to explain herself. She stood in the sun-filled kitchen and gawped like a deer caught in a huntsman's gaze.

"I must go," she muttered, abandoning her newly rolled pastry.

"Kitty, what ails you?" Lizzie called out after her, but Kitty was deaf to her pleading. She gathered her skirts and swept out of the room, her pulse racing.

The front parlour brought her no peace, nor did her bedchamber. Eventually she found herself wandering in the kitchen garden, deaf to the birdsong and blind to nature's bounty all around her. She walked around in circles, growing more confused with every turn until a familiar voice pierced her delirium.

"When Lizzie told me you were out here pacing up and down like a woman gone mad, I thought she was exaggerating," Rosalind declared.

Kitty glanced towards her sister, who was sitting on the back steps in a loose-fitting dress and hugging her knees. She opened her mouth to tell Rosalind to fetch a shawl against the chill, but then closed it again. The day carried only the slightest breeze. And besides that, Rosalind had proved herself well capable of making her own decisions.

It was Kitty who needed the advice.

"I don't know what to do." The words were ripped from her. She expected her sister to look surprised, but Rosalind merely smiled and drew her neat braid of hair down over one shoulder.

"So, my wise and sensible older sister finally admits that she doesn't have all the answers."

Kitty shot her a look, but couldn't take the time to formulate a proper response. Her mind was full of Guy. She shouldn't have left, not without expressing herself properly. He had told her he was falling in love with her. And she had allowed him to think that those feelings were not returned, when in fact her love for him filled every pore of her body.

Rosalind jumped up and took her arm with surprising strength. "Tell me," she ordered.

Kitty looked at her helplessly. When did her little sister grow so poised and lovely? Beside her, Kitty was like a wild woman with tangled hair and swollen eyes. "I've made so many mistakes," she whispered.

Rosalind reached up to stroke her dishevelled hair. "With love in your heart and purity of intention," she said, simply.

"But that doesn't make anything better." Kitty sat down, uncaring of the damp grass beneath her. Rosalind pursed her lips, then gathered her skirts to kneel gracefully by her side. "Don't sit there, the grass is wet," Kitty warned instinctively.

Rosalind gave a short bark of laughter. "Let us walk then, dear sister, and you can tell me what ails you." She got lightly to her feet and extended her hand. "You can tell me anything, you know. I'm practically an old married woman."

"Oh, Rosalind," Kitty exclaimed, her cheeks blushing pink for the second time, but her sister spun away laughing.

"I don't mean that."

"I should hope not." Kitty smoothed her skirts, painfully aware of her own double standards.

"Richard has kissed me though," Rosalind declared boldly. "And I let him. I even wanted him to. I love him, Kitty. And I can't describe how wonderful that makes me feel."

A lump lodged in Kitty's throat. "You don't have to describe it," she whispered, "I know it for myself."

Rosalind spun around to grasp both her hands. Her grip was warm and reassuring. "Really?"

"Really." Kitty wanted to smile but was closer to crying.

"With who?" Rosalind's eyes lit up with curiosity. "Who else was at the castle with you? Not another one of the servants, surely?"

Kitty's courage failed her, but why should she hide the truth from her sister of all people?

"With the Earl of Rossfarne," she whispered "Guy."

"The Earl of Rossfarne?" Rosalind shrieked so loudly that Kitty was sure the fishermen in the harbour must have heard. She shushed her urgently, but Rosalind merely shook her head, her long braid swinging from side to side. "You've been a little quiet these last few days, I did wonder if anything was wrong. But I never thought..." She trailed off, biting her lip in wonder. "I certainly never thought that anything would happen between you and *him*."

"If you met him, you would like him." Kitty swallowed, knowing such a meeting was unlikely to happen.

"The Earl of Rossfarne?" Rosalind repeated, at a more reasonable volume. "The man who took our jewels? The man who gambled with Father over *you*?" Her voice rose uncontrollably again.

Kitty grasped her sister's wrist and pulled her further away from the house. The last thing she wanted was for Lizzie or Alfred to hear her confession. "He tried to return the jewels," she said, pleased to tell this tale at last. "No one would answer the door to him."

"Oh." Rosalind's eyes were as round as saucers. "So that was what he wanted?"

Kitty nodded. "All the time I was there, I was trying to find a way to steal back the jewels. But if I'd just told him the truth from the start, he would have given them to me. I know that now. I was such a fool." She clutched her arms over her chest as if trying to keep hold of the grief that was spilling out of her.

Rosalind nibbled her lip thoughtfully as pigeons cooed from the fruit trees. "How could you have known though?" she asked after a pause.

"Because he only ever showed me kindness." Sorrow dragged down her limbs and she sniffed in a most unladylike manner.

Her sister stopped walking and looked at her enquiringly. "How so? He was the earl, and you were just a servant."

"We spoke, often. I even sang for him." A hard lump formed in her throat as she put it all into words. "He protected me from his uncle, the Earl of Darkmoor, when he came to visit. If Guy hadn't helped me, he would have…" Kitty shook her head, unwilling to go further. "He was suffering from an injury he sustained in battle, and I tended to his wounds." She gulped back tears as she tried to explain it all.

"And?" Rosalind raised her eyebrows, her expression wise beyond her years.

Kitty ducked away from her knowing gaze. "And so much more."

"You kissed him?" Rosalind's voice was breathless and her cheeks tinged with pink.

"I did." Kitty put her hands to her face, hiding her shame. She wouldn't say anything further to her innocent sister, though part of her longed to tell of how Guy had set her body on fire with his love-making. He made her feel things she'd never dreamed of. Sensations she would never again experience.

"Did he take advantage of you?" Rosalind asked, her face pointed and anxious.

"No." Kitty shook her head fervently. "Nothing like that. He told me he loved me." Tears were streaming down her face now. "And he said he would find a way for us to be together." Her voice broke at the memory, and she sniffed again. Her hands fumbled in her pockets for a handkerchief but came out empty.

Rosalind gasped, her eyes wide as she took it all in. "He told you he loved you?"

Kitty nodded, abandoning her search for a handkerchief and

using her sleeve instead.

"And do you love him?" Rosalind pursed her lips and pointedly handed over her own handkerchief.

"I do." The words came out on a wail of anguish as she finally admitted the truth in her heart, pressing her damp face into the lavender-scented folds of cloth.

"But Kitty, this is no cause for grief. If two people love each other, they can find a way to be together." Rosalind's voice was full of optimism. For her, life was so simple. They had reached the highest point of the garden, from here the land dipped down towards the sparkling sea. As if mindful of the painful memories it would bring, Rosalind turned them both around so they were facing the green sweep of lawn and the familiar outline of Shoreston.

"Not always," Kitty insisted, dabbing her eyes. "Not when one person has lied to the other." This was the crux of it. The act she would never forgive herself for. The black beams of her childhood home blurred in front of her. She was deaf to the melodic tweeting of the birds and oblivious to the golden slant of the sun's rays.

"Nonsense," Rosalind tutted impatiently. "Everyone makes mistakes."

Kitty shook her head. "I put my fear and distrust before everything else. He was so angry." She recalled the coldness in his voice when he ordered her to leave and she shivered, despite the warmth of the day.

Rosalind put her blonde head to one side and regarded her thoughtfully. "Won't he have had time to calm down, by now?"

"I couldn't go back." Kitty started pacing again, wringing her hands in agitation. "I couldn't face him."

"I think you're going to have to." Rosalind folded her arms decisively. "Or you'll spend the rest of your days regretting it. Come inside, I have an idea."

"HERE NOW." ROSALIND placed the dress reverently on the bed and stood back to admire the shimmering silk. A splash of colour in the otherwise plain bedchamber. "This will look beautiful on you," she declared.

Kitty felt flushed and untidy, but she couldn't help reaching down to run her hand over the rose-coloured gown. The silken fabric pooled beneath her fingers as she gently touched a row of impossibly tiny pearl buttons. This dress was from another age of happiness and wealth. It had belonged to their mother, worn only for the most special occasions. Since Isabella's death, Kitty had been keeping it safe for Rosalind. She'd imagined fetching it out for her sister's engagement ball.

"I couldn't wear it," she declared. "I'm too tall, and I'm the wrong shape as well." She snatched back her hand, embarrassed.

"You *will* wear it. And when the Earl of Rossfarne sees you, he will be so overcome he will sweep you into his arms and forgive you everything."

Kitty ignored such a romantic flight of fancy. "This dress is meant for someone dainty and elegant, like you." She was better suited to the servant's dress she'd worn in Rossfarne Castle.

Her sister pretended she hadn't spoken. "You need a pendant to go with it." She flicked a glance at Kitty. "Maybe one of the Answick jewels?"

"No." Kitty backed away and held up her hands as if warding off a curse. "Not them."

Rosalind let out a peal of laughter. "Maybe you're right," she conceded. "But we will find something. And before that, you will sit still and let me fix your hair. You won't leave this bedchamber until I've transformed you into the lady you were always meant to be."

Rosalind stood on tiptoe until she could reach Kitty's shoulders and lower her forcibly into a waiting chair. Kitty opened her mouth to protest but thought better of it. Her determination to eschew her mother's lineage hadn't brought her good fortune of any kind. A small part of her mind suggested that mayhap it was time to embrace it? Still, she couldn't help sighing deeply as Rosalind fussed over her.

"This doesn't feel right," she stated. Since Rosalind's birth, Kitty had been the one to stand in attendance.

Rosalind rolled her eyes, her mouth full of hairpins. "Stay still," she ordered.

Nerves flickered in Kitty's breast as Rosalind's deft fingers ran through her unruly locks of hair, pinning and securing it neatly on top of her head. She was to appear to Guy as Miss Katherine Alden, for the first time. She would claim her ancestry and her upbringing, meeting him not as an equal, far from it, but as a woman of some means, nonetheless.

If only she had done so from the start.

"There." Rosalind stepped back, triumphantly. "You look beautiful."

"In comparison to what?"

Her sister tutted, darting forwards to secure a stray curl which had escaped her ministrations. "You are beautiful, Kitty," she declared, matter-of-factly, "don't try and talk yourself out of it."

Kitty didn't believe her, but she could see that Rosalind spoke from a place of love. She clutched her hand. "Thank you," she said. "Thank you for understanding. And thank you for all of this." She gestured at the sumptuous gown before reaching up and patting her pinned hair. "I'm sure I shan't know myself." She fought a wave of self-consciousness. "I'm not used to it, that's all."

Rosalind's eyes were dancing. "Time for the dress," she declared. "Stand up."

Clad only in her chemise, Kitty stepped carefully into the silken gown and allowed Rosalind to button it behind her, smoothing out the creases and ensuring the expensive fabric flowed snugly over her curves. Kitty hardly dared to believe it, but the dress fit her perfectly. She turned around and it spun with her, flaring slightly at the back.

"It was made for you," smiled Rosalind.

"It was made for Mother," Kitty corrected her. "I never thought…" her voice trailed off.

"You never thought you could follow in her footsteps," Rosalind finished off for her. "You closed yourself off from the possibility of living a comfortable, respectable life, determined to see me become a lady, even as you scrubbed floors and mended stockings. But worse than that, you never allowed yourself to think of your own happiness." Rosalind frowned up at her. "I hope that's about to change."

Nerves assaulted Kitty afresh. "That depends on Guy," she whispered, emotions shooting through her at the feel of his name on her tongue.

"Fight for what you want," Rosalind said, lifting her silver chain over her head and fastening it around Kitty's neck. "For your sake, this time, not mine." She patted the chain. "This will bring you luck."

Kitty's fingers sought out her sister's. "I'll take all the luck I can get."

"Come then," Rosalind stood back. "You have an earl to woo."

Kitty flushed, remembering how it had felt to run her fingers over Guy's shoulders and see him responding to her touch. She had wooed him once, in a servant's cap and apron. Now she was dressed like a lady, but she had never felt more vulnerable. After a moment's thought, she tipped the small number of shining coins she'd earned at Rossfarne Castle into her mother's coin purse. It wouldn't hurt to be prepared.

"What about Lizzie and Alfred?" Kitty put a hand to her heart. As much as she loved them both, she couldn't bear to have them fussing over her wellbeing just now.

"It's alright. Lizzie is taking a nap and Alfred is busy in one of the barns. If we leave by the front door, no one will see us."

"Are you coming with me?" Kitty was both surprised and gratified.

"Are you seriously asking me that? This is the most fun I've ever had with my older sister." Rosalind nudged her playfully. "Although I'll leave the earl to you. I have to admit, the thought of him still terrifies me."

"That's because you don't know him," Kitty said earnestly.

"I believe you. But there's time enough for that. Today is about you and him." Rosalind squeezed her hand. "Are you ready?"

She wasn't. She would never be. But if she didn't go now, she may never get another chance.

"I'm ready."

THEY STOOD ON the beach, holding hands and biting their lips at the sight of the flooded causeway.

"We misjudged the tides," Rosalind said.

Kitty swallowed down a new lump in her throat. "Low tide won't come again until nightfall." She shrugged, as if this fact didn't cut her to the core.

"And the earl may be gone by tomorrow." Rosalind spoke the words that Kitty could not bring herself to.

All of Kitty's newfound courage faded away. "I am too late." Her voice trembled as emotion threatened to overwhelm her.

"No, never." Rosalind shook her head violently, her golden hair shimmering in the afternoon sunlight. "There is always a way."

Kitty knew a swell of envy at her younger sister, secure in a loving relationship and buoyed up with hope for the future.

"I am tired, Rosalind," she said, feeling it in every bone of her body. Though the gown she wore was beautiful, the restrictive bodice nipped her flesh and made her back ache. The skirts were heavy and her hair was tight against her scalp. She'd made herself into a lady for naught.

"The earl's boathouse," her sister exclaimed, tugging at her hand. "Let's ask there."

Shame gathered in her belly. "I couldn't," she hissed.

"Why not?" Rosalind raised her eyebrows. "You do know, you were only *pretending* to be a servant?"

Kitty shook her head, unable to articulate her reluctance, but Rosalind would not be dissuaded. She knocked at the small wooden door of the boathouse, then pushed it open without waiting for a response. Both of them blinked at the sudden gloom after the bright sunshine outside.

"I take orders from none but the Earl of Rossfarne," a deep, male voice boomed from inside the boathouse.

"The Earl of Rossfarne is a personal friend of my sister's," Rosalind declared, making Kitty wince with embarrassment. "She wishes to go across to the castle."

A tall, dark-haired man came into view. He was wiping his hands on an oily cloth and regarding them appraisingly. Behind him, Kitty could just make out a shingle track down to the sea and the sleek rowing boat adorned with the earl's coat of arms. The sight of it took her back to that dreadful night in the parlour and conversely, gave her a boost of courage. She had learned a lot since then.

She straightened her back and met the man's enquiring gaze. "That is correct."

The boatman shook his head. "I've heard nothing from the earl."

She inclined her head. "He is not expecting me."

"Well then." He threw the oily rag onto a pile and turned his back on them.

"Do you not know who you are speaking to?" Rosalind demanded imperiously.

"As I said, I take orders from none but the earl."

Rosalind went to speak up again, but Kitty held her back. She cleared her throat. "I may not be expected at the castle, but I will be welcomed there nonetheless."

"Is that so?" He turned to face her and instead of flinching beneath his condescension, she stood taller. Her dress may be unfamiliar and uncomfortable, but it was exquisitely cut from the finest cloth. She would not be cowed by a boatman.

She raised her eyes coolly to his. "I bring news of my uncle, the Duke of Answick."

The boatman blanched and Kitty channelled as much steely hauteur into her gaze as she could find.

"Very good, my lady," he acquiesced. "I'll take you now."

The boatman hauled the rowing boat down to the shallows, holding her gloved hand while she stepped inside and lowered herself carefully to a wooden bench. Now that this hurdle had been overcome, her stomach clenched with nerves for the ordeal still ahead.

She must face Guy and find a way to make him understand.

The boat rocked as the man clambered in and took up the oars.

"Goodbye, Kitty. Good luck." Rosalind stood on the shingled beach and waved her white handkerchief, the afternoon sun casting a golden halo around her.

Kitty waved back, wishing her sister could be beside her for this, the most frightening leg of her journey. But deep down, she knew this was something she must do alone.

The oars splashed rhythmically across the tranquil sea, sending a fine shower of spray into the air and taking Kitty back to her time at Rossfarne Castle, when the tang of sea salt was forever on her lips. The boat turned into the cove and she twisted her hands together at the sight of the beach where she had surrendered herself to Guy.

When she'd known heights of pleasure she'd never dreamed of. When she'd willingly given him all she had.

She lowered her head as tears threatened once more. But this was no time to weep. This was her chance to put things right.

She gripped the smooth sides of the boat as they scraped through the shallows. The boatman jumped out and hauled it further up the beach. Kitty rose to her feet, knees trembling, and allowed him to help her down.

"Would you like me to wait, my lady?"

She bit her lip, flooded with indecision. "Yes please."

He nodded sharply and set about securing the boat. Kitty took a deep breath, lifted her skirts and walked as gracefully as she could towards the gatehouse. Despite her fears, it felt like coming home. The jutting outline of the castle, once formidable, now seemed familiar and welcoming. A slight breeze ran over her skin like a caress. Confidence flowered inside her. She had come this far, maybe success was within her reach.

The marshal must have spied their arrival, for he was waiting for her outside the gatehouse. She lowered her skirts as she reached the stony path and reminded herself to stay calm.

He nodded a greeting. "How can I help you, my lady?"

The beautiful dress was as effective a disguise as her servant's attire. If the marshal recognised her, he didn't show it.

Kitty raised her chin. "Miss Katherine Alden, to see the Earl of Rossfarne."

The marshal pursed his lips. "I'm afraid that won't be possible, not today."

She folded her hands together to stop them shaking. "How so?"

"The earl has returned to the service of the king. He left this morning. I'm sorry to say, you've had a wasted journey."

His words sank through her like a stone. She was too late. Hot tears formed at the corners of her eyes and this time, she made no attempt to blink them away. It mattered not if she appeared like a composed lady or a dishevelled serving maid. The man she loved was not here.

He'd left, thinking her a thief. And now she would never get a chance to put things right.

Chapter Twenty

THE SUN WAS high in the sky when Guy left Rossfarne, but the skies began to darken as he travelled further up the coast. His horse was high-stepping and co-operative, carrying Guy back to the life he had once loved with long, unfaltering strides. Guy sat deep in the saddle and forced himself to focus on the future. He had grown accustomed to holding himself still, so as to protect his injured arm, but now there was no need for caution. He was whole and healthy, ready to serve the king to the best of his abilities.

Just weeks ago, this was all he'd wanted. To return to his band of brothers on the battlefield. To fight for king and country. To feel the adrenaline rush of excitement while charging towards an enemy, knowing that his fate rested in his skills with a sword and the unity of his fellow knights.

The Knights' Code was writ large in his memory. A motto he had learned in training, now as familiar to him as his own name.

"Without trust in one another, we are nothing."

Sorrow darted through him. He trusted the men he rode towards, but all trust in the woman he'd left behind was eroded.

He frowned with annoyance and tightened his grip on the reins. Would his thoughts forever be cursed to return to Kitty? Might there come a day when the memory of her smile did not bring him pain?

His horse's ears flickered backwards and forwards, as if listening to his internal debate. They were rounding a bend in the coastline when some sixth sense compelled him to twist in the saddle and look back in the direction he'd ridden from.

Shafts of slanting sunlight pierced the skies to illuminate the battlements of Rossfarne Castle, dark in the distance. If Guy shaded his eyes, he could make out the huddle of the village where the sparkling sea met the jutting cliffs.

Home.

He reined in his horse, shocked by his instinctive pull towards a place he still scarcely knew.

Not a place, a person.

It was no good. His inner turmoil could not be quietened. Guy cursed and swung himself down from the saddle, allowing his horse to crop at the grass while he stood amidst abundant purple heather and breathed deeply to calm his racing thoughts.

She had deceived him.

No matter how often he circled the matter, he couldn't get away from that one dreadful fact.

But could he not find it in his heart to forgive her?

Guy sighed deeply. His heart had been barricaded away for so long, he knew not what it was capable of. But as a trained knight, he realised that he would be no use on the battlefield until his mind was clear and focused.

Rossfarne Castle shimmered on the horizon, taunting him with all that could have been. Viewed from this distance, Guy was taken aback by its romantic beauty. The castle had been filled with darkness, yet it could be spectacular. For a brief time, while he held Kitty in his arms, he had entertained thoughts of banishing the gloom and making it a comfortable home, but it had been within his power to do so sooner.

Instead, when he first arrived in Rossfarne, he'd followed in the footsteps of his ancestors, clinging to the shadows and hiding behind the notoriety of his family name. On that cursed night in the tavern, he'd done nothing to shake the other men's assumption that he was as great a villain as his uncle.

Nay, he'd gone so far as to encourage it.

His family coat of arms had provided a foil for his temporary vulnerability.

Guy clenched his hand into a tight fist. If he had chosen a different approach, so much could have been different. But he could only deal with what was, not what could have been. He had regained his fitness and the future was his for the taking. This brief time in Rossfarne would soon be far behind him, but was that what he wanted?

Could he imagine living the rest of his life without Kitty? That was the crux of it. The question he hadn't allowed himself to ask. Because if she was guilty of distrust, of hiding behind a facade, so too was he.

The sun came out from behind a cloud, enveloping him in light and warmth. He tilted his face towards it and closed his eyes.

What would happen if he lowered his guard?

THEY ROWED BACK to the mainland in silence. The boatman was likely irked by her sudden return, but Kitty had no care for his opinion. The despair that had washed over her at the gatehouse had been replaced by a desperate, burning conviction.

She had to find Guy. She would do whatever it took.

Where once she had been determined to fight for her sister's future, now she would go into battle for her own. She may appear foolish, but what of it? Better a fool than a deceitful thief. Better to try and fail than spend the rest of her life immersed in regret for what might have been.

She thanked the boatman and pressed one of her hard-earned coins into his hand, the flash of which appeased him. He tugged at his forelock and wished her a pleasant afternoon. She turned her face towards the village and pondered her next move.

She could go home and change out of this cumbersome dress, but to do so would waste what little time she had left to her. The sun was already dipping in the sky. Within hours, it would be dark.

She needed a horse, but they had none at Shoreston. The carriage had gone soon after Mother died. She looked around impatiently. Was her only option the earl's own stable yard? He kept a pair of horses on the mainland. It was an option, but the prospect of bribing another of the earl's servants made her toes curl. As if in answer to a prayer, she heard the faint clopping of horse's hooves on the cliff road and with no thought to her elegant gown, Kitty began to run.

The slight young man with soft brown curls was open-mouthed in surprise to be accosted by a red-faced woman in a dress more suited to a ballroom than a cliff top.

"May I assist you, miss?" he asked, holding out an arm to steady her as she bounded around the corner towards him.

Kitty wheezed in her restrictive bodice. "Your horse," she spluttered, gesturing to the well-fed chestnut brown cob standing behind him. "I must borrow him."

"My horse?" He frowned. His face was finely drawn, she noticed. And there was something familiar about his hazel eyes.

"Don't worry. I have coin. I can pay you for your trouble." Kitty fished for her coin purse.

"It is no trouble." The boy stepped forwards to look her fully in the face. "Katherine Alden?"

Only hours earlier she would have flushed with shame at being recognised, but now she merely nodded.

A huge smile broke across his face. "Richard Erkine." He held out his hand. "It has been many years since we last met, but we are soon to be related."

She took his hand automatically, her mind racing to keep up. Richard Erkine. The neighbour so recently betrothed to her sister.

"It is good to see you again." He gave her a short bow.

It had been so long since anyone paid such an act of respect to Kitty that she simply stood and stared, before recovering her wits and dipping her head.

"The pleasure is mine, sir."

"Your sister speaks highly of you."

"And of you." Her eyes darted back to the horse. Richard Erkine appeared to have grown into a splendid young man, but she had no time for polite conversation.

He seemed to read her mind. "You are welcome to my horse," he paused. "Unless, of course, you would prefer to take my family's trap? Have you a long journey ahead of you?"

He was too well-mannered to question her intent. Kitty was not dressed for a journey of any kind, but she would press his well-bred reticence to her advantage.

"Not far, I assure you. And I give you my word that I do not usually rampage about the country in such a manner. I will greet you properly, Mr Erkine, on my return. Forgive my impatience to be gone." She put a hand on the animal's neck in what she hoped was not too proprietorial a gesture.

"There is nothing to forgive," he said smoothly. "I can see that events have, mayhap, overtaken you? Allow me." He cupped his hands to give her a leg-up, and after a moment's thought she placed the tip of her foot into his palms. "There we go."

She caught her breath as Richard Erkine launched her upwards, but found her seat more easily than she'd feared. The cob had a broad back and she could balance quite well, despite her cumbersome gown.

"Thank you," she said, still breathless from the speedy ascent. "Fear not, Mr. Erkine, I will take good care of him."

She urged the horse forward and soon settled into his smooth stride. It had been some years since she rode, but it all came back to her. A voice in her head cautioned that her mother's fine dress would be ruined within minutes. She knew a moment of doubt at the waste, but Rosalind's prospects were secure and her own hung in the balance.

Besides, she would have no need of fancy gowns if her quest did not succeed.

She trotted up the cliff road. As soon as it levelled out, she would break into a canter. She would find Guy, even if she must ride into the night.

But her courage began to falter as the shadows lengthened and the day's strong sunlight grew dim. The horse's ears flicked backwards and forwards uneasily and the tight bodice of her gown chafed her skin. Evening insects buzzed around her, buffeted by a salty breeze rolling off the sea. Soon it would be dark and cold. If Kitty wasn't dressed for riding, she most certainly wasn't dressed for riding in the dark. Besides, the horse may stumble and fall, or ruffians could set upon them.

Stifling a sob, Kitty drew back on the reins and brought the uneasy horse to a halt.

She must admit defeat. To continue was madness. She should never have set off in such a hurry.

She was both a thief and a fool.

"It's no good." She stroked the horse's hot neck. "We will turn back."

The rumble of wheels and a distant sound of horses' hooves brought a new chill to her bones. What fresh challenge was this? There was nowhere to hide on the clifftop. She must take her chances with whomever had presumed to follow her.

"Whoa," a man's voice carried on the breeze.

Kitty stiffened. She could urge her horse into a gallop, but would that be wise in the failing light, with the sheer cliff edge just feet away?

"Steady there."

She heard the approaching cart come to a stop. Breathing as deeply as her dress would allow, Kitty turned to face them.

A kind-faced old man held a lantern towards her.

"Miss Katherine, thank goodness I've found you."

"Alfred." She was weak with relief.

"Come here to me now. I've got a blanket and a flagon of mead to warm you."

She slid from the horse, leaning against its belly for support. Her aching legs threatened to buckle beneath her.

"Oh Alfred, I've been so rash."

"None of that now." He was behind her, wrapping the blanket around her shoulders and taking the reins from her hands.

"How did you know where I was?"

"Mr Erkine came to us with a story which Lizzie and myself found hard to credit. Miss Rosalind, though, said it may well be true. So here I am, in the Erkines' trap. And not before time, by the looks of things."

"You must think me a fool," she said, though she hardly cared. It was enough to be safe with the prospect of rest and warmth ahead of her.

"I think you are brave," he countered, stoutly. "But two heads are better than one."

"You're here to help me?" she sagged against the wooden trap as hope unfurled in her chest once more.

"If Miss Katherine Alden thinks there's a need to follow someone over the cliffs, then who am I to question it?" Alfred helped her up to the front of the trap and folded the blanket over her knees.

"You're very kind." She swallowed back tears as he hitched the cob to the back of the car.

Alfred swung himself up beside her and patted her knee. "I only hope the Earl of Rossfarne is worth all the trouble."

DAYLIGHT WAS FADING and the proximity of the cliff edge had reawakened the ghosts of his childhood, but he urged the horse on, encouraged by the twinkling lights of Rossfarne which grew closer with every stride.

Now that he had decided to turn back, he was seized with a frenzied impatience. He had to make things right with Kitty. To apologise for his anger and his hard-headedness.

He heard the approaching trap long before he saw it. He reined the horse in to wait for it to pass, but as soon as his eyes alighted on the familiar figure sitting up front, his twitching impatience ceased.

It was her. And yet it wasn't. The woman sitting in the trap was a lady in a beautiful silken gown. Her long red hair was scooped up elegantly on the top of her head. The old man handed her down from the cart as if he were escorting a queen.

Guy knew a rush of adrenaline, familiar from the battlefield. He dismounted from his horse, abandoned the reins and stepped towards her, hardly daring to believe she was not some wondrous mirage conjured by his fevered imagination.

This was the woman he had held in his arms. Those were the lips he had kissed. How had he found the courage? She was radiant, unattainable even.

"Guy?" she ventured, biting down on her top lip, a habit he recognised.

"Kitty." His voice wobbled. When last they met, she had worn the garb of a poor servant. She had bobbed her head to him and addressed him as "my lord," when all the time she was the daughter of a lady.

But hadn't he always known it? From her grace and her bearing, coin or no, Kitty had been a woman of importance.

Her green eyes arrested him. "Were you returning to Rossfarne?"

"Yes." *To see you*, his mind added, but his lips closed over the words. Her polish and poise had thrown him afresh. What right had he to profess his love to such a beauty?

What then, had he been riding into the night to achieve? Guy shook away the insecurities which had plagued him since childhood and summoned the confidence to step forward and take her gloved hands inside his.

"I realised I had forgotten something." His voice was strong again. He planted his feet apart and breathed deeply, even as her bewitching citrus fragrance washed over him.

"Oh yes?" Her face tilted towards his. Her rosebud lips parted. He fought an urge to lean down and kiss her. His body yearned for the feel of her pressed against him, but first he must put right what had gone wrong between them.

"You." He swallowed. "I could not ride away from you." She squeezed his hands. The smallest gesture of encouragement but it unleashed a damn inside him. "Forgive me, Kitty. I should not have spoken so harshly."

"No." She shook her head so violently a red-gold tendril of hair escaped to flutter around her shoulders. "It is I who must apologise. I should have told you the truth long before I did." Her voice was strong, but her heavy breathing betrayed her regret.

"You came out here to find me?" He hardly dared to believe it.

"First I ordered your boatman to row me across to the castle." A faint blush rose up to stain her cheeks but she pushed on with her tale. "When I discovered you had already left, I borrowed a horse to come after you."

"You rode out here, all alone?" He looked back at the waiting trap.

"For a while," she paused. "I acted in haste, but I would have done anything for the chance to see you one last time. To tell you how sorry I am. And to tell you…" Her words faltered.

"To tell me what?" He placed a hand in the small of her back, drawing her closer. It took iron self-control not to crush her into his arms.

She bit down on her lip. His thumb skimmed over her cheek, and she closed her eyes, leaning into his touch.

"To tell you that I love you," she said.

Her simple honesty floored him. It was as if he'd been waiting his whole life to hear those words.

"I love you too, Kitty," he whispered.

She smiled, a ray of sunshine through the darkness. "You told me after the storm that you were falling in love with me. I couldn't say it back, not when I was still deceiving you. But I couldn't let you leave without knowing how much you mean to me." She glanced back at the trap and the manservant who was studiously looking up at the clouds. "I guess that's what's happening, isn't it? You're going away? The castle is all shut up."

He shook his head. "I'm not going anywhere. Not if I have you to come back to."

"You do." She moved imperceptibly nearer to him, and he could no longer resist the compulsion to reach down, cup her face in his hands and kiss her.

But no sooner had their lips met than she pulled away. "But the king is waiting for you. Don't you have to return to his service?"

His hands travelled to her shoulders and skimmed the sides of her body down to her waist. He had never been less interested in the king.

"King Edward has many knights," he declared. "I think he can manage without me for a while longer. Although I may have to do some grovelling…"

"Oh, Guy." This time, she kissed him, standing on tiptoe and wrapping her arms around him until he was buffeted by desire. His fingers skimmed the pearl buttons of her dress. So many of them, he could never hope to undo them all.

The sound of the manservant clearing his throat brought Guy to his senses. However much he wanted Kitty, he couldn't take her here. Especially not before asking the question which burned on his lips.

"Kitty," he started, "or should I say, Miss Katherine Alden?" He pulled away from their embrace and she stumbled slightly on the uneven ground.

"Yes?"

He lowered himself onto one knee and grasped her dainty fingers.

"Will you marry me?"

Chapter Twenty-One

Two years later...

THE TINY, STONE-BUILT chapel was sweet with the fragrance of spring flowers, which the bride had artfully tied to the end of every wooden pew. Peeping through the heavy arched entrance doors, Guy concluded that he had never seen so many villagers come together to celebrate a wedding. Excited murmurs of anticipation rippled through the congregation, for the families of both bride and groom were well-loved in the village of Rossfarne.

Guy's gaze travelled to the tall, confident man standing near the altar, who couldn't resist turning frequently to check if the woman he was waiting for had arrived. Guy flashed him a smile. *She will come*, his eyes imparted. She had been counting down to this day for many months.

The rumble of an approaching carriage caught his ear, and Guy pulled back from the chapel interior, closing the heavy door behind him. Sunlight danced all around and it took a moment for his eyes to adjust after the cool shadows of the chapel. A well-groomed white horse made stately progress along the narrow country lane, pulling a smart but simple carriage behind him. Inside sat a lovely young woman clad in peach satin. She had roses entwined in her shining blonde hair and a posy clutched in her slender hands.

Guy smiled a greeting as the carriage rumbled to a halt beside him. "I have never seen you looking more beautiful, Rosalind."

She laughed, like a peal of bells. "Thank you, dear brother. 'Tis love and excitement for the day ahead."

He held out a hand to help her down and kissed her proffered cheek.

"Are you ready?"

She took his arm, graceful as ever, and more like her older sister than Kitty would ever allow. "Tell me, were you nervous on your wedding day?" she asked.

He paused for a moment to reflect on the happiest day of his life. Kitty and Guy had exchanged vows on a bright autumnal morning, when the glorious red and gold colours in the trees valiantly competed with the gleam of the polished carriage and the glinting highlights of Kitty's rippling hair. "No," he answered decisively. "I was filled with joy from sunrise to sunset." He cleared his throat and smiled down at the young woman in his charge. "I may be more nervous today."

"Thank you for giving me away in the absence of my father." She walked lightly around a puddle caused by last night's rain. A quick, heavy downpour, which had left the countryside looking washed and clean, ready for blue skies and bird song on this long-awaited day.

Guy was momentarily lost for words. It was typical bravery of Rosalind to confront a matter most would ignore. The truth was, Owain had taken up with a young widow who owned an inn near Dun Holme. Rumours had reached Rossfarne not long after his and Kitty's wedding, and Guy had ridden south himself to see if there was any truth to them. The charmless man he had once faced over a gaming table seemed little changed; still drinking, still gambling, and inexplicably still exerting some mystical hold over a hard-working woman of genuine worth who really should know better.

Guy had bought a drink and observed Owain for a while, one hand clenched around the bag of coin he had brought with him as a bribe. He was tempted to leave without making his presence known, but Kitty and Rosalind's instructions had been clear. Now Owain received regular payments on condition that he stayed away from his daughters.

Guy swallowed down his revulsion at the memory. Today was not for dwelling upon such times.

"The honour is mine," he declared, giving Rosalind a short bow, which made her laugh in surprise. Guy couldn't help his lips curling up into a smile. Kitty had broken through his barriers and as a consequence, he had both the love of a good woman and the wider family he'd never known. A younger sister, loyal retainers and soon the clever and kind young man named Richard Erkine.

He nudged open the chapel door and the congregation rose to their feet as a swell of music rippled through the stone building and out to meet them. Guy glanced down once more to check all was well with Rosalind, smiling again at her bright eyes and obvious happiness. She settled her hand more firmly in the crook of his arm and together they walked down the aisle towards the waiting groom. The eyes of everyone they approached were drawn to the young bride, resplendent in her wedding gown, but Guy was looking for someone else.

There she was, in a pew at the front of the chapel. Her red-gold hair hung in rippling curls down the back of a green taffeta dress. She turned to see them both and Guy knew the now familiar contraction in his heart.

His wife.

There were days when he could not believe his good fortune.

Kitty treated her sister to a wide, beaming smile and then flicked her eyes to his with a private message of approval.

Guy and Rosalind paused by the altar and Richard Erkine stepped forward to greet his bride. As Guy placed Rosalind's gloved hand onto Richard's arm, a shaft of sunlight burst through the stained-glass window like a blessing.

"Well done," Kitty whispered to him, when he had taken his place next to her in the pew.

He placed his arm over her shoulders and knew a flash of

desire as she moved imperceptibly closer to him. If he lowered his gaze, he could see a glimpse of creamy flesh where the embroidered bodice of her gown met her clavicle. Kitty bit down on her lower lip; no doubt aware of the direction of his thoughts.

His fingers beat a gentle rhythm on her arm. "You look beautiful in that dress," he murmured.

She looked up at him with dancing eyes. "I thought you'd like it."

He leaned closer and whispered directly into her ear. "I'll like it even more when I can take it off you."

He heard her breath quicken in response, but the look she shot him was one of calm admonishment. "Behave yourself."

"I'll try," he growled, obediently rising to his feet to sing the first hymn.

The bride and groom faced one another for their vows, both promising to love and care for one another until death should part them. Their voices were young and strong, their faces eager for the life ahead of them. At one time, Guy would have been uncomfortable with such unencumbered optimism, but now his smile was wide and genuine. He was happy. And he wanted happiness for those he loved as well.

The service ended with the couple proclaimed man and wife. Kitty squeezed his hand, and he brought her knuckles to his lips, remembering that pivotal moment in their own wedding. The day had carried an autumnal chill and Kitty had worn a gown of lace trimmed with fur, to stand beside him in the great hall of Rossfarne Castle and receive her countess's coronet. Candlelight had danced all around them and Guy had thought he might well dance for joy as well.

They followed the rest of the congregation out onto the sun-dappled village green to congratulate the newly wedded couple. Kitty flung her arms around her sister and Guy shook Richard's hand.

"Am I not the luckiest man in all of Christendom?" the young man demanded of him.

Guy smiled widely in return. "Mayhap you are, although I would contest you the title. Tell me, was it worth the wait?"

"At times, no," Richard laughed. "I thought the repairs to Shoreston would never be completed. These past two years passed with terrible slowness. But now I have a beautiful bride and a beautiful home to start our married life in."

"I know Rosalind is thrilled to be staying in the house where she grew up." Guy watched Rosalind and Kitty laughing excitedly together. "And Kitty is delighted that you shall both be near us." He clapped Richard on the shoulder. "Time now for feasting," he declared, pleased to be opening up Rossfarne Castle for such a joyous occasion.

Carriages were waiting to take the wedding party across the causeway to the castle. Once Guy had helped Kitty into theirs, and fastened the door closed behind them, he could wait no longer. The desire he'd held at bay throughout Rosalind's wedding surged in his veins, blurring his thoughts and making speech impossible. Kitty leaned back against the plush velvet, divining his intentions.

"Do we have enough time?" she asked, a smile flitting around her lips.

"Not to do what I want to do with you," growled Guy.

"Then we shall have to make the most of the time we have," Kitty smiled, a smile that would be his undoing. "But first, close the blinds." His hands trembled so much he struggled to secure the fastening. Kitty pushed him back onto the seat with a bejewelled hand. "Stay where you are," she ordered.

Guy had longed to take her in his arms, but her natural air of authority was impossible to resist. It made his desire for her even stronger. Kitty sank gracefully to her knees and ran her fingers down from his waist, dancing around the ties which only just constrained him. Her rings flashed in the narrow bands of sunlight filtering through the blinds. Guy leaned back his head and felt delicious desire ripple through him.

"Kitty," he whispered. Her name a caress. She didn't answer.

Her fingers were busy with the fastenings of his breeches. He gripped the edge of the seat as she released him. Then came her tongue, small and warm. He wanted her. Needed her. His hands went to her hair. "Don't make me wait," he begged.

He was powerless to act. All he knew was how much he wanted her. She pushed aside her skirts and straddled him, her mouth coming down to meet his own at the same time as he slid easily inside her. Her body was all around him, taking him deeply into her core and holding him a willing prisoner. She rocked her hips once, twice, and he was done for.

"Forgive me," he said, his lips pressed against her creamy flesh.

"Forgive you for wanting me?"

"For wanting you so much it strips away my self-control."

She laughed. "That was my plan all along."

"But now I must give you the same pleasure." He rained kisses down her neck, but Kitty reached out to lift a corner of the blind and shook her head.

"We are almost at the castle."

"No matter." He was focused only on her, on the dress that clung to her curves and must be removed. "We can send the driver round again."

"It is my sister's wedding feast," she admonished. "And we are the hosts. Besides," she bit her lip provocatively, "what I want from the Earl of Rossfarne can't be rushed."

Reality asserted itself. He was lord of the manor and must play the part. "Later then," he promised, his hand still caressing her curves.

"Later," she agreed, kissing him deeply. "I have something of a surprise for you."

ROSSFARNE CASTLE HAD been transformed over the last year.

Gone were the gloomy shadows and ghosts of its unhappy past. In their place hung glittering chandeliers, colourful tapestries and the soft light of hundreds of candles which illuminated comfortable furnishings and sparkling silverware. A band of musicians played from the dais in the great hall and the celebrating villagers spilled through the ground floor chambers, dancing, chatting and greeting one another gleefully. Guy's hand was grasped so many times he began to lose count. None could remember the previous Earl of Rossfarne opening the doors of the castle. None would have come even if he had, but now a new era dawned.

The older Erkines were a kindly couple who could hardly believe their son's wedding feast was being held in such a grand setting. Guy waved away their thanks.

"It is I who am grateful," he told them honestly. "This castle has been quiet and empty for too long. It needs life and merriment within its walls."

Rosalind claimed him for a dance and all stood back as he spun her around the room, his awkwardness on the dancefloor more than compensated by her bright smile and natural grace. Mead flowed, goblets were raised in a toast to the new couple and servants carried around platters of sweetmeats on groaning trays held high above their heads.

Guy scanned the crowd, desperate for a glimpse of his wife. He had barely seen her since they disembarked from the carriage. A journey he would have extended, if only Kitty had given him the chance.

A bright flash of auburn caught his eye. The Countess of Rossfarne was amidst a happy group of locals, all dressed in their finery. She stood by the fireplace, illuminated by candlelight, radiantly beautiful. Guy couldn't stay away from her for a moment longer. He left Rosalind in the careful attention of her new husband and crossed the stone-flagged floor. Kitty spied his progress and excused herself from the group.

"My lord," she greeted him with a show of formality.

"My lady," he returned the bow, then swung her into his

arms with a chuckle.

"Are you taking me for a turn on the dancefloor?"

He groaned quietly, breathing in her citrus fragrance. "I would rather not. I have already suffered that fate once, with your sister."

"I know, I was watching." Her fingers danced along his shoulders. "I thought you made a fine couple."

"She's a beautiful woman," he agreed. "Although not nearly so lovely as her older sister."

"Is that so?" She raised an eyebrow up at him.

"That is so." He spanned her waist, enjoying the sleekness of the taffeta beneath his fingers. "When can I get you alone?" he whispered.

"Not for many hours, I'm afraid."

"You torture me."

She raised herself up onto her tiptoes so her lips were inches from his. "It will be worth the wait," she promised.

"I already know that." Guy abandoned his scruples and pulled his wife towards him, swaying in time to the music.

"We're dancing," she said.

"Happiness will get me doing all kinds of things." He dropped a kiss onto her shining hair.

"Are you truly happy, Guy?" she pulled away from him, a haze of apprehension clouding her green eyes.

"Of course." He stilled his feet, puzzled by her sudden wariness. "Aren't you?"

"I'm so very happy." She returned to his arms, resting her head on his shoulder and half-closing her eyes as they danced together. A now-familiar feeling of peace and contentment settled over him.

"I have all I could ever want," he declared.

"Everything?" She looked questioningly up at him, and his stomach clenched. In truth, there was one thing that would make his happiness complete, but he didn't want Kitty to guess how he longed for it.

"Everything," he answered firmly. Kitty gave a sigh and leaned against him. He folded his arms around her as his heart thudded against his ribs. "What more could I possibly want?" he whispered into her ear.

He closed his eyes as the answer burned in his mind. There was something missing. An extra, wondrous gift that would take his present joy and elevate it into something even greater. It was something he had always wanted, but as the months of their marriage passed by, a nugget of doubt had seeded into his heart. Maybe it would never happen.

Maybe he would never hold a child of his own in his arms.

Sorrow darted through him, but Guy clenched his teeth and chased the thought away. He had already been blessed with more than any man deserved. How could he ask for anything more?

Kitty was in his arms, his life was full of love and light. It was more than enough.

Chapter Twenty-Two

KITTY WAITED FOR him on the wide canopied bed that stood at the centre of their bedchamber. Flames danced in the fireplace, sending a rosy glow about the room which had been beautifully furnished with hand-carved cabinets made especially for Rossfarne Castle. So many nights she had spent safely cocooned in Guy's strong embrace, but despite all of this, she was nervous.

Footsteps on the stone stairs indicated he was on his way. Kitty re-arranged her loose hair and leaned back on her elbows, aiming for nonchalance when she felt anything but.

He paused in the doorway, the narrow frame making his tall, muscular body appear even larger. A thrill of anticipation shot through her as his dark eyes raked over her white smock appreciatively. Their years together had done nothing to dull the magnetic pull of attraction between them.

His finely carved lips broke into a smile. "That's the view I've been waiting for."

He crossed the room in a bound and scooped her into his strong arms. Kitty's body folded into the natural curves of her husband's, but she turned her face away from his kiss, even as liquid desire pooled inside her. She must speak.

Guy's breath was warm against her cheek. She leaned her forehead against his solid chest and breathed in his masculine fragrance. Leather, sea salt and the essential scent of her husband. This was the man she loved. Why, then, was she so afraid?

His fingers splayed through her hair, a gesture of affection as well as longing. She nuzzled into his shoulders, suddenly desperate to prolong this period of not knowing. Alert to her mood, Guy changed the course of his hand, from skimming over her hip to cupping her face.

"I'm sorry," she whispered.

His thumb caressed her cheek. "What is it?"

His palm was warm and comforting. Kitty took a deep breath. Once she had said the words, there would be no going back. Her throat tightened, and she could only shake her head.

A concerned frown flicked over his dark brow. "You can tell me anything, you know?"

For two wonderful years, her life had been full of love and laughter. They had fortune, favour with the king and family nearby. Aside from a couple of short spells when Guy returned to the battlefield and she feared for his safe return, their days passed by in comfort while nights were studded with bliss. Guy had walked out of the shadows. But did he want what she was about to give him?

How would he take the news?

Earlier in the day, surrounded by the chatter and laughter of wedding guests, she had been filled with confidence. But now, alone with her husband, her doubts had resurfaced like ghosts from the past.

"I have something to tell you." She forced out the words, fixing her gaze over his shoulder so he wouldn't see the worry in her eyes.

Guy held her steady against him for a moment, in which all she could hear was the rhythmic beating of his heart and the spluttering of logs on the fire. Then he gently pulled away until he could see her face.

"Tell me," he repeated, an invitation, not an order.

"We have never spoken of it." The flickering light from the flames cast his face alternately into planes of light and dark.

"And you have never spoken in riddles before tonight."

She remembered the sorrowful tale of his younger brother. How his voice had broken in anguish as he relayed the harrowing events. *"It was my job to protect him, and I failed. I never want to feel that pain again,"* he had said.

It had been on the tip of her tongue to ask if that meant he did not wish for children, but their wedding day had been still ahead of them, and it had seemed pre-emptive. Then, for many months, there was no sign of pregnancy. She had thought it would not happen. Until now.

Guy pushed himself into an upright position and pulled her against him, holding her tight and safe inside the circle of his arms. His hands skimmed over the swell of her breasts to settle on her belly. His breath warmed the bare flesh of her shoulder as the hooting of an owl filtered through the half-open window.

"I can wait all night," he said, teeth nibbling gently at her earlobe.

It would be the easiest thing in the world to turn her face to his, entwine her fingers into his thick hair and give him the deep, passionate kiss they both craved. But she must speak.

"I am with child," she said, the words falling like raindrops all around them. A new reality which could no longer be denied.

His hands stilled against her smock, warming her flesh. But she knew a chill as his face lifted away from her. Silence enveloped them, sending a flurry of nerves outwards from her heart. She twisted against him, needing to see the expression in his eyes.

His face was shuttered and blank. A look she'd never wanted to be confronted with again.

"Guy?" she tried. Her throat constricted with alarm.

"With child?" he repeated. "Are you sure?"

She nodded once, not trusting her voice. "Quite sure," she whispered shakily.

Then came the smile. Sunshine after the darkest night. His handsome face became boyish. Cares stripped away. He cupped her cheeks and gazed down at her adoringly.

"A child."

She placed her hand over his. "Is it what you want?"

He blinked in surprise. "Of course."

"I was so scared."

"For what reason?"

She couldn't mar this happy occasion with terrible memories from the past. She merely shook her head, unable to tear her eyes from his.

"I wondered if it might not happen for us," he said slowly. "But I always hoped."

She nodded eagerly. "Me too, and now it has."

His hand went reverently to the slight curve of her belly, settling on her in the gentlest caress. "Our baby."

Her tears were tears of joy. "Yours and mine."

His lips pressed against her head. "I was happy before, but now you have made me the happiest man in England."

"Oh, Guy."

"I do not deserve it."

"No man deserves it more," she corrected him. Shadows danced on the wall behind him. Her handsome husband. "Will you kiss me properly now?"

He cupped her face in his large hands, drawing her towards him until their lips met in a featherlight kiss.

"Should we?" he asked against her cheek. "Can we?"

In answer she took hold of his hand and placed it firmly against her breast. A shot of longing made her limbs grow heavy. "We can and we should."

She sensed the moment he allowed his desire to surface. His breathing slowed, along with the practised movements of his hands on her willing flesh. His mouth went to her neck, and she arched against him, giving herself over to the first wave of pleasure. His fingers skimmed over the straps of her smock. A silent ask for permission in the face of this new dynamic between them.

Her answer was to hitch the lacy fabric up over her hips and then pull it over her head in one smooth movement. She shook her hair free, feeling the heat of his gaze travelling over her body, lingering on her bared breasts.

"Beautiful," he breathed.

Again, she brought his head towards her, thrilling to the sensation of his feather-light kisses. Heat gathered in her core as she moved beneath him, giving herself over to the sensual stroking of his hands, the warmth of his tongue, the teasing of his fingers. She reached for him, eager for the feel of his skin but encountering the soft linen of his shirt.

"You are still clothed," she managed.

"My attention is on you." His head was at her navel now. Kissing and nuzzling and making her writhe with pleasure.

"No." Her hands flailed against his muscular shoulders. Trembling fingers grasped for his buttons.

With a low growl he caught her wrists in one hand and pinned them above her head. "Be still, wife," he breathed.

She closed her eyes as his fluttering kisses travelled over her ribs, tickling and teasing as he moved lower. She pressed her head back into the pillow and let the sensuous waves wash over her.

He came up beside her, smiling at her pleasure. Her breathing slowed and she hooked her arms around his shoulders.

"I have been wanting to touch you like that all day," he said.

She snuggled closer to him. "It would not have been proper in the chapel."

"No indeed." He lifted her chin. "I hope you're not tired?"

The hint of worry in his voice made her choose to tease him. "It has been a long day." She mimed a yawn. Heard his resigned sigh.

"Very well." He settled himself more comfortably. Reached for her in a chaste embrace.

She gave herself away with her chuckle and her hands which still sought contact with his skin. In one swift movement, he pulled his shirt over his head, and she ran her fingers over his muscled chest in possessive delight. Every hard, defined ridge was familiar. He was all hers.

He stood to remove his breeches and she feasted her eyes on his athletic physique. His bronzed skin glowed in the light of the fire. At last, he was back on the bed beside her. Their bodies moved together, legs entwining, lips landing on exposed flesh, luxuriating in the feel of one another.

She reached for the maleness of him, relishing the hardness beneath her fingers. He groaned with barely suppressed pleasure, making her body once more open up with desire. He shifted against her, supporting himself on his elbow, one hand trailing a familiar path over her breasts and down to where she wanted him.

"Are you ready?"

In response, she wrapped her legs around his waist, drawing him down and deep inside her. His low growl of delight set her free. She rocked her hips against him, pushing, bringing him entirely into her core where he filled every bit of her. Hot waves of pleasure travelled up and down her body. No matter how many times they came together, she could never get enough of her husband, the feel of his skin against hers and that wonderful sensation of limbs aligning perfectly with one another.

When it was over, he rolled onto his back and held her close. Their hearts pounded as one. Her hair clung damply to her neck and she pushed it away, enjoying the cool air against her hot skin.

"I love you, Countess of Rossfarne," he said, his voice husky and spent.

"I love you, Earl of Rossfarne," she replied, every word resonating inside her heart.

"It is a marvellous feeling." He traced gentle circles on her back.

"Love?" She pushed herself onto her elbow, looking into his shining eyes.

"Love," he confirmed. "The most important thing."

Chapter Twenty-Three

THEY SLEPT ENTWINED in each other's arms, and Guy woke with the glow of contentment still upon him. As the morning sunlight crept through the shutters, he gazed down at his sleeping wife and placed a reverent hand on her gently curving belly. His heart leaped to know that beneath his fingers stirred a new life. Their child. One he could watch grow up, safe and happy in Rossfarne.

Kitty slept peacefully and he settled in beside her. Since their marriage, he had ridden north to join King Edward on two separate campaigns, but England knew peace for now. Guy could only hope that this peace would last, although his long experience as a knight threw this into doubt. If and when the next summons came, he would do his duty, with his new manservant, Arthur, by his side.

Despite the joy of the morning, his lips still tightened at the memory of how Thomas had double-crossed him. It was bitter irony that Guy had once commanded his manservant to search the castle for stolen jewels, whilst all along Thomas himself harboured purloined coin inside his own bedchamber. The surly servant had not masterminded the theft of Guy's coin on the battlefield, but he had taken a cut from the false coward who had done so. A cut which ensured Thomas's silence. More recently, his trusted position within Rossfarne Castle had given him all manner of chances to add to his stash; opportunities which he hadn't hesitated to avail himself of. He had grown too complacent at the last, leaving his chamber door open while he inspected his wealth at a time when the marshal was passing by.

A knock sounded on their wooden chamber door. Guy blinked in surprise, then shifted quickly to cover his nakedness with a robe and cross the room, before the knocking could disturb Kitty.

It was Arthur himself, pale-faced and yawning at the early hour.

"What is it?" Guy demanded quietly.

"Sorry to disturb, milord. 'Tis an urgent message for you. The boy said it couldn't wait."

He nodded his thanks and took the missive in his hands, his heart sinking at what this news might be. He must go down to the solar and open it, for the stairway was still in darkness, but he had no wish to wake his wife.

"Guy?" Her voice was heavy with sleep.

He ducked back into their bedchamber, smiling at the sight of her sitting up and rubbing her eyes, her beautiful red-gold hair tumbling down her back.

"Go back to sleep," he urged.

"What is it?" she persisted.

"Nothing that can't wait." He took three strides across the floor and dropped a kiss onto her forehead. "I'm sorry to wake you."

Kitty's dextrous fingers plucked the parchment from his hand before he could stop her. She raised her eyebrows. "An urgent message?"

Guy sighed and sat down on the bed. The sheets were crumpled and warm. "Apparently so."

She laid a hand on his knee and looked at him seriously. "Please open it."

The red seal looked familiar as he broke it and unfurled the parchment, his eyes skimming the words quickly. With every line he read, his heart beat faster and the knowledge he would have to leave Kitty's side dropped like a stone into his chest.

"It's Otto," he said bleakly. "Otto Sarragnac, son of the Earl of Darkmoor," he added, seeing her blank expression.

"Oh!" Her eyes opened wide. "The man who…?"

He nodded, pursing his lips at the unwelcome memory of how Lord Ulric had disrespected his wife. "His son, that is," he corrected.

"What does he want?"

Guy folded the parchment, wanting to treasure every moment of this domestic scene. Beyond the castle walls he could hear gulls crying and waves breaking upon the cliffs. The white-washed walls of the bedchamber were patterned with sunlight and Kitty herself was a vision of loveliness. A beautiful woman, carrying his child.

He took a deep breath. "I must leave you, for a short while," he said. "I promise, it is the last thing I want."

Her hand touched his, warm and comforting. "Tell me what has happened?"

"It is all Otto's worst fears come to pass. His father, Lord Ulric, has died in battle. Now Darkmoor is plunged into unrest and my cousin needs a man he can trust by his side. When he was last here, I promised him he could call on me at such a time."

Kitty's sea-green eyes flashed with understanding. "Of course, you must go," she said bravely, nodding once.

Guy cupped her face with his palm. "Thank you for understanding."

She shrugged, smiling. "I married a knight," she said simply. "And I love you for that. I would not change who you are."

"A knight with a wife to come home to, and a child on the way." He placed his hand against the curve of her belly, before pulling her into a tight embrace. "There is no luckier man in the land."

THE END

About the Author

Elizabeth grew up in a rambling old farmhouse high on the Yorkshire moors, where a sense of history was never far away. She studied English at university, specialising in mythology and folklore and often bemoaning the lack of sword-wielding heroines. After graduating, she spent several years moving between northern France, southern Germany and London, where she worked in travel publishing and PR.

She now lives a stone's throw from her childhood home, with her husband, children and a feisty black cat who enjoys interrupting her writing. She plots most of her novels while walking in the rugged Yorkshire countryside, finding endless inspiration in the rolling hills.

www.ingramcontent.com/pod-product-compliance
Lightning Source LLC
Chambersburg PA
CBHW060442310726
48977CB00001B/287